Outlaw's Bride

Grizzlies MC Romance

Nicole Snow

Content copyright © Nicole Snow. All rights reserved.
Published in the United States of America.
First published in June, 2015.

Disclaimer: The following book is a work of fiction. Any resemblance characters in this story may have to real people is only coincidental.

Please respect this author's hard work! No section of this book may be reproduced or copied without permission. Exception for brief quotations used in reviews or promotions. This book is licensed for your personal enjoyment only. Thanks!

Cover Design - LJ Anderson - Mayhem Cover Creations
Formatting –Polgarus Studio

Description

I HAD AN OUTLAW'S BABY AND KEPT IT A SECRET...

SALLY

He's going to kill me when he finds out. I should've left Roman behind after our unforgettable fling two summers ago. I wasn't supposed to end up having his kid, always looking over my shoulder for the last man in the world meant to be a father.

But danger has a funny way of betraying a woman's best kept secrets, and reigniting old flames that should've died on a hot summer night.

Now, he's hellbent on claiming me in all the explosive ways that make my heart stop and my head spin. I'm losing it, or maybe just my panties. *Every single pair.*

An arranged marriage with the Grizzlies MC's biggest badass? I shouldn't want this so bad...

ROMAN

Forgive and forget? F*ck no.

I tried like hell to push her away, spent every waking

minute on whores and booze. Then I found out what she'd hidden, and I lost my damned mind.

Sally's lies stole more years off my life than prison did. She owes me big. I'm taking her for payment, and I don't care what she's got to say about wearing my brand.

No chick makes a fool outta me. And I'm not fooling when I tell her I'll get my perfect wife, even if we're faking it all the way to the altar.

Give me a week. I'll conquer her spitfire tongue and remind her what it's like to ache desire. I'm not stopping 'til her lips are on mine, making her squirm the way she used to, begging me for more…

The Outlaw Love books are stand alone romance novels featuring unique lovers and happy endings. No cliffhangers! This is Roman and Sally's story in the Grizzlies MC series.

I: A Piece of Him (Sally)

I remembered him like it was only yesterday.

The heat of his kiss, the raw power in his arms as he pushed me down in the back seat, fisting my hair and making me scream when he sucked along my throat. He was going to be my first. I never dreamed in a thousand years he'd be my last.

He conquered me, and I fucking let him. I loved it. I didn't love him – at least not *yet* – but I lived giving him my innocence.

Sex came natural to him. He forced me to recognize his awesome talent in everything he did, from the way he shoved himself inside me for the first time, to the cadence of his voice, growling in my ear, twisting my head perfectly to bring my ear to his rough lips.

"Follow my lead, Sally. You're too damned hot to tell me fucking doesn't come natural." He paused, flicking his tongue over my earlobe until I squirmed. "Just watch and feel and learn. Every time I push my dick deep, you grind back. Meet my hips. Fuck me like you mean it, babe. Fuck me like you want it. Keep going 'til it feels like you're gonna blow, and I'll give you the final push. I'll teach you how to use that hot cunt between your legs to suck every drop of come outta a man's balls. Especially *mine*."

God.

And just like that, he fucked me. My best fuck, my *only* fuck. Roman shook the whole truck with his thrusts as he plowed into me, sending me screaming toward the sultry release.

I didn't know him, and it didn't matter. I was too deep in the pleasure zone after about five seconds to even care.

The way he handled me…sweet baby Jesus.

I hadn't meant to lose it this easy. Sure, I wanted to, but I didn't know this would be the day until he started pulling off my clothes.

I went down easy. One kiss was all it took to seal my fate forever.

Maybe it was his strength, or just the rogue good looks in his massive, tattooed body and chiseled face. His dark eyes told me he knew *exactly* what to do with a woman like me in every glance.

And I listened. I melted. I surrendered.

I'd never been a small girl. Growing up on my Uncle's ranch left me strong and well rounded beneath my curves. Stronger than the skinny twigs with palm sized boobs most of the biker boys in this town brought to bed, anyway.

I was pretty voluptuous, actually, which made it all the more amazing when Roman followed through on his promises.

It started with him walking me into the back, showing off the work he'd done on my Uncle's truck. He'd done the job quickly and efficiently, just like a good mechanic could, and I was gawking at him like a schoolgirl with a bad crush every time I twisted in the machine, pointing out some gear or strut.

My thoughts went everywhere. Mostly, just wondering what those big, thick hands could do besides tuning up vehicles in record time.

If only I'd just wondered, fantasized, and left it at that.

I shouldn't have let him pull me inside for a closer look. All alone too – nobody else was in the garage. It must've been a light day for the Grizzlies Motorcycle Club, or maybe his brothers had other business.

I should've put up a fight, especially when his hands grabbed mine, bringing my trembling fingers to his lips. It couldn't possibly mean anything good except some incredible sex.

I was young, but I wasn't stupid. I knew the average badass wearing the Grizzlies MC patch offered nothing except a heart stopping romp between the sheets – or maybe somewhere wilder.

These boys didn't do relationships and dinner dates. They flirted, they fucked, and they moved onto the next hot ass within grabbing distance.

I knew better, and I didn't listen to common sense. The second we locked lips, lust did all the talking.

Maybe I shouldn't look back and be so hard on myself.

After all, it's hard to say no when you're twenty-one

years old and still a virgin, and suddenly the biggest badass in all of Redding has his hands reaching for your bra clasp. And it's even harder when a tattooed giant like Roman shoves his fingers on your thigh and squeezes until it hurts because you want it so bad.

Lust never lies. We melded, a perfect fit, even before he maneuvered his huge frame between my legs, pressing the swollen cock behind his jeans to my panties. The honest *need* in his body fed hunger in mine.

Nature took over. Before I knew what was happening, my shirt was off, and the seat flopped back, leaving ample space for me to open my legs.

The things he did with his mouth set my pussy on fire. When he shoved his hands between my thighs and brushed my wetness, asking me if I'd ever been with a man like him before, I couldn't hide it. I told him I'd never been with any man.

The look he gave me was like a wild animal locking onto its prey. He told me not to worry. He'd take care of everything. He'd teach me all about pleasure, the flesh, *fucking.*

Lesson number one didn't truly sink in until he stripped me naked, shoved his broad face between my thighs, and ripped down my panties with one rough hand. I creamed the instant he started sucking my clit.

Sure, I'd read about the wonderful things a man's tongue can do in dirty romance books and even seen it in some porn. But it was *nothing* compared to having him there, shaking his huge head from side to side, pulling my clit between his teeth and crashing his tongue against it until my entire body exploded.

I came so fucking hard I almost went blind.

Five minutes later, I'd barely come down from the high, and he'd flipped me over in my stupor. One hand pulled me open, baring my virgin slit for his cock. His pants were off, and I caught a quick glimpse of his rock hard, throbbing, insanely huge dick.

I didn't know how he'd ever fit. He didn't care.

There wasn't time for any questions before he pushed himself inside me, all the way, stretching everything wide open for his cock. He sank deep, held it for a moment, shaping my pussy to fit his length.

It didn't hurt much. After several seconds, it started feeling pretty damned good actually, and then *fucking amazing* when his thrusts picked up speed. A dozen strokes in with my legs splayed wide, taking his massive cock, and I couldn't think straight.

I couldn't bother with right or wrong, or what time Uncle Ralph wanted me back with his workhorse on wheels, or even the fact that I couldn't check if the outlaw between my legs rolled on a condom first. Roman taught me a lot that day, especially about losing my mind.

Good sex was worse than good whiskey.

A woman couldn't think about *anything* when her nerves were on fire, blowing all her circuits. I stopped trying when he rocked my body harder, shaking the truck along with it, quaking my whole fucking world apart.

The things that came out of my mouth probably made

mama spin in her grave. Especially when he slowed his thrusts, just enough to let me form words, urging me on.

"You like that, woman? Fucking tell me you do. I wanna hear you beg for this dick. Start talking. You'd better practice talking dirty awful fast if you don't want me to pull out right now and shoot my load on your tits." Then his hand came down, slapping my butt for emphasis.

"Oh, don't stop! Please don't pull out. Please *keep fucking me.*" If only I would've known those words sealed my fate.

"Fuck you like what, babe? I don't give a shit if you're a virgin. I don't do gentle. I don't do slow. I only know how to fuck sluts."

"Then fuck me like one." His hand reached around and cupped my breast. Pushing into his palm, I moaned, praying he'd understand my body's needs.

"Bullshit. You're a good girl, Sally. I've never seen you so much as hanging around a hog roast out here before. You're not a biker bitch. You're not a club whore. I can't fuck you like one unless you make me believe it." Growling, he pulled out, resting his cock between my ass and rubbing it up and down.

"Anything. Do you want this?" My cheeks burned bright red as I shoved my ass cheeks against him. Yes, he had me so drunk on his body I offered him everything that moment, and I would've given it to him too – anything to bring him back to the fire he'd kindled inside my pussy.

Silence. Until I heard the thunder building in his throat. With a snarl, he titled my head to the side, jerking my hair in one fist, pushing his lips close to my ear again.

"You're lucky the thought of fucking a virgin cunt no man's ever been in makes my dick pulse lava, blondie. Turn the fuck over. I'll take all your holes another night." Another slap on the ass, and I obeyed.

I was so vulnerable, so exposed beneath him. His dark hazel eyes flashed. He took a good long look, bathing me in his hungry gaze.

"Lock those legs around my waist, and don't you fucking let up when I make you come. Consider this a test. We'll see if you're worth more than one fuck. I hardly ever do girls twice, and never when they've got hooks on 'em, trying to pull me into some shit. I'm a *free* man. You hear me, babe? You down with that? I'm looking for a fuck. Not a girlfriend."

My eyes narrowed. I can't say he didn't give me many chances to run. He told me straight up he was the world's biggest asshole with a gladiator's body and a tiger's stripes going up his arms. The roaring bear inked in the middle of his rock hard chest should've been warning enough.

I ignored it all. I wanted him that bad. I'd play along to keep this going, to feel him shaking me again. I'd already gone too deep, and now I wanted my virgin innocence obliterated.

For one night, I just wanted to feel his cock inside me as many times as I could. I'd deal with the guilt in the morning.

Reaching up, I ran my fingers down his chest, stopping just above his throbbing cock. Steam shot out my pores when I really *felt* how hard he was. *Holy shit.*

"You talk a lot about wild and free, don't you, Roman? Why don't you shut up and show me what that means?" God, I sounded nervous, but I managed.

I hooked my legs around his waist and gave him a squeeze. I teased him, and I loved it.

His cock jerked, letting out a steady trickle of pre-come. For several seconds, I watched the thick, pearly liquid dribble down to my soft belly. Then, I reached down and swirled my finger through it, instinctively raising it to my lips.

One drop was all I needed to be addicted to his taste. And apparently, one stunt like that was all it took to tease the animal inside him, the beast that took hold of his body while he pushed his magnificent cock deep into my virgin wetness again.

"Fucking shit." He shook his head, sliding in to the balls. "Don't you know you're playing with fire, baby girl?"

"Mm. I guess I'll just have to be your pyro for the night."

His whole body shifted forward. Taking my wrists in both hands, he slammed them onto the leather seat beneath me, holding them over my head. Then his hips moved, and he resumed thrusting. He pistoned in and out a little easier this time because I was twice as wet.

He melted me alive, or at least turned everything below my waist into napalm.

I came apart. Panting. Pleading. Impossibly wet and

hot and wanting, ready to blow up the entire biker clubhouse attached to this garage if he refused to finish fucking my brains out.

Thankfully, he did.

Roman throttled my whole body. His deep, hard strokes shook my breasts and vibrated through my bones. My lips popped open, forming an O, a release valve for the fireball exploding around my clit. I barely had time to reach up and wrap my hands around his neck before it went through me, scorching everything, promising an earthquake.

"Roman!"

"Come on, babe. Keep it the fuck going." As if it was so damned easy. "I wanna feel you clenching this dick 'til I blow."

Hugging his powerful ass, I lost it. I thought I knew what an orgasm felt like from using my vibrator, but having my pussy wrapped around his dick drilled it into my brain, introduced me to a new sensation a thousand light years from earth.

It's different. It's incredible. Shit, I think I'm addicted.

I could've said the same about him – not just the sex. Something about being fucked by an outlaw giant three times my size fueled the hormones blazing in my veins.

I couldn't hold back. I didn't try. I came as hard as he commanded, throwing my head back and screaming my lungs out, so loud I wondered if any of the other rough bastards inside the clubhouse would come storming out to find out what all the commotion was.

Nothing would've stopped them from seeing us tangled together through the half-fogged windows, locked in ecstasy.

Roman's hips didn't stop either. If anything, they fucked harder, deeper, so fast and relentless I started to worry something would break in our bodies. But then his hips jerked to a stop, and he pressed me deep into the leather with all his weight.

"Goddamn, you're *fucking tight*." One more ragged breath and Roman couldn't speak. "This pussy's mine. *Mine*."

His cock pulsed, buried deep against my womb, making me feel him swell and twitch. He came with the same raging intensity. The deluge instantly fed my own orgasm like kerosene, and my legs squeezed his waist so hard they hurt.

His come flooded me in molten jets. Pulse after pulse hit my womb, so hot and powerful I swore I could feel it. I came so fucking hard, so long, I didn't know if I'd ever be able to walk straight again. I wondered if he'd left me paralyzed.

A small eternity slipped by in the heaving, rocking, sweating mess of us pinched together. My pussy refused to let go until he began to soften, and then I started my long glide down from the high, awakening to his salty lips on mine.

"You fuck pretty hot for a girl who's never done this before. You sure you're not bullshitting me about that virgin thing?" he asked, gently pulling out and wiping his dick. "Never felt a pussy ramp up to a hundred degrees and stay so damned tight."

Smiling, I caressed his legs with mine, feeling his seed trickle down from my middle. Ugh. I should've been worried, but I told myself there was plenty of time for that later. I'd been taking my birth control as steady as I could, hoping for the big day, and now I could finally put the pills to use.

I couldn't worry. The deed was done. I just wanted to enjoy the moment, the hazy afterglow we'd left in the truck, the smell and warmth of smoking sex.

"Fuck me," he growled, cupping my mound and feeling our cream pouring out into his hand. "I think I'm in love with this pussy."

"Yeah? Does that mean I get a second date?"

Roman looked at me, wiped his brow, and laughed. "You gotta be shitting me. You think fucking in an old truck's some kinda date?"

My cheeks flushed and I looked down. Of course not.

How dumb could I be? Dumb enough to entertain love-at-first-fuck, I guess. Suddenly, I wasn't so keen on being so naked before this man.

Embarrassed, I started reaching for my clothes, somewhere in a heap on the floor, when he put his hand on my cheek. "Ah, what's this? I'm just fucking around, Sally. Come on, get dressed and we'll go have some grub. Every chick deserves a sit down date when it's her first time."

The next week defied belief. The fun didn't end with a late night breakfast and another romp at his place.

I *dated* a bad boy, an outlaw, a man who'd probably strangled guys almost as big and bad as he was with his bare hands.

Roman picked me up a couple days later for a ride on his Harley, and the sweet autumn breeze blew through my hair. Having my hands wrapped around his body was sheer heaven. On his bike, holding him close, all my problems faded into a big fog of masculine spice and rippling muscle.

Roman saved me from having to think. With him, I didn't have to worry about the bad economy, my pissed off cousin, or hurtling toward permanent farm girl status.

I didn't fret skipping college, or feel my stomach twisting in knots when I remembered the only places hiring in Redding were even scarcer and lower paying than Uncle Ralph's ranch.

Him and his bike took me away from all that. He teleported me to an alternate universe of motor oil, dark inks, and pounding hearts, a paradise so awesome I never wanted to come back.

One evening became two, and then an entire week of hard riding, hard fucking, quality time together.

Roman picked me up every sunset, and we tore through the countryside on his bike, occasionally stopping in town for drinks or food. It always ended the same way – my bare ass bouncing beneath him in the bed, or sometimes in the tall, cool grass.

We fucked our way to happiness. We used sex to wipe ourselves clean. Me, with my boredom and mundane worries. Him, with his dark biker obligations, his mysteries, the scary warrior bloodlust I saw darkening his hazel eyes.

Club business, he said, warning me not to wander too deep into his world. And I didn't because when we were alone, the only business he had was me.

We fucked underneath the stars and in his little apartment. We kissed until each other's taste was inscribed on our brains forever. We fucked until neither of us knew night from day, right from wrong, heaven from hell.

One day, he woke me up early at his place. I wiped the sleep from my eyes, and realized he'd just ended a call.

"Get moving, babe. I gotta get you home." The tension in his strong face told me something was wrong, but he wouldn't say what.

I kept pressing him about it the whole ride home. My heart thudded like never before on the bike, and it had nothing to do with the road tearing by underneath us.

I was scared for him, terrified at his silence.

When we pulled up the dirt path to my family's farmhouse, he ripped off my helmet, and told me he'd call me later. I couldn't let him leave without trying one more time.

"Roman, please…what's the big secret?" I asked, frustration heating my blood. He gave me the same icy stare and looked away, mumbling something about it being nothing I needed to worry about.

I grit my teeth. "Fine then, keep it to yourself. Guess you can tell me now, or I'll just find out later when I come by the clubhouse."

Shaking his head, he got off his bike, and grabbed me by the shoulders. Then he shook me – and I mean *really* shook me – so hard I stumbled back scared.

"Don't you fucking *dare*," he growled. "Not now. I told you the rules our first night out – I come to you, Sally. Never the other way around. There's a damned good reason for that, and I need you to fucking listen."

"Listen to *what*? How can I trust you if you won't tell me what's going on?"

"It's club business," he snapped, making me hate that two word sucker punch for the first time. "Not yours. I've gotta put my brothers first, second, and third. That's what a man does when he's in the Grizzlies MC."

Thanks, I thought, feeling the chill realization of how far down the ladder I must be.

"I swore an oath to this patch." His right hand formed a fist and slapped his chest, right where he wore the roaring bear tattoo underneath his shirt. "What's going on today's between brothers *only*. You've gotta understand that. Look, you know I like you a lot, but I can't fucking bring you into a world where you don't belong. I'm not gonna be responsible for you getting hurt."

Hurt? So, it was just as bad as I thought. Maybe worse.

Without another word, he turned his back, and began revving his engine.

Fuck it. I went after him, too upset to worry about the

loud motorcycle drawing Uncle Ralph's attention from the fields. He'd look at me with horror if he knew I'd been hanging with a Grizzlies MC man for more than a week.

But it didn't matter. Him leaving did, especially when the chill current swept up my spine, telling me this could be it.

Whatever was going on threatened to pull him away from me forever. It scared me senseless.

"Wait!" I yelled, stepping in front of the bike before he could dart away. "Will I see you alive again? Just tell me the truth. Just that. Please, Roman, don't do anything that'll get you killed. *Please.*"

Frustration stormed in his eyes. "You'll see me in one piece if you step outta the way *right fucking now.* I'm going, babe. Don't make me run you over. I've got my orders. Yours are to calm the hell down and let me go. I'll be back for you. Promise. Right now, there's shit I have to do, and nobody's standing in my way. Not even you." His cold, angry voice chilled me.

I wilted. My feet dragged on the ground as I reluctantly stepped away, watching as he sped off without so much as a wave goodbye.

I thought it was the last glimpse of him I'd ever have. Forever.

Turns out, forever was actually a little under two years.

Weeks rolled by, and there was no call. No note in the mailbox. No breaking news in the paper or on TV about a bloody battle that left men dead anywhere in NorCal.

Nothing.

I couldn't take it. I had to find out what happened.

My next visit to the clubhouse was a fucking disaster. I drove in about a month after he disappeared, circling past the gruff faced guards by the gate, hoping I'd see some sign of him.

But if I did, that would've been worse. If he'd chosen *this* way to dump me...

I bit my lip, trying to keep it together, especially around all these scary, rough strangers.

An older man with long gray hair named Blackjack answered all my questions. Thank God, because he was the most approachable of the bunch. He told me Roman was in prison, part of his service to the club for...God only knew what.

"Club business," the weathered warrior said.

I hated those two words before, and now I fucking loathed them. For any woman unfortunate enough to be in the Grizzlies MC's orbit, it was like having the door slammed in her face.

Of course, I broke down in my car. I wasn't just chasing him because I wanted to find out he was still breathing, though that was a big part of it.

I had something to tell him, a slow motion disaster building by the second.

"Why are you crying, girl? Look at me." Blackjack's eyes were surprisingly soft, far kinder than any ruthless killer's had any business being. Looking at the ENFORCER patch on his cut told me he ranked higher than Roman, which probably meant he'd been into even darker things for far longer.

"That's *my* business," I said. "Mine and Roman's. Is there an address where I can reach him? Maybe visiting hours or something?"

Blackjack shook his head. "It's too dangerous. Where he's going, rival gangs use visiting time to sneak up on a man and cut his throat. He knows to keep his head down, refuse everybody, even from the club. Sure, the guards will come in blazing, but by the time they break up the fight, he'll be bled out like a slaughtered hog if somebody gets a lucky stab."

Jesus. Telling him in person would've been hard enough.

Now, this old vulture was telling me I wouldn't get a single chance for nearly *two years?* If ever?

"Stay there a second," Blackjack said after a moment, watching new tears pulling at my eyes. "I'll get some paper and pass along a PO box where you can send him letters."

I hated sitting there and staring at the clubhouse wall. A huge mural of a ferocious grizzly bear leered out from the side, its mouth stretched wide, ready to devour everything. Right now, it was chewing my world apart, piece by bloody piece.

I barely knew the club, and I hated it. I certainly wouldn't be the first in Redding to feel that way. Uncle Ralph told me they were no good, though my cousin, Norman, always said they were the only thing stopping even bigger rotten apples from rolling into town and taking over.

My Uncle only had me take the truck to their shell repair shop because the other guys in town screwed him over one too many times. Talk about a dismal situation when the most honest mechanics around were honest-to-God outlaws, smugglers, and possibly murderers.

It was surreal. A few weeks ago, I'd been scared to death over Roman going off for an evening, wondering if he'd come home alive. Now, after hearing about jail, I knew I'd be feeling my nerves burning out for the next twenty-two months.

He's not the only one in prison. You're going to pay for your mistake, I thought.

Karma's come to collect her debt, and it's him. He's gone. You're going to do this alone, whether you see him alive again or not.

My thoughts pulled knots in my intestines. Or maybe it was just the changes in my body, the shadow left in my flesh by too many unforgettable nights with a bad boy.

"Here you go," Blackjack said, sticking his hand through my car's open window. I felt so tiny in my own crappy rust bucket after driving Uncle Ralph's truck most days. "Write him anytime. I'm sure he'll answer you. Remember, the boys who run that place read everything before it gets to him. My number's there too. You really ought to call it if you need anything, rather than coming to the clubhouse. It's a bad time for too many outsiders."

I blinked. Blackjack put both hands on the window's frame and leaned in. "There's things going on in this club right now. That's why our boy's in jail. We're not interested in babysitting civilians, or receiving them at all unless it's absolutely necessary. You look like a smart girl, and I know he wouldn't want you fucked over by any bad business that isn't yours. Stay away from this patch for awhile, Sally. If you care about him at all, you'll listen."

I didn't say another word. Neither did he.

A crater blew open in my heart. Two years. No contact. No way to reach him at all except a note by pigeon that would be intercepted and poured over by the guards before it ever made it through.

No privacy. No help. No more loving – if I could call whatever we had that without being totally delusional.

As soon as Blackjack walked back into the garage, I turned my car around and waved to the prospects manning the gate. I couldn't wait for it to slide all the way open before I gunned it out of there, fighting the fiery tears in my eyes.

I was alone. The sooner I learned to accept it, the better.

I didn't send a single letter the entire time. I couldn't bring myself to pick up the pen, couldn't put my hands on the keyboard. It would've written the lamest note in the world, and also the one guaranteed to stop my heart when I thought about how he'd react.

Two long years passed in a painful haze. I tried to forget, at least until he got out. *IF* he got out…

We never spoke once. Not until last week, when I

finally mustered up the courage to walk into the clubhouse and try to tell him everything I'd been terrified to say by letter.

He'd only been free for a few weeks. His twenty-two months in prison were a lifetime to me.

I'd heard the rumors around town. The Grizzlies were fighting for their lives the past few years. They'd been warring with everybody across the wild west, rival MCs like the Prairie Devils up in Montana, and bigger worries closer to home. Nothing hit them harder than the Mexican cartels coming north, muscling in on the territory they'd held for decades.

Every other week, there was a new gruesome headline. Missing people on both sides of the border, bombings and gunfights in every major city, especially Sacramento and LA. Thankfully, the war zone hadn't really hit Redding yet.

Oh, except for the club's infighting. Their old President, the notorious old thug named Fang, was deposed. Blackjack took over the entire national organization, and he'd made Redding the MC's permanent headquarters.

Change was in the air, and nobody on the outside knew what it meant. Not yet.

Now shops funded by the Grizzlies MC sprang up all over, gun shops and strip clubs and biker bars. They cleaned up other dirty clubhouses as far as Klamath Falls and San Diego, and even ran a few charity events.

No one was going to roll over and call these guy

heroes. Honestly, it didn't take a perfect vision to see through the PR stunts, and some of the new businesses they'd helped set up were likely fronts for money laundering.

Other things stayed the same.

Their cartel wars weren't over. New violence somewhere in the state cropped up every week, except now it sounded like the Grizzlies were beginning to gain the upper hand.

Me? I stayed out of it.

There was plenty to keep busy. I'd never grown beyond the ranch, and now I was managing a lot more of it since a stroke took Uncle Ralph's life last year. Cousin Norman and I shared the farm, managing the machines and the family's old employees, including a few younger guys who'd become hangarounds with the Grizzlies MC.

They were my source for most of the rumors. I never contacted Blackjack or anyone close to Roman, deciding to keep my distance until I was good and ready, and Roman was free.

Days passed. I heard he was back in town, and apparently the club's Enforcer now.

It took an entire summer week to gather my courage. I let Norman know I was going into town for a few things, but really, I was heading for the clubhouse.

The fresh paint on the place instantly looked brighter when I pulled up. Two prospects were guarding the gate, and I struggled to explain who I was while they gave me cold, skeptical stares.

But as soon as I said "Roman," the man who's name patch said Stryker walked over and punched the button. The gate slid open, and I walked through it, leaving my car parked on the curb.

It was early evening. Two men were arguing over drinks at the bar. I'd never been inside the place before, and it was about what I expected. Dark, smoky, dizzying.

The sharp stink of booze and testosterone clung to the air, and I stumbled forward along a narrow corridor, trying to get my wits.

"Sonofabitch!" A man growled. "Hey, lady! Look out!"

Something sharp whizzed past my face. There wasn't time to dodge, or even wonder if it was a bullet. It smacked the wall just a few inches from my head, a long metallic dart, lodged in the wood like a stray missile.

An angry looking bald man looked at me, straightening his cut. When he saw it hadn't taken out an eye, he spun around to face his partner, a strong, younger man I'd seen riding around town.

"Asshole! What the fuck is wrong with you? Are you trying to get somebody *killed?*" Baldie slapped both hands against his brother's chest.

The other man took a swing, missed, and drunkenly hit the floor. Before I knew it, I was watching a mini-biker brawl, two men on the floor cursing and throwing fists.

Ugh. Not exactly how I wanted to re-introduce myself to Roman and his friends. I was about to say something and try to ease the scuffle when I heard footsteps.

I looked up, and there he was, coming toward me. My

heart thudded like a bomb's aftershock, and it didn't let up until he'd closed the gap between us, two fucking years apart.

Roman and I locked eyes. The words I'd practiced so many times died on my tongue.

I couldn't believe it. I couldn't believe how he'd changed. Could I even believe my own eyes?

Was he always so huge – or did prison add a few inches to his bulging muscles? His face looked tougher too, accented by a few more lines in his forehead, a sharper angle to his powerful jaw. He'd probably just passed his thirtieth birthday in jail, and he had all the insanely hot finishes of a man aging into his prime.

Jesus. Before I came here, I told myself over and over I wouldn't feel the old heat. This was going to be business like, personal, but I wouldn't let my old attraction take over. Not before I saw what he was like.

Yeah, good luck with that.

As soon as his dark hazel eyes sucked me in, I lost it. The tattoos on his muscular arms rippled in my peripheral vision, forcing me to remember those hands on my body. They'd held me down so tight while he fucked me, fingered me, warming me up for that battering ram between his legs.

The men stopped fighting when they saw him coming. The young guy with the sandy hair helped himself up, holding onto the bar, nursing his ribs after they took some cringe-worthy kicks from Baldie. One look at Roman, and he started shaking, making excuses.

The bald guy retreated behind the bar, fixing himself a drink. Roman stormed right past his beaten up brother, giving him a quick shove, muttering when he tried to stand up. "Get the fuck outta my way."

I'd stolen all his interest. While we stood there staring at each other, lost in our memories, everything else in the clubhouse might as well have been happening on the dark side of the moon.

"Sally." I flattened myself against the wall the instant he said my name.

It wasn't just his body changing behind bars. Prison or age deepened his voice, given it a smoky richness to go with the deep baritone he'd had before. My mind went wild, recognizing the same wicked cadence and thunder I heard that summer when he growled into my ear, ordered me to suck his cock, to come each time he fucked me senseless.

"What the fuck are you doing here?"

Good question. My lips tasted bitter against my tongue, as if they didn't want to move, didn't want me to remember why the hell I'd come to confront him.

"I had to see you. I heard you were out of jail."

"Yeah, word spreads fast." He folded his huge arms, and his biceps bulged so thick I swore they'd bust his seams. "What the fuck is this? I'm surprised you showed up. Pretty sure you'd forgotten my ass when I didn't hear from you. It's been – what? – two goddamned years?"

Ouch. Steeling myself for this crap before I walked through the door was completely different from actually facing him. The lump in my throat didn't want to go down, and it had to before I could form words.

"I'm sorry, Roman. When I heard the news from Blackjack, I didn't know what to do. He said I couldn't see you in person, told me it wouldn't be good to visit you –"

His hand shot up, right in front of my face. "And he was right. You were wise to stay the fuck away. This world's not for you, babe. If I'm not worth writing to, then I'm sure as shit not worth your time now that I'm out."

I sucked in a sharp breath. *No, no, you don't understand.* I couldn't force the words out, and he just kept talking.

"What? Don't give me that fucking look. You always had a good head on your shoulders, woman, and it's time for you to put it to use. You know it's too late, too far gone for us. Mistakes were made, and they weren't fixed. If you've got any sense, you'll pick those long legs up, turn around, and walk out that door."

I froze. The cold energy in his eyes danced over me, sucking the life out of me. "What? *Why?*"

"Because what happened that summer two years ago was a big goddamned mistake. I'm sorry the memory's left you hanging. If you're still wrapped up in me, then I don't know who the hell you are. I don't wanna know. I should be ancient history by now, and you should be settled down with some civilian and a couple kids. This clubhouse never was a place for a real lady."

Real lady? Was he patronizing me, or just trying to let

me down easy? Shit, the fact that he was letting me down at all hit me in the chest and shredded my heart.

Before I could say anything else, he turned, heading for the bar. "Wait! Roman!"

The blade he'd pushed into my chest just sank deeper when I heard myself saying those fucking words. *Wait.*

Haven't I been doing it for twenty-two fucking months? All alone, hiding my memories at the ranch, suffering in silence?

My brain flipped to a different mode. I couldn't let him get away from me again like this. I had to get his attention – *now.*

Running after him, I grabbed a bottle off the bar and threw it.

I wasn't trying to hit him, but the glass made a hell of a noise when it hit the floor, right by his boot. Roman whirled.

How could those eyes that were so sexy and full of life be so dead and glacial? I stared back at him, hoping he caught pure hell in my dark blue eyes. Maybe I'd see a spark of something that was still alive.

My temper took over. This wasn't the man I knew, even if this stranger had the same incredible body, the same face I'd imagined night after night.

"Go ahead and walk the fuck away again, you coward!" I screamed, my voice surprisingly steady. "At least this time I know it's not the prisons and the courts holding you back! You're not man enough to handle *us.*"

Christ, that idea scared me too. But I still said it, I still offered it to him, even after all this time.

I expected him to strike back, shove me to the wall, get in my face. Instead, he just turned around and kept going.

He left me alone. I was about to storm out when the brother who'd taken a beating with the bald guy stepped in front of me.

A few minutes later, I sat with him at the bar. I let Rabid – what a ridiculous name, right? – pour me a shot of whiskey. We talked about bad luck and love.

He was nice enough, and I actually felt better by the time I had a couple drinks. We must've sat and talked for hours. If he wasn't so hooked on some redhead he was chasing, I might've leaned over and kissed him just to spite Roman.

Maybe to spite myself for being so stupid, thinking this would be easy.

"Good luck, baby," Rabid said, just before I gathered up my purse to leave. "Try coming by in a few weeks. Maybe then we'll have sorted through some of our shit."

""I hope so," I told him. "Thanks, Rabid. I've got a feeling you'll sort whatever's got you by the balls just fine."

His chances were definitely better than mine, anyway. When I left the clubhouse, the only thought rattling around in my head was how much I never wanted to see that overgrown asshole, Roman, ever again.

If only it were that simple.

At home, the reason why I practically walked over broken glass to see him at the clubhouse sat in my arms, soft and sleepy.

Soon, Caleb would be growing into a real toddler. I've tried like hell to raise my son alone, to forget about Roman and walk the fuck away, never looking back.

But every time I looked into my son's dark brown eyes and saw the same powerful jawline forming on him, I knew. I understood what he deserved, what he needed.

The kid had to have his father – even if the man who shared his DNA turned my heart to ice.

No, no, I couldn't give up this easy. God help me, I was the only one who could bring Roman into his life, or else I'd keep them apart forever.

II: Longing (Roman)

Prison changes a man. It makes him leery, anxious, and ready to fucking fight every second his body isn't so damned exhausted it makes him stay still.

We'd only been in church for five minutes, and I was getting goddamned antsy.

"Beam. Stryker." Blackjack stood at the head of the table, staring at our two prospects like he was about to anoint them with holy oil. "You've proven yourselves. You've spilled blood and licked dirt for this club, and now you're going to do it some more."

The room was dead silent. The two men looked at each other, nervous as hell. It would've been funny if I didn't have so much shit on my mind.

"The difference is, this time we'll be calling you our brothers. Welcome to the fold, boys. You've earned your bottom rockers, and the vote was unanimous." The Prez stopped and looked at me. "Roman?"

My cue to get up and hand them the patches I've been sitting on since we got into the room. The boys stared at me like their damned eyeballs were about to melt.

They probably couldn't believe how quickly they'd been patched in. Well, there's more of that these days, especially with good men dropping like fucking flies along the border.

Before we really started to tango with the cartel, we were the biggest MC west of the Mississippi. Flash forward a couple years, and we'd lost hundreds, rivers of blood spilled to gain the upper hand over those bastards from Mexico. Not to mention some of our own brothers, who'd turned this club into such a shithole it was too weak to push the invaders back where they belonged in the first place.

"Congratulations, brother." I shook Stryker's hand, a tall man, former soldier.

Then I moved to Beam and offered the same thing. He had more of a punk ass skateboarder's look, but whatever. Seeing dudes with weird styles was nothing outta the ordinary in any MC.

"Take your seats, brothers. We've got business." We all nodded and found our places while Blackjack limped back to his.

The Prez's bum leg probably wouldn't ever heal. He'd taken a bullet when the boys fought Fang, our old fuck of a Prez, not long before I got outta jail. When I showed up for duty with the new and improved Grizzlies MC, I wasn't sure what to expect. Luckily, the past few months have proven it's a big improvement.

Anything beat the old group of thugs, killers, and honorable outlaws getting their asses kicked by the cartel. I went away after killing for the brothers I trusted. Since I took the Enforcer promotion, it was my job to make damned sure no man sat at this table or wore this patch who couldn't be called a brother in the fullest sense of the word.

Once everybody was seated, Blackjack looked at Brass, our VP, waiting for him to deliver the latest war report.

"We're still struggling with these ambushes, Prez. The Devils are working with the Oregon crew, helping hold things down up north. But they hit us every week in LA and San Diego. Sacramento's got spots we don't control, even after several months." He paused, as if he didn't want to say the next part. "They're still going after men's families. They beheaded a brother's old lady last week in SoCal."

Fuck. Christ.

Hands went up and slapped the table. Men shook their heads. My guts spooled up like a goddamned chain getting ready to snap.

The brothers who've got women they've claimed looked the worst. At our table, that was Brass and Rabid, but several other guys were just as pissed. I felt it too – an iron hot fire making me wanna hit the road and strangle a few cartel soldiers myself.

Thinking about those fucks butchering an old lady only fed the shit running through my head. It wasn't just about the dead chick – it was the ultimate slap in the face, the ultimate way for those cocksuckers to squat on us and take a steaming dump on the entire club.

For a split second, it made me think about *her,* before I shoved Sally outta my skull for the dozenth time that day.

"Christ." Blackjack's lips twitched angrily, taking a few seconds to collect his words. "All the more reason to end this thing before Christmas."

"I hope it's that easy, Prez," Rabid said, breaking in. "Shit, I'd give up Jack all winter if we didn't have to worry about those fucks breathing down our throats."

"Quit bullshitting, brother. I'd settle just for the Mexicans breathing down our threats, instead of fucking cutting them." Brass stared at his friend across the table.

"Enough. You know why we're here." Blackjack peered out at all of us, one by one, stopping on me dead last. "We need manpower. The two brothers we've just patched in are just the beginning. Roman, you're going to choose three new hangarounds by the end of the week. Make them prospects. Make sure they're ready to face hell for this brotherhood."

A few guys exchanged icy glances. The club's power structure was too damned new for a lot of 'em to openly grumble to the Prez. Not me.

I couldn't slack off when the stakes were this high – even if the Prez was wrong.

"Prez, I told you last week we can't be flipping through these strangers like a revolving door. Hell, this isn't the army where we can snap our fingers and draft a bunch of bastards from Redding just looking for a little action and some mean tattoos. We can't pick up every motherfucking kid fresh outta high school who likes Harleys and thinks wearing this patch'll show all the ladies his balls have dropped."

A few guys snickered. Brass gave me a nod, then looked at the Prez.

"Roman's right. Look, Prez, I do all the background checks I can on these guys, but I can't catch everything. One of them could be some plant wearing a badge, trying to get into our operation, or even some fucker working for one of the cartels."

Several guys started at the Veep in disbelief. "It happens. Believe it, or don't. Better you hear it from me than find out the fucking hard way."

Thank fuck. Maybe hearing it from the VP would make the Prez see the light. Then Asphalt piped up, his bald head shining, reminding everybody the asshole's the biggest hothead at this table.

"Yeah? Excuse me, Veep, but what fucking good's that gonna do if we're all dead? The cartel's picking guys off one by one. Sure, we've made progress, but just wait 'til they call for reinforcements in the spring. These bastards are *huge*. They've got shit stretching all the way down to Colombia, and if they think we're a big enough problem, they'll bring in reinforcements."

Damn if I didn't want to grab his head and bounce it off the table like a goddamned basketball. "You're thinking short term, Asphalt. And that's being pretty fucking generous. How bad do you think we'll have it if this club gets caught between some DEA mole and the cartel's shit? We can barely keep the bribes flowing now to make sure the Feds look the other way with all the blood turning this state red. Shit, next year, we've got an election coming up, and all the money in the world might not save us if those peacocks in their suits latch onto it." I let my fists hit the table. "Think harder, *brother.*"

Yeah, that last part was an afterthought. I didn't give a shit when he started eyeballing me neither. Too bad the Prez started doing the same thing.

"You know we're in a desperate situation, son," Blackjack said. "If we hadn't spent so much time and effort sorting out our own problems in this club, the cartel wouldn't be tightening its hold at all. The stakes have never been this high."

Several guys coughed. I was the only man in the room who could take the Prez head on, while everybody else just wilted underneath his sorcerer's gaze. I never had trouble seeing why Blackjack held the Enforcer spot before me under Fang. Shit, he'd been cracking skulls for this club since most of us were kids.

"Imagine it's you. Your families, brothers. I know there's nobody wearing this patch who'd hesitate to shed sweat and blood for the bear, but no man ought to risk his lifeblood, his woman, his kids. We protect our old ladies and our children as viciously as we backup as any man with our patch. If that means we've got to bring in a few more good, eager soldiers faster than we'd like, then you'd better believe I'll fucking do it." His fist came down hard.

The old table was probably gonna take a lot more punches before the meeting ended.

"You know what the revised charter says. It's every full patch member's right to call for a vote, and we'll go by majority rule." Furrowing his brow, he folded his arms. "Do it. I can't have dissent when we're fighting for our goddamned lives. If anyone here disagrees, call the vote. We'll sort out your objections without any hard feelings."

My hand twitched. I wanted to fucking do it bad. Of course, I didn't. Gauging club politics came easy to me. I'd been through enough tense church sessions like this one to know I'd be on the losing side.

That's the thing about democracy. It only fucking works when the votes go your way.

"Well? Nobody?" Blackjack paused. "Good. Then we've aired our objections and we can move forward like men. Roman, you have your orders."

My hands balled into fists. All I could do not to give the Prez the world's most sarcastic-as-fuck salute.

"I'll make sure the new recruits are up to speed," I said. And I meant it too.

I'd been in the life long enough to know Prezes and Veeps don't always make perfect decisions. But brothers like Blackjack and Brass deserved my respect, and I was damned sure going to give it to them – even at the cost of bringing down more shit for this club we'd all have to clean up.

Church ended on a high note. Several brothers hit the bar with our newest full patch members, laughing and serving them shots. I kept my distance like always.

Evening rolled in, and the guys with old ladies invited them to join the celebration. The whores and club sluts began to show up too.

I needed to keep my ass glued to the bottle. So, I sat, watching Rabid and Brass hug their women close. Every time they kissed their girls, there was love in those lips, the only kind that comes from a man putting his brand on his old lady.

I couldn't decide what the fuck was worse – the lovey-dovey shit with the old ladies, or watching dudes like Asphalt, Stryker, and Beam slobbering all over tonight's easy pussy.

Even old Southpaw was getting in on the action at the edge of the bar. The big, gray haired blockhead looked up and grinned at me over the shoulder of some nameless bitch straddling his lap.

My dick jerked hard. I'd been clean for too fucking long, stuffed away in prison, a desert without tits and ass if there ever was one.

Fuck. My hand tightened on my glass, thinking about Sally. I reached for the bottle, adding another big splash of Jack to my beer. I downed the shit in one big gulp and started all over again.

Back when I was behind bars, I told myself getting fucked up was first on the list as a free man. As it turned out, there hadn't been time for that crap since I got to the clubhouse.

Rabid and his new old lady, that bouncy redhead on his lap named Christa, caused us a world of shit just a few weeks ago. She'd hidden her blood debts to our brothers up in Oregon 'til it all came screaming outta the closet – and the crew in Klamath Falls was rotten to the core. We found out real fast who our brothers really were in that group. The rest were dead and buried, rotting underneath ten feet of thick concrete.

Of course, Sally picked the worst time in the world to show up during that fuckery. Seeing her after two damned years of silence blew my brains out my skull.

Did she really expect to just pick up where we'd left off after I'd given her more than any other woman that summer? Did she think I'd forget she hadn't said boo for two fucking years while I lived in that pit?

When she whipped that bottle at my boots and cursed me for walking away, she tore my heart in half.

One part wanted to march right back, throw her over my shoulder, and fuck her goddamned brains out. That chick warmed my blood like nobody before.

The other half wanted me to spit in her face, tell her what a bitch she was for walking away, leaving me high and dry like a goddamned chump.

No, it wasn't just the dry spell in prison driving me up the wall. Even when I touched her a couple weeks ago, it was like a fucking jolt. Sandpaper scratched my veins, and molten blood pooled straight in my dick, turning it into a hammer ready and willing to bust holes in the walls.

I couldn't deal with that shit, that firestorm in my blood leaving me in a stupor.

I took another swig, feeling relief from bad memories

when it hit my guts and burned. Every glance around the clubhouse hurt my eyes. Too bad there was no relief as long as I was stuck here.

A few minutes more, watching brothers on the verge of getting their dicks wet, and I couldn't fucking take it. I jumped off my seat, carrying my new beer and whiskey cocktail with me, wandering toward the room in the back where I always crashed for the night.

I just wanted to pass the fuck out and find some peace for a few hours. Soon as I flicked on the lights and kicked the door shut behind me, I got an eyeful that lit my dick up like a fucking bottle rocket.

Twinkie was on the floor next to my bed, naked from the waist down. Her arms sprawled out above her blonde pigtails, a half-burnt joint between her fingers. She twisted her head, staring at me with those bright hooded eyes – dangerously similar to Sally's.

Do it, do it, do it, motherfucker.

My cock's lightning hit my brain, and I heard its pleas crystal clear. At first, she looked scared, startled. She knew damned well she wasn't supposed to be in a brother's room without his permission.

Normally, that shit got these whores an ass tanning or an angry shove back where they belonged That night, I had something different on my mind, and there was no fucking way I was shutting my sex starved dick up.

"Oh, Christ. Hold up, Roman, I'm on my way out!" she moaned, staggering to her feet, her eyes going wide and alert when she saw me coming toward her. "I didn't take anything, honest. I just wanted a spot to relax by myself, and I know there's never anybody in your –"

I didn't let her finish.

Five seconds later, she was up against the wall, my lips covering her mouth. I couldn't wait to start humping her bare cunt before I snapped off my belt and pushed down my pants.

"Roman!" she groaned, soon as I brushed her clit, breaking the kiss. "Holy shit."

Yeah. Holy shit.

I barely had time to stoop down to my pocket for a condom. I had to get the fuck inside this chick, before my balls exploded, before the booze in my system stopped clouding my brain long enough to think.

I couldn't fuck her if I felt the guilt tugging at my heart. And just thinking about the guilt at all pissed me the fuck off.

Sally and me weren't shit. Fuck, she didn't even write me once while I was in the pen, and seeing her show up without telling me what the hell she really wanted poured salt in the gashes she'd left behind.

No woman's got any business doing that shit to me. And the only way they'd get away with it was if I let 'em.

I had to put a stop to it by fucking myself blind. I had to get back in the game, get my cock good and wet, pump my loads into a pussy or two that didn't mean shit to me, and never would.

Thank fuck for Twinkie.

Snarling, I grabbed her pig tails, jerking her head up

over my shoulder while I slid inside her. My hips hit autopilot as soon as her hot cunt swallowed me up.

Surprisingly tight for a whore. It would do, and I'd do her, use her pussy to medicate myself for the night with a little help from Doctor Jack.

I pistoned hard and fast, feeling the fire building in my balls. It took her a minute to fully process the fact that I was fucking her. Yeah, me, the six foot five, totally silent asshole who never had one night with a whore in this clubhouse in all the weeks he'd been home.

Her fingernails wrapped around my shoulders, just below the blades, digging in little by little. These girls were used to getting fucked. Showing them new tricks wasn't easy.

Fuck if I didn't make her come, though. Maybe she blew her gasket on the novelty of fucking me, or maybe it was because I was just that goddamned good.

She moaned my name a couple more times, sucked at my throat, making me growl like a demon in her ear while my hips went berserk. Her ass slapped the wall over and over, and I seriously wondered if I'd put her butt through the goddamned sheetrock.

Didn't stop me. Didn't make me give up a single second. It'd take a raging bull to stop me after this, buried balls deep, the first cunt I'd had in almost two fucking years. The first one I had since...

Sally.

Her name crackled into my fucked up brain like a phantom, ruining it just as Twinkie's pussy tightened like a rubber band around my cock.

Fuck, fuck, fuck.

She convulsed. I couldn't hold back. I pinned her down, straining the wall worse than ever, listening to her breath hitch while my balls throbbed, ready for release.

I came into the condom, trying like hell to squeeze the rage outta my body. But it wouldn't fucking leave. She'd buried it too fucking deep, and emptying my nuts in this whore wasn't doing shit except scratching a temporary itch.

Damn if I didn't scratch it raw. My body slapped hers against the wall 'til I couldn't see, couldn't feel anything except the wave of fire, hate, and frustration rippling through me, but never leaving me as easy as the seed flowing into that sheath wrapped around my length.

Fuck me.

Her hips were still trembling against mine when I pulled out. I let go, watching her sink to the floor, knocked into a sex coma.

Okay, maybe there was a little pride in that. Just not enough to scrub the dirt from my skull.

"Get up," I growled. "Clean up in the bathroom and get the fuck out. I need to sleep."

"Wait, what? You don't want me spending the night?" Those big blue eyes made me wanna punch the wall.

Cruel fucking reminders. That was exactly what they were, dark gems telling me she'd never be the chick I really wanted wrapped around my dick, even if they had a few things in common.

"You heard me. Go." Grabbing her pants off the floor, I threw them at her, and pointed to the small bathroom attached to my room.

She pouted. I watched her turn around and pull up her panties, then the torn jeans she always wore around the clubhouse.

That hollow feeling hit me as I eyeballed her all the way to the door. Before closing it, she shot me one last pitiful look, as if to say *asshole* and *is this it?* all at once.

"Yeah, it's fucking it," I growled back quietly, once the door clicked shut. "That's all I've got to give. You're just another fuck. Everything she should've been too."

I walked to my bathroom and ripped the small door underneath the sink open. There was a third of amber whiskey left in the bottle there. I popped the cap and guzzled it, relived there was still some sweet fire in this world that could numb the bullshit.

Maybe I fucked up giving Sally the cold shoulder. She definitely did keeping her distance for two goddamned years, when every fucking day was a struggle to watch my back and stay breathing.

Prison doesn't give a man do-overs. You either play it careful, work the gangs inside, and avoid the bloodthirsty fucks who wanna shank your guts in the shower, or you leave in a body bag.

I walked out without a scratch. I'd never had much use for all that touchy-feely bullshit about emotional trauma, but damn if I couldn't feel the damage underneath my skin. Prickly, savage, and relentless.

I had to let go. I needed to get the fuck on with my own life. I understood crazy, and being obsessed with Sally was fucking it.

Staying wrapped up in some chick I had a messy fling with almost two years ago was nothing short of downright *loco*. I didn't give a shit how many empty whores I'd fuck, how many bottles of Jack I'd suck down, or how many times I'd feel my dick twitching with a hunger that wouldn't be satisfied by anything less than Sally's hot cunt tucked around it.

I'd screw my head on straight and serve this club. The Grizzlies MC marked the beginning and the end of my entire life, and pouring all my focus into it hadn't failed me yet.

The show had to go on. I'd fight like hell for my brothers before I fought for her after she stabbed me in the back.

And if spilling more cartel blood wouldn't silence the stir crazy ache in my veins, then I'd sure as shit find something that would. Crawling back to the woman I was dead set on walking away from forever wasn't an option.

III: Corralled (Sally)

"Sally! Turn that damned thing off!" I barely heard Norman shouting over the tractor's rumble.

It wasn't until he ran right in front of me that I slammed on the breaks.

Jesus. The machine snorted, jerking to a stop less than a foot away from him – too damned close for comfort.

My cousin just grinned like we were playing a game of bumper cars and waved. "Come on. Get off that thing. We need to talk."

I hoped to God he wasn't going to ride me about coming out here an hour late again – especially when I'd been up with Caleb half the night. My rambunctious baby still woke up at the craziest times. This past year, I'd forgotten what it was like to sleep through a solid eight hours, much less a whole night.

We didn't have time for petty arguments. Harvest was just around the corner, and soon we'd be prepping, packaging everything we could for the market, and then winterizing the place.

"What's up?"

The smile on my cousin's face melted. Crap, now I knew something was wrong. He was rarely this serious, and whatever had him ruffled probably didn't involve me dragging my feet on too little sleep.

"Norm? Is something going on?" I prodded him when he didn't answer.

"It's Greg, our rodeo boy. You know how he spends a lot of time out camping in Modoch?"

Of course. I didn't understand what the hell he was getting at with our best guy, unless…*oh god.*

My stomach dropped about a thousand feet. Had he screwed off too much? Did my cousin want to fire him?

Surely, he wouldn't be that crazy. It wasn't like Greg lit the field on fire or something. We'd be sunk without his cattle experience.

I couldn't take the suspense. I had to take him down from disaster.

I shot Norm a cold look and pursed my lips. "Don't tell me – you want him out? What's he done?"

Norman cocked his head. "Nah, it's nothing like that. The kid's doing a wonderful job when he's actually punching the clock."

"Then?"

"It's what he's seen up there that I'm interested in. The kid's been seeing lots of crap flying at night. Foreign guys prowling around, burying shit in the forests. Those parks are arid and sparse, let me tell you, but they make damned good hiding places because they're so isolated. If he hadn't been up there, I wouldn't have known how to make heads or tails of anything."

"Huh?" Confusion fogged my brain. "I don't get it. What's that got to do with our farm?"

Norman shot me a stern glance, tight lipped as ever. "Walk with me."

I had no choice but to follow him. He acted like he was sitting on the biggest secret in the world, and something about that turned my stomach into knots.

We got in the truck – the same clunker still chugging away after Roman's repair that fateful summer so long ago – and drove down the narrow path leading to our property's edge. We hardly ever came out here.

The fields were no good for growing or grazing past a certain point. This was dead land, and we'd never had the time or resources to till it up and revive it.

"There!" He hit the brake, and the truck jerked to a stop next to a dusty field full of brittle weeds. Norman rolled down the window and stuck his hand out, pointing furiously at the ground, right where it formed a ditch between the rusted barbed wire and the no man's land beyond.

I strain in my seat to sit up, scanning the ground. When I saw it, I felt like I'd taken a turn down Weird Street.

Something resembling a trap door laid in the ground, covered only by a thin layer of sandy Redding dust.

"What the hell?" I popped the door and clambered out, crossing the road, approaching the strange compartment I'd never seen before.

It shouldn't have been there. It shouldn't have been *real.*

Norm couldn't reach me before I crouched on the ground and ripped it open. I had to jerk hard, tugging with both hands, until the pressure holding it shut gave.

The cavern below was surprisingly deep. Dark, too. My eyes needed a few seconds to adjust, peering through the cobwebs and dust.

I didn't see anything obviously dangerous. It should've been a relief, but it wasn't. I reached in, feeling around. The pit was deep, about the right dimensions for a grave, and my arm burned before my fingers brushed the ground.

I slid forward, digging my toes into the earth for support. Deeper, deeper…both hands touched something, got a hold, and pulled. I jerked myself up with a small box, and the rattle inside it said it wasn't empty.

"Shit! Be careful!" Norm must've said it about five times. "You're gonna fall in."

I ignored him.

About a minute later, the contents were sprawled out in a small circle around me.

Old, wrinkled pages torn from an atlas. A sturdy hunting knife. A simple flip phone from the early 2000s, and it looked worn enough to really be that old too. A small booklet was taped to the map. I pulled it off and thumbed through it, seeing a few basic phrases in English and Spanish.

All of them were things like *hands up, down on the ground, don't move, don't make me shoot.* If I had to guess, it'd say it came from the Mexican military, judging by the big blocky text and sharp looking crests on the front and back.

Of course, there was no good reason for legitimate soldiers to be out here in northern California. Everything here was too fresh to be a time capsule, and too weird to be anything official. The only thing that made sense turned my blood to ice.

Cartel. Nothing else made sense.

"Sally, Christ! Be careful with that junk." Norman panted. "Greg already showed me everything this morning. There's no guns or grenades in there, but hell, it'd be nice if you gave me a chance to tell you."

"Sorry, Norm." I looked up. "What's the deal? You're acting like you want to leave this crap in the ground, on *our* property."

My cousin shook his head, his salt and pepper hair bobbing in the summer breeze. "You're damned right I do. This stuff could've been hiding underneath our noses for months. We don't know if or when the owners are coming back. What do you think they'll do if they realize we've been screwing around with their stuff?"

Damn. My heart beat five times faster when his words sunk in.

Jesus, if this was what it looked like, the cartel on the prowl, then our farm wasn't safe anymore. I'd read enough brutal stories to know what happened to anyone who got in their way, or just ended up in the wrong place at the wrong time.

Whoever buried this crap out here wanted to keep it a secret. I didn't know much about the criminal underworld, but I understood men who killed and smuggled for a living would do *anything* to stay in the shadows.

They wouldn't hesitate to hurt me, Norm, or – God forbid – my Caleb. I thought about shadows descending on his crib late one night, all while a dark hand smothered me, pulled me away from my son, an ice cold knife pressed to my throat.

Jesus, no. I can't let it happen. I won't.

Swallowing the lump in my throat, I boxed up everything, and then pushed the crap back into the spider hole. I flipped the door shut, listening to the loud *bang* as it hit the frame.

Norm threw his hands up. "Dammit, Sally, you've gotta be more careful than that! Just looking at that stuff might tip somebody off. We've been poking our noses where we shouldn't, and if those bastards find out…"

He didn't need to say it, and he knew it. We'd both imaged about a dozen brutal possibilities by now.

"I'm just following your example, cousin. You said yourself you'd looked in there before I did. Maybe you should take your own advice before you decide to get up my ass."

He opened his mouth, and then promptly closed it. He hated being wrong, especially when it was the family's black sheep who pointed it out.

If I'd learned anything about growing up here since

Uncle Ralph took me in, it was Norm's twenty years on me hadn't really made him any wiser. Of course, his mistakes were little ones. He'd hit the bottle and gotten a couple DUIs after Jenny died, a tragic end to a barren, strained marriage.

I was the reckless bitch who'd screwed up big time and gotten myself knocked up by an outlaw. That was far worse, and everybody except my dearly departed Uncle made me feel it every fucking day.

"Fair enough," he said at last, deciding to let it go. "Still, we need to be very careful here. This is serious business, Sally. This *could* get us killed."

I rolled my eyes. "Uh, yeah, you're repeating yourself, Farmer Obvious. Should we both go to the police, or do you want me to make the run by myself? I'm not letting anybody here get their head cut off. I'm dealing with it."

We'd almost reached his truck when I said it. Then Norman froze, glaring at me like I'd just said the stupidest thing imaginable.

"*What?* Don't give me that look – not unless you've got some awesome plan from your years of dealing with Mexican drug lords."

My sarcasm tightened his face. "Look, it's not that easy. Going to the police is just as bad as taking that shit out of the ground and pouring concrete in the hole. What do you think they'll *do* out here exactly, Sally? Assign us a national guard platoon to guard the ranch?"

"Of course not! But they'd at least look into it, wouldn't they? Maybe send a few guys on patrol at night to catch anybody prowling around?" I paused and shook my head. "Am I just speaking a different language?"

Norm's lips twitched in a bitter smile. "Yeah, Sally. You're speaking Pollyanna. I don't think you realize we're dealing with stone cold criminals here. You've seen the news. These guys chop entire family's heads off just because they looked at one their goons the wrong way. Greg says –"

"Greg says a lot of shit," I snapped. "He's not an expert anymore than you, Norm. Jesus, I've hung around more dyed in the wool outlaws than any of you. Remember who Uncle Ralph always sent to see the Grizzlies when one of these old rigs needed a repair?"

I slapped the truck on the side before climbing in. Norm slowly joined me, hauling himself up into the driver's seat. Turning his head to face me, he gave me the dark look I'd seen a thousand times. *Oh yeah, the Grizzlies. You mean the biker bastards who knocked you up.*

I'd never admitted anything. I never would. FATHER UNKNOWN was listed on Caleb's birth certificate, and I'd hold to it for the rest of my life.

Especially when it looked like Roman wasn't coming around anytime soon.

Truthfully, it was nobody's fucking business except my own. But that didn't mean Norm and everybody else couldn't put two and two together. Or maybe just one naïve, virgin farm girl plus one vicious biker thug who'd always fuck anything with curves.

I knew the solution to that equation – two big messes.

Two ruined lives, maybe three once Caleb grew up and started asking questions. I lived every sick struggle that came after the equals sign.

"And that's the whole point here, Sally," Norm said softly, after all. "Your connections, I mean. You can help out here. Greg just feeds me information from all his travels and the guys he talks to. But he doesn't have an in like you do."

"Connection? In? What the hell are you talking about?"

His fingers reached up and twisted the key. The truck snorted to life, and slowly we headed back to our work area, away from the borderlands and their dirty little secret.

Norm wouldn't answer. Somewhere about a mile or two down the road, it hit me. *Oh, no.*

No, no, no, no.

No.

"You're talking about the MC, aren't you? Jesus, if you think I've got some special connection there, some people I'd call my friends, you're out of your fucking mind." I had to kill this plan *now*.

It wasn't happening.

"Sally, I'm not saying you do. All I know is, you've been around them before. They know you. And they're also at war with the cartel. Don't you listen to the radio?"

I wasn't going to answer him. Not until he stopped treating me like a total idiot, or a damned tool he could throw around anywhere he pleased.

"You ever heard the phrase, 'the enemy of my enemy is my friend?'" Norman asked.

"Jesus, Norm. Have you ever been off this farm?" I had to stop before I bit my tongue in rage. "Are you listening to your own plan right now? I mean, really fucking listening? We've got prowlers hiding crap on our land who belong to a terrorist gang – and your solution is to invite *another* one here?"

"Come on, you know it's not like that," he insisted, drumming his fingers on the steering wheel. "The club's cleaned up their act from the rumors I hear. They're really helping people in the town now. Yeah, this cartel fight's part of that. They're selfish sons of bitches – they always were – but I think anybody wearing their patch is a whole lot less likely to shovel us into a shallow grave if we see something we shouldn't. They don't go for civilians. You stack 'em side by side with the cartel and tell me who's the lesser evil."

Does it matter when you still wind up with evil? Pushing the thoughts away, I stopped and stared at my cousin.

"Come on. They're not that bad, girl. The drugs and whoring's all over from what I've heard."

"Oh, I'm supposed to know that? I don't really read the papers, and I'm not best buddies with Greg either."

He snorted. We drove on for awhile in silence. Of course, I wracked my brain the entire time, trying to find a better solution.

The sanest one was running into the house, packing my things, and taking Caleb away, then heading as far north as we could possibly get.

We could handle the Washington rain and winters far easier than the danger here in Redding. If only we had the cash.

Money was always the wall. So was my background – or lack thereof. Farming alone didn't offer a great big world of opportunities. And besides, who'd hire a single mother without blood relations obliging them to?

I bit my lip. *God damn it.*

Much as my cousin was playing with fire, toying with quite possibly the worst idea in the world, there really wasn't a better alternative.

"Look, why don't we take the day to hash this out? I'm sure this isn't the night they'll be coming back to check up on the stuff they left in that hole," he said, pulling up near our main storage shed.

"No need. We can't waste any time. I'll do it." I looked at him. "Just give me a day or two to call the clubhouse before I head over there. I'm supposed to give them advanced warning before I show up."

I hadn't called Blackjack last time before I'd marched in and confronted Roman. I wouldn't tell my cousin that two days was the minimum I needed to walk in without screaming, without losing my mind after he'd slammed the door in my face.

"What the hell?" Norm stretched back in his seat, looking stunned. "What brought you around so fast?"

"Caleb," I said. "He's all that really matters here, more than the farm."

We shared a heavy look. His eyes were dark, understanding, sympathetic. For the first time that day, maybe my cousin wasn't such an enormous asshole after all.

A few days later, I stopped in front of the MC's clubhouse gates. None of the prospects recognized me from a couple weeks ago, and I didn't recognize them.

They mumbled something about having to check with a full patch member. Mentioning Blackjack's name gave me a shred of leeway. Probably the only reason they didn't tell me to fuck off.

What the hell's going on? Why all the strange new faces? Was the club running through men like a bad retail job?

I recognized a couple locals wearing the prospect cuts. None of them nodded or gave me the smallest wave. They were all too busy looking tough and manly. Guess they feared their dicks would shrink an inch or something if they said hello to a neighbor.

There were definitely things I'd never grasp about the MC life.

"You again? Shit, I didn't think you'd be back so soon!" The tough guy named Rabid shouted to me when he was only a few steps away behind the gate. "Let her the fuck in."

A couple seconds later, the high metal bars pulled open. I drove through the gap, parked, and got out, staring at the clubhouse with dread.

Maybe I'd get lucky. Maybe Roman wouldn't be inside if they've sent him on a run or something.

"Sally, right?" Rabid said, stepping up to me with another man at his side.

"Good memory. You're Rabid. Can't forget a name like that." We exchanged a smile, and then he pointed at the new man.

"This is my brother, Beam. He's gonna take care of whatever you need inside. I'd handle it myself, but I'm about to head out on a run with our Veep." He started walking toward the big garage where they kept their bikes, but then he turned around to add one more thing. "Give Goliath some hell in there. The poor bastard could use it. Knock some fucking sense into him."

Beam chuckled at my side, leading me toward the main door. My heart thudded at about a hundred miles per hour in my chest, running on a vile anger and anxiety hybrid fuel.

The thought of coming face to face with Roman again turned my stomach. After what he did, growling in my face and pushing me away, he didn't *deserve* to see me, much less speak to me.

We'd already said everything we needed to. He'd proven he wasn't worthy to see his son.

I couldn't imagine ever introducing my boy to his father. For some reason, the cold reality it would never happen hurt like hell too. As screwed up as my family had been, they've always been there for me.

Uncle Ralph bailed me out when I was fifteen, right

after mom overdosed on shitty sleeping pills. He finished raising me, turned me into a country girl, probably the only thing that saved me from following mom's filthy footsteps. Norm, as insufferable as he was, taught me a lot about hard work. And the extended family was always happy to pitch in, babysitting Caleb when I needed them to, or just making me feel like a human being at our holiday dinners.

No, it wasn't perfect. I'd never been incredibly close to anyone. I probably never would be.

That's the price when you're a black sheep, the girl who threw her youth away making a baby with a badass who wasn't fit to be a dad. But I'd be crazy to leave the only kin I had – reason number one hundred and one I couldn't seriously dream about fleeing to another state to escape the hell coming down.

"Shit, baby," Beam said when we got to the door, catching my attention. "I think you're about to be the best dressed lady we've had in this clubhouse for months."

His grin made me stand up straight. He looked me up and down, a slow hunger in his eyes like I hadn't seen since my long lost summer paradise with Roman.

Holy shit. A man was giving me the kinda attention I hadn't had for eons. I couldn't decide whether to smile sweetly or slap him across the face.

He was kind of cute, in his own weird way. Short spiky hair trimmed a little too close on the sides, almost like a rock star, or an overgrown skater kid. His lean, hard muscles weren't hard on the eyes either, even if they weren't as massive as Romans.

He definitely had the biker bad boy vibe, the wild energy that makes a woman want to crawl on the back of a Harley anytime, even if it led straight to his bed.

Hell, maybe *especially* if it led to his bed.

But however sexy he looked, I wasn't buying it.

I wouldn't make the same mistake again. Not with another Grizzlies MC boy. Not when the wounds Roman left on my heart were still bleeding, drowning in salt.

Instead, I straightened my top, trying to make it a little less revealing in case anyone else inside wanted to throw their eyes on my cleavage.

"Thanks," I whispered, the only curt, diplomatic answer that fit. "I don't want to be a bother. I just want to get in, talk to your President, and get out."

"Keeping busy? We're cool with that. Come on. We don't waste anybody's time." He held the door open for me, and I followed him in.

The place wasn't any brighter in the day light. It always looked like nighttime at the bar, where there were a couple guys drinking, staring at the counter as the neon lights behind them cast their shadowy glow.

My eyes flicked to the spot where I'd hurled the broken bottle at Roman. My heart throbbed venom through my veins. It happened weeks ago, but it might as well have been yesterday.

Why the fuck did he disappoint me? *Why?*

This all could've gone down so differently. I could've had a family. I could've had a life.

We headed toward a dark brown door with the Grizzlies iconic bear carved in it. Beam's heavy fist pounded the wood. The big gold rings on his fingers echoed through the clubhouse.

"It's open!" a gruff voice I vaguely remembered yelled from the other side.

Blackjack stood up as soon as we walked in. I hadn't seen him for years, and he'd become even more imposing. Long gray hair hung down his shoulders, and his cut clung to him like a vest of armor, the PRESIDENT tag stitched ominously on his chest, along with several wicked looking symbols only the club would understand.

Several seconds passed before he recognized me. "I'll be damned. You're Roman's girl. Christ, what's he done now?"

Beam's eyes bulged. Thank God we were alone so nobody else would find out my dirty little secret.

"Sally, isn't it?" Blackjck mused, remembering my name. "You're here for him, aren't you?"

"Not anymore," I said coldly. "I'm here to talk business, Blackjack. This isn't about Roman."

His eyes narrowed, and he cocked his head. "Grab a seat. Just you and me."

Blackjack waved Beam outside. I sat and spilled everything, trying to focus on his face in the cramped office. It wasn't easy because my eyes kept falling to the patches on his leather. There were claws and daggers and bright red streaks that looked like droplets of blood.

Roman had similar patches and inks on his chest. But I

never gave them this much attention before. They'd never frozen my blood until now.

Jesus. You were really naive when you fucked him, weren't you? These men handle life and death like it's mowing crops.

Your business is farming. Theirs is blood.

I talked, told him about the trap door, the eerie little toolbox I found in the dirt. Blackjack stared at me with his arms folded, silent as stone. When it was all over and my lips stopped moving, he leaned forward.

"You're right. This is fucking serious. You came to the right place," Blackjack said. "I can't tell you much about what we do, but I'll say this is the first I've heard about cartel activity in our own backyard since early summer."

I nodded. "You can come and check it out yourselves. My cousin owns the ranch too, but he's cool with you guys. Bringing you in was his idea."

"Smart man. He's right, you know. A lot of good people *will* get hurt if they're allowed to operate in Redding, brothers and civilians alike." He paused, gathering his thoughts. "I'll send my boys out tomorrow to check on the spider hole and make sure your perimeter's secure."

"And what about after? Can you have men around the ranch permanently? I need to know we're safe if we're going to be letting your men ride free on our land."

I kept thinking about Caleb. His safety came first, second, and third. If anything happened to him because of my mistakes, my oversight, I'd die. And I'd deserve it too.

He didn't answer me at first. I leaned forward, pressing

my hands on the cool table.

"Blackjack, *please.* I need you on board. If you're coming into my home, you're going to protect it too."

"Yeah, all right," he growled at last. "We'll add your place to the regular patrols I have my crew do around town. We've got a lot in the balance right now. My men have a lot of obligations beyond your farm, Sally."

"I know. I have some idea what goes on in MCs. You're not just fixing Harleys and doing charity runs."

Blackjack's lips pulled up in a knowing smile, and then it faded just as quickly. "One more thing –

there's a chance you'll be seeing him. Roman's my Enforcer, Sergeant-at-Arms for this charter. He's the toughest sonofabitch I've got, and he's my agent in the field when I can't be there myself. You really okay with having him on your clay?"

Damn. I hadn't really thought about it until now, but there was no way around it.

Whatever. I couldn't run from the asshole forever. I'd just keep my distance, stay out in the fields or indoors whenever it was his turn to comb our property.

"I'll handle it fine," I said slowly. "I'm a big girl. I've dealt with worse."

Yeah, like raising the son of the last bastard in the world I want to see snooping around my house, I thought.

"Good. I'll have Beam walk you through the details about what to expect before you leave. He knows all the logistics of a job like this. You still got my number?" Blackjack reached into his pocket, pulled out a cigarette, and lit it.

I nodded. He stuck out his hand, and I gave it a shake. His tough leather palm caressed my hand, thickened rough by decades of doing only God knew what.

"Then we've got ourselves a deal, woman. Call me if anything comes up. Your place is under our protection now."

The weight of the world was lifting off my chest as I stepped out into the hallway, closing the door behind me. I didn't see Beam anywhere waiting for me, so I started to walk.

Damn, I had to find him and get out of here.

The clubhouse was way bigger than it looked on the outside. A long hall branched off toward what looked like a bunch of rooms. The other way led back where I came, past the spacious bar and the eating area.

I headed there first. "Beam?"

A couple guys looked up from their benches. The bald brother named Asphalt stood up, twisting a beer bottle in one hand. "He's back in storage. Told me to send you down there if you needed anything."

"I do."

"Here, let me show you. Fucking shit." Asphalt staggered over his own boots and swore, obviously a little too tipsy from his drinking. He led me to the same corridor by Blackjack's office, where he stopped and pointed. "It's straight down and to your right. You'll see a big steel door. Knock if it's closed. Fucking thing rattles like a tin can. He'll hear you."

The biker hiccuped, covered his mouth, and then left me all alone. Ugh, I wanted to get the hell out of there. The sooner, the better.

The hall was just as long as it looked. Several doors were half-open. Most of the rooms were empty, but a couple brothers were inside others, passed out and snoring in their beds. A little more than halfway to the section where it hooked left and right, there was another door, wide open and lighter than the others.

My eyes caught a naked woman snoozing on the ground, ass up, a massive arm around her with wicked black ink I'd recognize anywhere.

Roman. There he was, buck naked, passed out on the floor with her nasty looking pigtails draped over his barrel chest, an empty bottle of whiskey slipping from his other hand.

My knees stopped working. I jerked to a halt and stared at the unholy sight, shaking my head, trying not to have an instant meltdown.

I knew he was a bastard after our last run in. But seeing this…

Hot, painful tears stabbed the corners of my eyes. My voice hitched as I strained to catch my breath, too damned loudly for my own good. I couldn't flee before he was wide awake, couldn't escape before his huge, naked body stood up and stomped toward me.

"Fuck me with a torch," he grunted, wiping his forehead, not even bothering to hide his nudity as he stumbled through the opening, pushing me against the wall. "What the hell are you doing here, babe?"

God. I tried to cover my ears. He really had the nerve to call me that after…after *this?*

"I'm not your babe, and it's none of your fucking business!"

"The fuck it isn't," he growled. Grabbing my wrists he threw them over my head. "You're in this clubhouse. That *is* my business, seeing how I'm the Enforcer, and I didn't tell anybody to let you in!"

"Blackjack did, and he doesn't need your permission." A tiny hint of satisfaction rolled through me as I watched his eyes widen.

His grip weakened, just enough for me to snatch my wrists away and slide out underneath him. It would've been a lot more satisfying if he weren't standing there totally exposed, teasing me with his statuesque muscles and furious tattoos.

Damn it all. Straight to hell. I couldn't force myself to process how a man who looked so perfect could be so fucking evil.

Just then, the whore decided to trot up to his side, barely covering her breasts. "What's going on, baby? Who's she?"

Roman's head snapped around. I seriously wondered if he was about to break her neck.

"Go back inside. This shit doesn't concern you." Their eyes were locked for several seconds before she finally shrugged, and went back into his room, closing the door behind her.

"You should've fucking called me. The Prez should've come to me. We've got history, babe. You can't just waltz in here like this." He took another step forward, toward me, doing absolutely nothing to hide his fuckable body.

I wasn't sure how I managed to stay angry. Somehow, I forced myself to keep my eyes glued to his face. I didn't even sneak a glimpse at the massive package swinging between his legs, the tool he used to fuck away all my senses, leaving me with a kid he knew nothing about.

And it's going to stay that way, too. You blew it, you drinking, whoring, lying asshole.

Latching onto that fire deep in my belly was the easy part. Holding on? Not so much, but I did.

"Get away from me, Roman. I need to find Beam. I don't need you. Get out of my way and go hang with your new girlfriend."

Anger wrinkled his huge face. "You fucking around? Girlfriend? She's nothing to me. Just another club whore. Something to empty my balls in when I've had a few drinks and I wanna kick back."

"Oh, so just like me?" My voice hardened to a harsh whisper. "That's all I was to you, right? Just another dumb blonde whore."

His nostrils flared. Shaking his head, he lifted his fists, then turned around and banged them on the wall. The insane energy in those huge muscles made it sound like someone fired a gun point blank inside the clubhouse.

"It's not like that, Sally, and you fucking know it!" His

fist shot up, pointing a raging finger at me. "You knew damned well what we started, and you decided to throw it in the goddamned trash. You could've dropped me a line any hour, any second, any fucking day, and you *didn't*. You drove me to these pigtailed skanks warming my bed – you pushed me the fuck away and I'm picking up the pieces. Don't you dare blame me for any of this horseshit. We could've had something. I gave you that chance, and you made your choice. *You* decided we were just a midsummer casual fuck. Not me."

Ouch. Another dagger in the chest, and it sank deep.

There were no innocents here. We'd made our mistakes, we were both guilty. I'd lied, and he was dirty. Tainted. Destroyed.

That wasn't on me – was it?

"Yeah, it's all my fault," I spat. Sarcasm helped keep my tears in check, steadied my voice. "I never cared. You're totally right. I was a cold blooded bitch, just looking for a nice warm dick, right? It was just a summer fling. You telling me to basically shut up and mind my own business while you rode into a situation that could've gotten you killed is *my* fault. Got it."

His rich dark eyes turned about ten shades darker. "Come on. *Come. The. Fuck. On, woman.* You know that's nothing but –"

Bullshit? I thought. *No. Not that easy.*

"Club business." I finished for him. "I get it. You chose what really mattered to you, and it wasn't me. You chose this life. Go live with your choice behind that door. She's waiting."

I tossed my hair, looking past him, into the clubhouse. I pointed at the room he'd walked out of, where the skank was probably in bed, counting down the seconds until he came back and fucked her.

It wasn't just her either. It was the club.

What would things have been like if he weren't sucked into all this? Would I have ever tingled for him at all without those dark inks licking his muscles, without the edge cut into his soul screaming *danger*?

He was the ultimate double-edged sword. I'd only realized too late that both ends were bound to cut me to pieces, unless I threw him away forever.

Roman stood there seething for several seconds. I couldn't believe I'd actually rendered him speechless.

Surprisingly, it didn't make me feel good. What little satisfaction I had for a second quickly faded.

There was nothing except emptiness between us, and even the emotional tension evaporated like dew on a hot morning.

"Sally? Roman?" I jumped when I heard Beam's voice. He'd snuck up behind me, then took several steps between us, confusion spreading across his face as he looked at Roman. "What the hell's going on here, brother?"

"Nothing you gotta be worried about," Roman said sharply, pouring ice on his anger. "Help her with whatever the fuck the Prez said, and get her the fuck out. She doesn't belong here. Next time somebody comes into this clubhouse unannounced, you let me know too. Got it?"

Beam nodded glumly.

Roman turned. I caught one more flash of his chiseled back before he thundered away into his room, slamming the door shut behind him so hard the walls rattled.

"Christ. What did you say to him?" Beam grinned ear-to-ear.

"It's not important. We've got history, but that's all it is." I said, feeling the heat on my cheeks. "He's right about one thing – it's nothing anybody needs to worry about. I'm here for business with the club. Nothing else."

Beam's smiled turned into smug determination. He nodded. "Got it. Come on, I'll walk you to your car."

My quick transit through the clubhouse felt ice cold. Roman should've left me burning hot after screaming in my face, naked as the day our bodies tangled together, leaving me a piece of him forever.

But thinking about Caleb brought winter to my veins. I just wanted to leave this fucked up place forever, forget about the bikes and their bad manners.

Lucky me, that wasn't an option. Thanks to the cartel, I was going to be locked into seeing the Grizzlies patch a lot more, but at least I wouldn't have to come to this clubhouse.

"Will Roman stay back when Blackjack sends his guys to our property?" I asked, as soon as we were back in the garages.

Beam shrugged. "Totally up to the Prez, baby."

Cold. I listened to him rattle off a few more basic safety tips – all the usual things about going out in groups, never leaving anybody alone at night, etc.

I was ready to climb into my car, when he stuck out a hand and grabbed me by the wrist, pulling me close. It was so sudden lightning rolled through my body.

"Just between you and me, I'll make sure he keeps his distance. Don't have a clue what went down with this bastard in the past, but he shouldn't talk to you like that. You're not his slut, and you sure as shit ain't his old lady neither." When he pulled his lips back from my ear, I saw anger brimming in his face, mixed with something else.

Oh, God. The look. I hadn't seen it since those unforgettable nights with Roman, when a big, tattooed badass pulled me into his arms, rocked me underneath him like a toy, fucked me until I was nothing but a steaming, sated mess.

Beam couldn't hide it. And I couldn't hide the fact that I saw everything. Saw it, and shuddered.

"Thank you," I whispered, gently stumbling around with my hand on the car door handle. "I can handle Roman myself, Beam. But I appreciate you for keeping an eye out. Really, I do."

Another understanding nod, and he turned. I started my car and drove toward the gates, while he motioned to the prospects standing guard to open up. Beam's eyes never left me once, locked onto my face as I pumped the pedal.

No lying – deep down inside, being admired by another brutal badass made me prickle, sweat, and flush. He brought back the memories I wanted to forget most, everything that big, rough, tattooed wave did to me two summers ago.

He was a walking, talking, dangerous temptation. Everything dirty and so fucking good I could have all over again, if only I wanted to roll the dice on inviting biker badass number two into my bed.

I drove on, gripping the steering wheel so hard my knuckles turned white. Jesus. Seeing Roman naked was one thing, but knowing yet another brother wanted my panties as trophy?

I wasn't sure I'd survive the autumn harvest. Something told me I'd soon be seeing *a lot* more of Beam once their patrols started, and I had to keep my distance. Even if the sexual tension surging in my blood wanted to chew me up and spit me out.

No sex was good enough to risk another kid without a father. And no man with that patch would *ever* be loving or responsible or worth it.

Deep down inside, they were all flawed. Maybe a few grew up, guys like Rabid, who had a hard-on for one girl so bad they let go of the whoring, the drinking, the senseless killing.

My visit proved they were rare, and also drove a stake through the heart of my expectations forever. I couldn't unsee the bitter truth.

Roman would never be father material, much less my boyfriend. We were too damaged, too hurt, too adrift in two very different worlds. And brothers like Beam were the same, except they'd never miss anything outside the bedroom.

I swore then and there to batten down the hatches and seal them tight. I'd survive.

Everything. I'd keep my son safe, keep the cartel away from our farm, and keep my head while the bastards with the bear patch roared into my life.

I knew I could do it, as long as I hung onto all my good senses. Even if I had to get a chastity belt and lock myself up tight.

IV: Bang, Crash, Boom (Roman)

I fucked Twinkie 'til she couldn't even walk over the next week. She was nothing but a hot warm hole for me, a stress ball with tits and ass and long blonde pigtails. Whenever she whined or asked me about the strange chick who'd given me shit, I stuffed her panties in her mouth, pinned her down, and railed her cunt 'til she forgot all about it.

But on the sixth or seventh day, I kicked her outta my damned bed and picked up the bottle.

Fucking couldn't cure everything, no matter how many times I busted my nuts. Truth was, Sally gave me one helluva kick in the balls without even raising her foot.

Shit, just seeing her again did that. But having her talk back to me, trying to make excuses for abandoning me while I was in prison? I didn't know whether to slam her against the wall, shove my lips on hers, and suck every last molecule of air outta her lungs, or hold her down and spank her ass 'til she gave me a proper apology.

And if goddamned Beam hadn't shown up a second too early, I would've done it too.

Instead, I walked the fuck away with my tail between my legs.

Or did I? I told Sally everything I had to say. I bled and ached behind bars to forget her, and it was only slightly harder having her get in my face.

I could live without her, go on doing the same shit I'd always done since I put on this patch. I'd done it for almost two years.

Serving this brotherhood the best way I knew how was all that mattered. Pussy came and went. The patch was forever.

Easy words. Harder to believe them.

No matter how much I drank, pumped iron, and fucked the closest whore I could grab with golden locks, I couldn't make myself believe shit. Sally haunted my fucking head.

I had to forget. Again.

I told myself I'd get the fuck over it, make her fade like a phantom. Enough time could do anything.

Then I saw her face at night in my dreams, her perfect body, remembering the way she rode my cock and turned my nerves to steel, the fever hit me like a junkie missing his dope.

Yeah, I'd cut Sally outta my life like a cancer. But I'd suffer first, rage and sweat and bellow, the same way an addict does when he's lost a hit that sends him up to heaven.

Next week, Blackjack ordered us to start our runs, the

latest patrols in the endless cartel war, now threatening to bite us on our own turf. Prez split the crew in half. He must've sensed Sally's reluctance to let me on her land – or maybe the bitch said something to him herself – who the fuck knew.

Regardless, the Prez had other plans for me. I rode with him, Brass, Asphalt, and a couple prospects out to the old warehouse, while the rest of the crew took care of playing guard dog at the Jennings' farm.

We had a bigger prize waiting for us inside the run down place where we got our intel. It had been a heavy industrial complex back in the day, now it was more like a ghostly slaughterhouse. We'd skinned more than few sorry bastards alive and paved their carcasses with concrete here, and now there was one more pig on the docket.

"Star talking, Alejandro. That's your name, isn't it?" Cool and collected as always, Blackjack eyed the beat up cartel goon strapped to the chair, slowly lightning a cigarette and taking a long pull.

Fucker sat there like a bulldog. He was a bit older than most of the sloppy thugs we normally brought in, scrawny kids too young to drink, but old enough to kill for their border spanning mafia.

Those shitheads begged for their lives when they realized we were gonna snuff out their short lives of sin. Not one ever got their wish.

Our new buddy, Alejandro, just stared in silence, giving the Prez the evil eye. Asphalt shot me a wide eyed look as I took a step forward, my fists balled into mallets.

These hands were fucking hungry. Since prison, I couldn't shake the overwhelming desire to feel a man's bones snap, crackle, and bleed beneath these knuckles, and Sally's shit last week made the need twice as strong.

"Let's not bullshit. We both know you're here to die, boy," Blackjack said, breathing smoke in his face. "We're giving you one final choice – the kindest choice this world ever offers anybody in our biz. You cooperate, answer a few questions, and you'll go out of this world quick and clean. Feed us more bullshit, and we'll make sure you choke on your screams before the bear opens his mouth and drags you down to hell. Understand?"

Alejandro didn't even flinch. Gotta admit, the fucker had balls. Blackjack's always been an imposing SOB. He'd been a natural Enforcer in the old days. As Prez, he commanded our respect – no ifs, ands, or buts about it.

I saw the Prez's lips twitch with frustration. He pulled out his smoke, dropped it to the floor, and ground it into the concrete with his boot.

"Who's the rat? We know you've got one embedded in my club." Pausing, the Prez locked eyes with the prisoner, drowning him in an icy stare. "You can't save yourself, boy, but it's not too late to save your friends. The sooner we shut this thing down, the quicker we stop killing each other. Your friends don't have to end up buried beneath ten feet of concrete too. Flapping your gums just might save a few lives."

For a second, the bastard's eyes lit up. I wanted to believe he'd talk, but they were never so altruistic. The average cartel soldier was a selfish, violent little shit. They didn't have a code like the average MC. It was all business to them, and their whole damned enterprise was killing.

Besides, I didn't like the energy going on there, especially the way he looked at the Prez like he was doing him some great favor.

Sweet terms never mattered to these fucks. Nobody's ever happy about going to their grave. They either scream for a mercy we'll never give 'em, or fight us 'til the bitter end.

No compromise.

The Mexican squirmed in his restraints, making some noise like he was about to talk. Blackjack leaned down, holding his ear closer to the asshole's face.

Shit, I didn't fucking like this. Two steps forward, and Asphalt started shaking his head, warning me to back the fuck off before the Prez found out I was treating him like a goddamned idiot.

He knows what's he doing, asshole! Asphalt's eyes said. *You're out of line.*

Brass' look was even worse. He mouthed a few words, and pointed to the spot next to him, right where I'd been standing before.

I blew the Veep off. Only needed a couple more seconds to know whether or not this was gonna go how I expected.

Alejandro coughed, mumbled something that sounded like *go to hell* in a thick accent. Then the fucker jerked like a fish leaping up to catch a bug, caught the Prez's ear, and sank his dirty teeth in.

Growling, Blackjack held his ground, punched the fucker in the face. The cartel boy had a grip like a gator, and I had my nine millimeter out in a heartbeat, pressed to his temple.

"No, son!" Blackjack roared. "Don't you fucking –"

Too late. The blast of my bullet going through Alejandro's rotten brain shattered the Prez's words. The dead thug slumped in his chair, and the Prez pulled his bloody ear away, holding a hand to the side of his head.

Asphalt and the prospects surrounded us, staring at the grisly scene in disbelief. Prez looked at me, disappointment shining in his eyes. Brass walked up, and before I knew it, his fist nailed me in the face like a heavy stone.

"Asshole! We were all reaching for his throat, and you know it. There was no reason to blow his goddamned brains out." The Veep's lips twitched, his face creased so angry he looked at least ten years older. "What the fuck you were thinking, Roman? Tell us!"

I turned my back, refusing to say shit. Didn't help that I barely had a clean answer myself.

Why'd I do it? Because my fists were hungry, and the cartel turd beginning to rot in his chair was wasting our fucking time.

"Boys, clean this miserable piece of shit up and take him to the bone yard out back. Make sure he's buried deep, VP. Roman, you're with me."

I fucked up. It wasn't like I didn't know it. But the

Prez was making a big mistake if he meant to give me a long lecture.

Yeah, I'd let my bloodlust do the talking, but I'd saved his damned ear too. The punk asshole never would've cracked, not after twelve hours of torture. I'd seen his type too many times to count.

We could've carved that fucker up, piece by sloppy piece, and he'd still spit in our faces, maybe try to take somebody's nose off too, if we didn't rip out his teeth first.

Soon as we got out back, the Prez threw his full weight into me. I hit the wall with an *oomph*. He'd always be smaller and older than me, but he was one mean bastard when he wanted to be, and no man in this club ever got over the shock of having the Prez get physical.

"What the fuck's your malfunction? You could've saved your bullets for another day, and you know it. I'm disappointed, son. These asshole informants don't grow like plums. You just trashed our best chance this month to find the vermin embedded in our own house."

His voice hit me in a harsh whisper. Angry, intense, and so fucking disappointed. Only the last one really got to me.

I tensed up, stood as straight as I could, and lowered my fists. "He had your ear, Prez. I had to step in. You know my job's to keep order, inside the club and out. I gotta protect you, even when you think you can protect yourself."

"Your job's keeping this club *safe*. If that means pulling brothers off each others' throats, or turning up the traitors who'd like to put a dagger in our backs, you know your duty. You know it so damned well I don't need to remind you. Just like I don't need to tell you I know how to protect my own body – he'd have never ripped my ear off. Somebody would've beaten him out cold first if you hadn't fired that popgun." Blackjack relaxed his death grip on my cut, spun around, and turned back after a minute of collecting his breath. "I thought keeping you away from the Jennings place would do us all some good. Clearly, I'm mistaken."

My guts twisted up in knots. "What? Come the fuck on, Prez. This shit's not about her. That motherfucker I blasted would've strung us around for hours. He wasn't like the other bitch boys who tense up and cry because they've got nothing valuable to tell us. I've seen his type before. He'd let us wreck him before he told us shit."

"Maybe," Blackjack said, narrowing his eyes "Or maybe we would've gotten him so delirious he'd sing like a goddamned rock star. Killing him wasn't your call, son. Unless he's got a gun to a brothers' head, that's mine, and mine alone. You went over the chain of command."

I lowered my eyes. Fuck. There was nothing to say to that when it was true.

"I want you to look at me and *admit* you're having trouble dealing with your old flame. Because if it's not her screwing up your skull, we just might have a bigger problem. No man who's drunk or hooked on the shadier shit deserves to be my Enforcer. And if it's not her scrambling your brain, I'm going to assume it's something worse."

"It's not that. I never touched that shit, and I drink half as much as the other fucks hanging around the clubhouse on a good night. I'm not a goddamned junkie, Prez."

Blackjack nodded, but he didn't take his eyes off me.

Fucker wanted me to say the rest. Admit the way she'd twisted me up in knots, sent me into a fury of fucking and drinking and storming tempers that still hadn't settled down.

I refused. I'd let him slice my tongue out before I admitted how bad Sally busted my balls, leaving me ringing with the aftershocks.

"Okay. We both know what happens from here." Without looking away, he stepped back, reaching into his pocket for a fresh smoke. "Pack up your shit and head out to the Jennings' place. You're gonna trade places with Rabid and oversee the little crew out there on patrol."

Fuck! I wasn't sure if he'd just realized my worst fear, or granted me some fucked up secret wish that wouldn't quit humming in the back of my skull.

I shrugged, tightening the impassable mask I called my face. "An order's an order. I'll be there. Put me wherever I'll make you happy, Prez. Just don't treat me like you're trying to save me from your own damned fate. It's not the same. I'm not getting back with her. The woman hates my fucking guts, and the feeling's mutual."

No, not quite. Fuck if I'll ever admit it, though.

His face darkened, and he gave me a stern look, tearing

the cig outta his mouth. "You're flying very close to the sun, and you're going to burn if you don't stop talking. Of course it's different. I can control my own damned business, and you can't. Your little crush is what's threatening the club's integrity right now. You're the only one standing here who's got to prove you can get a grip, iron out your own ugly bumps, son."

"You think it's really gonna make shit better? Boxing us in like two angry animals?"

"You'll come to terms, one way or another. Honestly, I don't give a shit what you say to her, as long as you give the girl her distance when she wants it. You're there to protect the property and dig into cartel spider holes. Don't pretend there's more here than there really is. And if you start implying I'm moving you around like a pawn to smooth my own past, I'll clock you on your ass. That's a promise."

That was the real trouble, wasn't it? The Prez and I knew each other too well. I'd had a glimpse into his life no other brother had before I went to the pen.

Too bad he had the upper hand this time, sending me onto blondie's turf to turn my balls blue. And jabbing his evil ass about the chick he'd lost a decade ago wouldn't change a damned thing.

Distance? Fucking *distance?* I'd give it to her in spades. I had to, or else I'd crash my bike into her barn. Seeing her was dangerous – worse than when she came to the clubhouse.

I knew the second I did, I'd start remembering how

nice it felt to fist those soft gold locks, how soft I made her perky tits in my mouth, how tight her pussy clenched around my cock each time I unloaded in her...

Fuck. Her body did scary, black magic shit to mine. Eyeing her tits and ass did more than just stir up old lust. Sally's body made me so drunk it hurt not to fuck her, and that kinda blinding, wanton pain caused a man to make mistakes. We'd already entered a situation where every little blip was fatal too.

I couldn't think dirty. I couldn't think about her lips, her ass, her pussy. I had to just buckle down and do my damned job, ignoring what we had, blind to everything I still wanted to do to her.

Not that I expected much outta playing pretend. Hell, I craved her wrapped around me like a fucking madman, but I'd never have pussy that good again.

I could forgive the hot hourglass shape she carried around, but there was no way in hell I'd forget about the woman behind it. She'd spat in my damned face in slow motion for two fucking years while I rotted in the slammer, and then tried to waltz back into my life like nothing ever happened.

No chick did that shit to me and got a second chance. *No one* – even if she made me heave and come like a bull on crack.

I'd watch her through the thick glacier wall between us, but I wouldn't fucking wonder. I'd jack my dick off in every nameless whore in California before I forgave Sally and hauled her into bed again, and *nothing* in this world was gonna change it.

Some old flames are meant to be smothered out forever.

I didn't see her for the first couple days. Not directly, anyway. I made sure to send Beam and Stryker up near the farmhouse. They did the talking when she was out, or else with her stubborn ass cousin, Norm.

Damn if I didn't look when she was moving her lips, though, standing with my boys. I stared across the fields like my eyes were fucking binoculars, following her dark, shapely silhouette across the fields when sun passed across the sky.

For a busy farm girl, she sure made a lot of trips back inside that house, sometimes for hours at a time before coming out and getting back to work.

Whatever, it was none of my business.

Mine was staring at me from the dirt. We'd found a couple more spider holes around their property, and an even bigger one beyond it on state owned grounds, tucked back behind a drainage ditch just beyond a large field.

We found it on day three, just as the bright September sun was gliding low in the sky. Fucking thing was so dark I couldn't see shit without a flashlight and lowering myself into it.

Stryker had to bring me a ladder to get down into it. Predictably, the Mexicans left nothing down there except empty shelves and some stray packaging. I picked the shit up and held it under the light, scanning for familiar markings, serial numbers, anything that would tell me what the fuck was down here.

Kevlar. I saw the familiar word and nodded to myself.

It made sense. This place could've easily held a small arsenal at one time, including body armor.

Only question left was whether the bastards were done and gone. Was this just a staging area for an attack – one they still had coming? Or were we looking at the ruins of an empire they'd already abandoned?

Smuggling up front could do wonders for an assault. Nothing was easier than bringing men over the border, and then driving the long haul to NorCal.

If they had another route for their weapons, or maybe brought them from suppliers already in the States, they'd have all the shit they'd need to fund a kill team to hit us where it hurt.

Fuck. I thought about the rats inside the club. Whoever the fuck they were, they'd be feeding heavy intel the whole damned time, guiding their bullets and bombs straight toward our clubhouse with surgical precision.

That shit only had one solution – we needed to make our move *first*. Snarling, I stuffed the body armor tag in my pocket and climbed the ladder.

Stryker frowned as soon as I told him what I'd found. "Fuck. The Prez needs to get more guys out here. What if there's more? We can't comb all these fields ourselves. There's too many acres out here. You got any idea how big and remote it gets on this property?"

"Yeah, but you're getting ahead of yourself. We've

gotta talk to the owners first. We're dealing with civilians, and the Prez isn't gonna risk butting heads over going into their fields for a closer inspection."

"Shit, you kidding? There could be a whole lot more out here, brother! This one's empty, but what if there's a fucking arsenal half a field away?"

I gave him an icy stare 'til he broke eye contact. Stryker was a hungry new pup with his patch, sure, but that didn't mean he'd get away with disrespecting the top dogs who'd been here for years.

"Call Blackjack. I'll talk to Sally or Norm myself."

His eyes widened. "You sure, Roman? The girl might be less cooperative if you –"

This time, my eyes turned his ass to stone faster than a fucking Medusa. I shot him a look so dirty his lips stopped dead. Stryker grunted, turned around, and started heading for his bike to phone it in.

That's what I thought. I grabbed my bike and rode down the road toward the center of the farm, where they had all the family shit.

It was a clear night, and the high silvery stars were coming out. They hung like shrapnel in the sky, reminding me one wrong move with Sally could shred my world to even tinier fragments.

Fucking hell. Part of me hoped I'd hash it out with Norm, and the other half hoped to see Sally. Shit, *see her?*

No, that was a lie. That part of me hoped to grab her, slam her against the nearest wall, and make her apologize for the pile of shit she'd laid on me at the clubhouse. Then

I'd twist her chin 'til her lips were open, ready to be sucked, teased, and bitten. I'd rob every oxygen molecule outta this chick's lungs, leave her tasting me for the next week.

Big surprise, my dick throbbed by the time I pulled up and killed the engine. I yanked on my jeans and headed for the door, hoping the damned wood between my legs went down before it turned me dumb.

A couple other bikers were there in front of the house. Old Southpaw stood near their garden on the hill, having a smoke. He saw me, nodded, and returned to gazing across the fields.

I'd seen him sling lead a few times before. He was roughly Blackjack's age, and even less spry, but he'd survived club life long enough to know a few nasty tricks. He'd be useful if any cartel parasites were stupid enough to show their faces.

Running up the short cement staircase, I saw the light on in the kitchen through the screen, and banged on it with my fists. No answer after twenty seconds, so I pounded it again.

Nothing.

"Sally? Norm? Come the fuck out. We gotta talk!" I cupped my hands over my mouth and yelled the last part.

Still no movement. Thankfully, the screen wasn't locked, but that shit wouldn't have stopped me when I ripped it open.

It banged shut behind me, and I marched into the house, one hand on the holster near my hip. The

Mexicans were sneaky motherfuckers, and I doubted they'd be able to get through our patrols unnoticed, but uglier things had happened in this business before.

Fuck, it was quiet in the farmhouse. Too damned quiet.

Where the hell was Beam? And Sally?

Something moved outside the window in the fields outta the corner of my eye. I whipped around and saw Norm with his salt and pepper hair moving near the garden, winding up a hose.

One accounted for. Two more missing.

The kitchen opened into a big living area, and at first it looked just as empty as everything else. I turned to head up the rickety old staircase, before I heard the laugh coming from the nook next to it.

I heard a wet smacking sound, recognized it instantly. Finding some cartel asshole with his dagger to my girl's throat would've only hit me a little harder.

My girl? Fuck no, she wasn't. Not with her lips on another brother.

Still, that didn't mean I was gonna shrug and walk away the second I saw Beam holding her against the wall, his punk ass crop of hair flopping as he moved his lips against hers.

Sally's eyes were huge, and they turned into big blue moons the second she saw me. Our eyes locked. Rage steamed through every drop of blood in my veins. She didn't take her eyes off me for a second, deepening her kiss, suddenly shifting her hips into his.

No way. No goddamned fuckin' way. She's not teasing me like this and getting the hell away with it.

"Thieving jackass – get the fuck off!" Everything happened in a blur.

I moved so fucking fast, all on auto-pilot, that I barely realized what my hands were doing before they clutched Beam's throat, twisted him around, and threw him against the fucking staircase. He hit the banister with a sick pop, about the time Sally screamed.

Beam roared, kicked, and twisted on the ground, bounding back on his feet. Okay, so the blow hadn't cracked his spine. Why the fuck did that disappoint me so much?

"What the fuck are you doing!?" They both screamed it simultaneously, like getting hot and heavy had linked their minds or something.

I ignored her and started heading for the fuck cornered by the banister. Growling, he took a predictable swing when I was about a foot away. I caught his wrist and twisted it with ease, bending it backward like fucking putty.

"You're here to do a job, asshole. Not make a move on the woman who owns this place. You step the fuck away right now, maybe I won't have to break your good riding wrist."

"Fuck you, Roman," Beam snarled, pain narrowing his eyes. "Where do you get off? You're not the Prez. You've got no right!"

"Whatever. Keep talking, asshole. I'll let you explain

your broken paw to Blackjack."

I wasn't serious. Snapping a brother's wrist would land me in a world of shit.

But I bent his hand to the limits, making him double over with rage and hurt, all while Sally finally caught up to me, beating on my back and screaming incoherently.

"Let him fucking go, Roman! This isn't your business! It's my house!"

If only it were so easy to ignore her the rest of the time. I didn't let up the death grip on his wrist 'til his knees hit the floor, and he became a gibbering mess, begging me to let go.

"Last chance, brother." That last word dripped sarcasm all over the fucking place. "You gonna be a good boy and behave yourself, or do I have to get papa involved?"

One more tug on the wrist. Beam grunted, then forced his eyes open, staring at me with the beaten hatred I'd seen on men when I remind them who's the strongest bastard in the room.

"Let go. Please. I'll bounce."

All I needed to hear. My hands released and I stopped backward. It took the fuck a few seconds to collect himself and stand up again. Turning, I finally looked at Sally, and she shook her head, tears bright in her beautiful eyes.

It was hard as fuck not to go after Beam. Christ, how long were they at it? Did he feel her tits? Her hot wet pussy?

Everything making me lose my goddamned mind for years? Everything I wanted to suck and own and fuck, even after she'd spat in my face several times over?

"Sally…" She looked away when I reached for her, whipping her head around to hide the tears. "You gotta talk to me, babe. I came in here on business. Honest. Seeing my boy fucking around like that wasn't part of the plan."

"Your plan doesn't rule my life!" she snapped. "None of this does. We're supposed to be done, Roman. I knew I should've taken this upstairs…"

"No, you never should've kissed this asshole. Period. You outta see him at the clubhouse. Our new brother goes through a new slut every week, and you were about to be his latest toy." My turn to shake my head. "Fucking shit, Sally. We both know you're better than a casual fuck."

"Am I?" Her blue eyes cut right through me, laser beams running on bald faced hate. "Casual's all we were, wasn't it? We made our mistakes and trashed what we had. I'm moving on, and you don't have any say. Besides, you want to talk about poor Beam going casual? Let's talk about what I saw *you* doing at the clubhouse, Roman. You're the manwhore. You're the one who came out naked, that pigtailed slut hanging on your arm, bawling me out for some crap I never even did!"

"You can kill the high and mighty shit, babe." Fuck, she didn't get it. "This is all club business. That's why I'm standing here. It's not about us. I'm not letting you ride Beam's dick, and that's got nothing to do with our ancient history."

"No? Then why barge in here and look at me like

you're so fucking jealous you can hardly stand it? I saw the way you went after him, Roman. That's not business – not even *club business.*"

Fuck, she was playing with fire. My fists burned, begging me to grab her, throw her against the wall, and shut those hot lips up for good. I'd show her what a real man could do with her lips, put that little pissant with the goofy haircut to shame for good.

Remind her how much better I am, in every single way, and always fucking would be.

"Whatever, babe. You leave the protection racket to me and feed your horses. My job's to keep shit under control, and if that's making you listen to common sense, or pulling my horny ass brother off you, I'm gonna do it. I really don't give a shit what the hell you think, and I don't need your permission."

Sharp, angry laughter burst outta her throat. "Finally! It's about time…thanks for saying everything we figured out weeks ago, probably longer. What the hell's so important that you had to come into this house anyway? You know you're not supposed to be in here."

She had me there. Technically, none of the brothers were supposed to enter, not unless there was a damned good reason. Beam sweet talking his way between her legs didn't count, and neither did me preventing that from happening.

Too bad. Ignoring her shit, I grabbed her by the hand and walked her over to the nearest couch. She squirmed the whole time.

Didn't matter. I had to sit her down for this, make her understand how goddamned serious shit really was, now that the family ranch had become a viper's den.

"God, you're obnoxious," she hissed, jerking her hand away when I finally let her. "I can't believe I ever cared about you."

I didn't even twitch. I looked at her dead on, ignoring the urge to stare at her huge, memorable tits poking outta her v-cut top. She wasn't gonna rip my heart out, or tie up my tongue.

"Babe, if you give a fuck at all about your relatives, kindly shut the fuck up. Listen." Her cheeks got redder, but she didn't say another word. "Earlier today, Stryker and me found more spider holes. That shit you and your cousin stumbled on last week's not just a one-off hiding place. They're using this whole area as a staging ground for shipments. Probably something that's gonna try scorching my club for good."

The rage lining her face melted. "Jesus. Staging area...what are you talking about?"

"I'm talking about arsenals, smuggling, shit as big as a shipping container. Bombs, guns, body armor, the whole nine yards. All underground, tucked back on your fields, and probably several more around here. They've done this thing before. Last year, just outside LA, they took over abandoned houses and moved their shit in ahead of their men. They whacked eighty percent of the Grizzlies charter down there, and started pushing their shit on the streets before the last brother's blood dried the following week.

They're sneaky sonsofbitches, but they do it seamlessly."

Sally ran a hand through her golden hair, and I noticed the unsteady tremor in her fingertips. Fear crept into her eyes. For the first time since I'd stormed into the house, my heart got heavier in my chest.

"Lay it on me, then," she said sadly. "What does this mean for my farm?"

"It's not safe. We'll beef up our patrols, but you and your cousin are both sitting on a ticking time bomb." She opened her mouth to protest, and I held up a finger. "Don't act like this shit's business as usual. It isn't. With the activity going on right under your noses, you're goddamned lucky you haven't collided with the cartel assholes out in those fields. They could've killed you any day, and they still might, as long as you're both here."

"I don't get it. We can't leave now. It's fall. Having the Grizzlies here so we could carry on was the whole point."

Clenching my teeth, I tried to pull back, tried like absolute hell not to let the growl creep into my voice. Total fucking failure.

"Babe, when you met with Blackjack, you turned security over to us. That means protecting *you*, not just the ranch. I'm telling you to pull the fuck out, and it's the same damned thing I'd tell you if I saw you walking toward a burning car. The cartel doesn't ignore civilians like the MCs – especially not when they're out here in bumfuck nowhere. If you or Norm run into them, you're dead. Simple as that."

We both shared a long look. Finally, her eyes flashed,

denial lighting up her baby blues.

"I'll talk to Norm." I waited for her to finish, but nothing else came.

Okay, now she was pissing me off.

"Unless you're gonna do a better job convincing him to get off his tractor and hit the road, don't bother. We'll handle this. That's why you brought us in. I won't let those fuckers hurt you."

"Roman..." She stopped and pursed her lips, winding up like a generator about to explode. "Don't make me bring Blackjack in on this. He'd give us more time to talk, or maybe help us figure out a way to stay. You don't get it. This is our livelihood. If we walk away now, we're losing *thousands*. This is when our work breaks a profit so we can pay our bills, instead of just sinking money into the farm."

"The Prez told you we're light on manpower, didn't he? Shit, even if we step up our patrols, we'd be lucky to secure your house, and that'd only be for a few hours. We can't leave half the crew hanging around here for fucking days. And if the cartel comes looking for blood, you'll be caught in the middle. You're not getting your head mounted on a stake on my watch."

Her hands moved fast. Before I realized what the fuck she was doing, she had a phone in her hands, angrily tapping on the screen, rolling through her contacts.

Christ. She was really serious about talking to the Prez.

"Put that shit down, babe. Not gonna ask again."

I meant every fucking word. We started off stepping in it the second I yanked Beam off her, but I tried hard to keep it diplomatic. That shit was gonna end if her fingers didn't stop moving.

"Goddamn it, Sally." Lunging, I moved to the couch, hauling her onto my lap while she struggled to keep the phone away from me.

Fuck. The woman was surprisingly nimble. It was easy to forget that when we'd fucked a million years ago, but this bullshit wrestling match reminded me what she could do.

Hell, suddenly, we were closer than we'd been since that last night two years ago, pounding into her, making her scream my name as I emptied my balls inside her, marking her as mine.

She sunk her teeth into my throat when she came. I fucking loved it.

"Stop – stop!" Getting the upper hand didn't take long.

One more pull, and the phone was in my hands. I stuffed it into my pocket, trying not to break the screen, reluctantly untangling myself from her arms and legs.

"Bastard!" she spat, aiming her foot at my chest.

I moved aside just in time. She missed me and kicked the end table instead, hard enough to send the lamp there crashing to the floor.

The fucking thing hit hard, exploding into a million pieces. I stood up, surveyed the damage, and let out a low whistle.

"You've got a fuck of a temper, babe. I don't blame you for being pissed, but you gotta stop fighting me. It's bad for your blood pressure."

The look she gave me caused a double take. I wondered where the hell my blonde, blue-eyed beauty went. Some demon replaced her, and she was gonna fly like a rocket and scratch my damned eyes out if I didn't smooth shit over.

Our ears ringing from the glass lamp shattering must've been the only thing holding her back. There was still a high, grating sound – so intense I needed a few seconds to realize it wasn't just broken glass rumbling my eardrum.

Something upstairs. Something crying.

A baby. For the second time since I stepped into the house, my jaw almost hit the floor.

"What the fuck? You got a kid in here, babe?"

Sally's bitter defeat vanished in a heartbeat. Her eyes went huge, saucer-like, as if I sprouted a second fucking head outta my shoulder.

I turned toward the staircase just as she started babbling. "Roman, wait...you can't go up there."

Can't? Who the fuck does she think she's kidding?

I had to find out what the hell she was hiding. Hundred year old floorboards creaked beneath my boots as I crossed the short distance to the stairs, then took those fuckers two at a time.

She couldn't catch up in time, screaming and crying after me. My heart went nuclear, throbbing pure venom in my veins. I couldn't imagine what the fuck had her so upset.

Actually, I could, but it couldn't be. No fucking way. God wouldn't be so cruel – not even to a bastard biker like me.

Upstairs, I tore the simple white door wide open and stepped inside. There was a cradle, a loud cry, and then the most familiar face I'd ever seen outside Ma's old photo book.

Seeing the kid was like looking into an old photograph. *Holyyyy fuck.*

My heart was fucking gone, not even in the same universe. I reached up and banged a fist on my chest to restart it, keep it from dying outta shock before I met my son up close.

Sally was right behind me, hyperventilating through her tears, panicked as all hell. And yeah, she fucking should've been.

I'd already decided what to do to the bitch who'd shut me outta his life. But first, I had something more important to take care of.

V: Furious (Sally)

My whole world ended the instant I forced myself upstairs and saw him standing over Caleb's cradle. I wasn't sure where the hell I was standing, but it definitely wasn't the same planet I was on ten seconds ago.

I could deal with that one. I could handle the cartel and the club, taking Roman's crap and flinging it back at him, muddling along as a single mother farm girl. I could even take the infuriating way he barged into my life and took control, shaming me, sticking his nose where it didn't belong.

But watching the strange new reality rising up in front of me...how could I even *start* to understand it, much less deal with it?

He knew. My best kept secret, destroyed, wrecked in the blink of an eye by shattering glass and a hungry baby rudely awakened from his nap.

All ruined by one mistaken kiss.

I knew I shouldn't have let Beam get so close. I shouldn't have invited him in for water. And there's no fucking way I should've let him put his glass down, walk me into the other room, push me against the wall and take my lips.

Now karma was coming to pay, and she was a bitch so mean she'd hold me down, make me lick her bitter tasting boots.

"Fucking shit." The harsh words coming out of Roman's mouth didn't sound angry.

They sounded…stunned. For a second, he stood next to the cradle like he'd just found a winning lottery ticket inside it. Everything beneath my waist went numb, terrified to move, anguish setting in as his huge hands reached inside and picked up my son.

His son.

"Fuck, you're mine," he growled, keeping his back to me the whole time. "Mine. My son…"

Tears stung my eyes like napalm. Something about watching the biggest asshole in the entire club go to pieces the second he held the kid reached up through my stomach and gutted me.

Roman was a bastard. An irresponsible jackass. A man who couldn't keep it in his pants for a million bucks.

But he was also a father. And I'd robbed him of that for more than a year.

Slowly, agonizingly, the feeling returned to my toes. I forced myself to move through what felt like concrete, inching toward him. If only I could form words from the desert my mouth had become.

Why wasn't Caleb crying? My baby boy was usually cranky after he woke up, but not now. Nobody except me and the babysitters normally held him. He always squirmed when cousin Norm did too.

The baby cooed, smacked his lips, and laid his head against Roman's palm.

Nothing made sense. He cried with almost everyone except me – everyone! – everybody except for this cruel, inked up, mountain of a man rocking Caleb's tiny body in his massive arms.

"Roman," I managed, calling to him when I was less than a foot away. "Please put him down. We'll go downstairs, talk this over. I'll explain –"

"Explain what?"

Shit. The rumble in his throat was just like a volcano winding up to explode. Slowly, he turned toward me, cradling Caleb tighter against his chest.

"I'm not interested in a goddamned thing you've got to say. You lost the right to tell me shit the second you decided to keep my own son a secret."

Fuck. I couldn't hold the tears in anymore. They went spilling down my cheeks. Apparently for nothing because Roman's face didn't soften a bit.

His honey colored eyes – the same beautiful hazel gems in Caleb's face – beamed total disgust. Hatred. I wondered where to find the closest cartel spider hole so I could crawl into it and die.

"Roman!" Fear caused my voice to crack. "Don't do this. Please, whatever it is you need to say to me, just put the baby down. I don't want to see him upset."

"Upset?" His lips pulled up in a savage grin. "I'll never

upset this amazing little bastard unless there's a damned good reason. Shit, what am I saying? The boy's not a bastard anymore. His father's here, and I'm sure as fuck gonna set things right. I'd say that's cause for celebration – how 'bout you?"

I didn't have to strain to detect the venom rising in his voice. Oh, God. I'd be lucky to see Caleb or anything else again.

With the way he was looking at me, I'd be *really* lucky to end up in a spider hole, and not just a remote ditch where nobody would ever find my body. My heart skipped every other beat, and I stepped backwards, shaking my head, putting my hands behind me to steady my failing knees against the wall.

"I'm so, *so* fucking sorry, Roman. You've got to believe me! I never meant to hurt you. I never meant to keep him away forever. I didn't know you'd get out alive, or what you'd even gone away for. I just –"

"Shut up."

My lips clamped shut. Roman stepped forward, softly stroking his son's brow. The soft, fatherly touch contrasted wickedly with his killer stare, devouring me piece by piece.

With two words, he turned me to stone. I stood and watched, trying to remember to breathe, as Roman walked past. He headed for my bedroom.

What the fuck? Caleb!

I didn't seriously believe he'd hurt the baby, especially after he just gushed all over his new son. But the banging starting in the other room scared the hell out of me.

"Hey! What're you doing in here?" I watched in disbelief as his huge hands ripped my closet open, tearing clothes off the hangers.

Jesus. I imagined him building a huge bonfire out of my things, razing the entire farm to the ground.

I wasn't blind to an outlaw biker's nature. They became total bloodthirsty barbarians under the right circumstances. And yeah, keeping his one year old son under wraps just might flip his murder, destroy, and burn switch.

"Stop!" I screamed, getting in his face as clothes started flying out behind him. Caleb moaned in his arms, and he pushed me away. "You can't fucking do this, Roman. Give him back. Just give me my baby and tell me what you're going to do to us!"

"He's coming with me, babe, and so are you." Snarling, he pushed the baby back into my arms.

Tears filled my eyes as I clutched him close, feeling his softness, praying it wouldn't be the very last time. I had to leave. I had to get out while I still could.

Oh, except Roman blocked the door, kicking it shut. He stood like a sentinel, arms folded. He waited for me to fuck up, do something that would give him another chance to rip our child away.

"You behave yourself, and I'll let you keep holding him. I'll tell you exactly what's gonna happen here, babe. You're gonna rifle through all that shit I just laid out on the bed and stuff it in a bag. Don't give a fuck if it's a suitcase, backpack, gun case, or garbage bag. Just get your fucking shit together as fast as your hands and feet can move. Now."

I blinked, then beamed every ounce of rage throttling my bloodstream at him. No effect. His cold, unmoving eyes pierced right through me, forcing me to turn toward the mess on the bed.

Fuck him for doing this. Fuck him for finding out about Caleb. *Fuck him* for reminding me I had zero control over what happened next now that my worst nightmare was coming true.

With a sigh, I gently put Caleb on the bed next to me and wiped my sore, wet eyes. Roman had already flung my big duffel bag out on the floor next to me, and I picked it up, remembering it used to belong to Uncle Ralph.

What the hell would he say if he saw me now? Using the same bag we lugged along on our happy family camping trips to be taken hostage, without even putting up a fight?

If only. Fighting wasn't an option. Not now.

Roman would rip me apart if I resisted, take Caleb away from me forever. The hellfire in his eyes said his tolerance for bullshit had plummeted to zero.

So, I packed in silence, trying not to look too closely at my baby or anything that would bring on more tears. By the time my bag was half full, I wanted to laugh.

It would've been funny in a dark, twisted way if it weren't so awful. I wanted to laugh at the irony. It wasn't the cartel threatening to ruin my life for good.

No, it was the man I once thought I loved, the bastard

I never should've kissed, much less had a kid with. And now, that same utter bastard had his eyes glued to me like an eagle soaring over a desert rat.

My judge, jury, and executioner, all in one.

"Come on. Hurry it the fuck up, woman. I wanna be outta here by nightfall."

Where are you going to take me? A shallow grave?

I honestly had no idea. I wouldn't put anything past him and the club. The penalty for some random bitch stealing a man's kid must be high, even if Blackjack seemed like a wise and reasonable man. There was no denying I'd wronged his a brother in his club, and he wouldn't be protecting me.

Thankfully, dead women didn't pack bags. That gave me a shred of hope.

When I finally stuffed my last few pairs of panties in and zipped it shut, I couldn't stand it anymore. I turned toward him and flinched. The same icy, hateful stare on his strong face hadn't lessened a bit.

"Pick up the kid. Let's go," he growled, flinging the door open, holding out one arm for me to pass like the world's evilest gentleman.

Women and children first, right?

"Just tell me one thing." I swallowed the heavy lump in my throat. "Promise me you won't take away my baby. Not unless you kill me first."

He chuckled. Throaty. Raw. Infuriating.

"Everybody in this room's coming with me alive, including you. I'm not the demon you think I am. We're gonna work through our issues, Sally. I've neglected this shit for far too long. I tried to walk the fuck away and forget. I'd have never done that if you'd told me the truth, and now, it's staring right at me." He looked at Caleb, resting his head on my shoulder.

"What issues? What are you saying?" Bikers don't do group therapy.

Stepping forward, he backed me against the wall in the hallway, slowly and deliberately so Caleb wouldn't scream. "I'm giving you another chance because you're fucking hot and you've kept my kid safe. I'm not blind. You've been the biggest bitch in the world to me, but that's not a death sentence – not yet. You get *one* more try, babe. One more shot. *Only one.*"

His hot, raging lips touched the edge of my ear. I shuddered.

"We're gonna be one big, happy family, or I'm doing this shit on my own. You'll learn to smile real big and be the best old lady a man's ever had in the entire Grizzlies MC. I hope to fuck you packed something that'll make my dick throb on our honeymoon."

Honeymoon? Family? Old lady?!

I wasn't sure if the lightning in his words hit my head or my heart first. All I remembered was breaking, sliding down along the wall, and sitting there while Roman took out his phone and dialed his guys.

Half an hour later, the older man named Southpaw had Caleb in an SUV ahead of us, and we followed behind him, mounted on Roman's bike.

The crisp autumn air normally caressed my cheeks, but out here, heading into Redding, it was like a slap in the face. Everything burned, especially my fingers. They wouldn't stop shaking no matter how tight I clung to his rock hard abs.

Hating them. Loving them. Sick to death that this asshole's body could still make me feel *anything* except an urge to drive a sharp object into his throat.

I'd never been into the psychic, superstitious stuff, but as we neared the clubhouse, I saw the future so clear it was like a prophecy.

The worst chapter of my life was about to start, and it might easily be my last.

Roman and Southpaw led us through the dark clubhouse, straight to his room. He never said a word, just shoved me inside, took one last look at his son, and closed the door.

"Make sure they stay put. I've gotta go out and get the shit I need to set this place up," I heard him mutter through the door. The older man chuckled.

"Talk to Brass' old lady. I'm sure she knows a thing or two about kids, seeing how her little sis babysits for some coin."

"Whatever. Just get her whatever she needs, brother. I'm gone."

"Hey!" Southpaw yelled back, so loud through the walls I covered Caleb's ears. "What do I tell the Prez if he finds out?"

"Tell him the fucking truth!" Roman yelled, his voice

further away. "We're keeping them safe. The farm's crawling with head chopping assholes. That's no place for a kid. We're doing the boy a favor, getting him outta the danger zone. That's all the Prez needs to know for now."

My kid. I could practically hear him thinking it. Jesus, had he even broken the news that he was a father to the brothers yet? I wonder if Southpaw even knew why he'd dragged us both in?

Shaking my head, my son stirred. I lay back on the biker's thick bed and stroked him, mostly to calm myself.

He'd been amazingly well behaved through this, but he'd need food soon. I had a couple containers stuffed in my suitcase, but as for his favorites, much less all the other things I needed to care for him here…

Damn it. If only I hadn't been in such shock, I would've told Roman exactly what we needed to prolong my imprisonment.

At some point, I managed to fall asleep. Putting in a full day's work on the farm, letting Beam give me a jolt of pleasure, and then getting taken prisoner by Roman completely sapped my energy.

I woke up to the sound of a heavy box hitting the floor.

My hands were empty. I bolted up, only to see Roman holding Caleb, while Asphalt picked up the crib he'd dropped on the floor. There was a woman with them too, a girl with brunette hair around my own age.

"Jesus, be careful!" she hissed. "All the noise around here will upset the baby."

"I know how to handle my son, Missy," Roman said,

shooting her a dirty look.

The woman rolled her eyes. "Oh, please. You know about as much as Brass, but I guess you haven't upset him yet. So, there's that."

I rubbed my eyes and stood up. Everybody turned toward me, as if I was a total afterthought.

"What the hell's going on here? Give me my baby!" I reached toward Roman angrily, expecting him to rip the child away from me.

Surprisingly, he gave in and passed me Caleb, even if he shot me one more look from hell. "Missy's here to help set this shit up, and make sure you two are comfortable. She'll help you get used to clubhouse, make sure you don't do anything fucking stupid too."

"Oh, good. Lord knows I've made enough mistakes. It's nice to have somebody to save me from myself. Is that all, *daddy,* or do you want to tell me how to cuddle my son too?"

Roman's jaw tensed. I nuzzled my nose against Caleb's as the kid snoozed. Meanwhile, Missy laughed, walking toward me, getting between me and Mister Badass.

"Come on, lady. I'll give you a hand." She turned to Roman. "Why don't you go deal with your club business? Brass will be by soon."

Roman gave me one more look, then nodded to Asphalt. "Let's fucking go. I'll be back later to see what's going down."

The door slammed shut behind them, making my little son stir. I covered his ears and pulled him close, returning to the bed while Missy walked around the room, taking everything in.

"Wow. This seems awfully familiar," she mused. With her back to me, I saw the huge PROPERTY OF BRASS on her leather jacket. It was a lot like the cuts the guys wore, except with long sleeves, and somehow girlier. Maybe it was just the size.

"Huh?" I murmured, wondering what she meant.

She spun around, beaming. "Nothing. Sally, right? I'm Missy, the Veep's old lady, and I guess I volunteered to help you get settled in."

"He wants us cooped up in his room? How long?"

"It's not so bad," Missy said with a smile. The uneasy tremor in her voice told me she knew she was lying. "Well…I'll do everything I can to spruce this up. Hopefully it's not for long. The big guy said it's only temporary. I don't think he'd dream of keeping you caged in like this for too long."

"Doesn't sound like it," I said with a sigh, fishing into my suitcase for Caleb's baby food.

"He's a good man. Mostly." Not very convincing. "Look, last time I checked, my old man ranks higher than yours. If Roman gives you too much crap, come to me. I'll get Brass or Blackjack on him right away."

"Old man," I said, popping the lid on some carrot flavored stuff and sitting Caleb on my lap. "You're helping me, so let's get one thing straight – I'm not here willingly. Roman told me about the cartel, and all but forced us here when he found out about Caleb…"

"Oh?" she said, ripping into the crib's box and pulling out an oversized instruction sheet. "Wait, what about him?"

She looked up from the instructions, her eyes huge.

Fuck. Apparently, nobody else knew the depth of our relationship. And just then, I really wished *I* was in the dark too.

"Nothing," I said sharply, the word that summarized everything about my life colliding with his.

Nothing good came from our summer fling. Absolutely *nothing* except for the little boy in my arms, gingerly taking small bites of baby food off my spoon.

Missy cleared her throat. "Uh, not my business anyway. Jeez, why do they make these things like hieroglyphics? Hang on, I'm going to get Asphalt in here to help."

She threw the crib instructions down on Roman's dresser and walked out, leaving me alone with Caleb. I stared at my son, guiding another bite softly into his mouth.

"One day, we'll laugh about this, little robin. I promise."

Caleb drooled a little food and laughed, breaking into a smile. Despite the shitty circumstances, I grinned back, and it wasn't even completely fake.

When I focused on the baby's smile, I could almost forget about being a prisoner. It wasn't hard to forget him, if only for a few seconds, the bastard who had the key to my entire future. And for a second, I didn't have to worry about whether or not he'd force me to be his whore next.

"Sally? Hey, open the fuck up."

It was late. Or was it early?

I sat up, quickly checking Caleb on the way to the door. It felt like we'd slept through the whole night, ever since Asphalt finished setting up the baby's crib, grunting and swearing quietly to himself the whole time, while Missy and I watched.

Roman hadn't returned, and the voice behind the door definitely wasn't him. I nervously crept toward the door, and did a double take when I saw who was on the other side.

"*Jesus.* You shouldn't be here after what happened…"

Beam stared at me, his eyes soft. "I don't care. Roman's not pushing me around. I'm a full patch member, baby, and I'm here to make sure you're all right. Let me in."

He pushed his way inside, and I didn't stop him. Not that he'd have let me. He stopped, folded his arms, and surveyed the room, fixing his eyes on Caleb, asleep in his cradle.

"Damn, there's our little man." A small smile curled Beam's lips, and I followed him several steps over to the cradle. "Is he really Roman's? I've heard the rumors…"

"I don't know." Shame flushed my cheeks.

Unearthing the secret I'd tried to keep buried yesterday was bad enough. Now, it was just a matter of time before the entire club knew. *Then what?*

"That overgrown motherfucker's not fit to be Enforcer, much less a dad. Shit, they outta put you somewhere more comfortable. This room's a goddamned dive." He looked at the open closet, which probably looked worse than before with all the extra baby boxes spilling out.

"What're you gonna do?" Beam reached into his pocket and plucked out a cigarette. "They can't keep you caged up with the kid like a fucking rat. I'll bring it to a vote if I have to. It's a risk, pissing off my brothers, but I'll do it for you."

My heart drummed. I cocked my head and gave him a serious look. Maybe I had a guardian angel here after all, if angels were tall, dark, and wore the world's most ridiculous punk rock haircut.

"Why are you trying to get in the middle of this? I appreciate your help, Beam, but Roman's right about one thing – it's between him and me. Nobody else. I brought this crap down on myself, trying to keep secrets I should've dealt with years ago."

"Bullshit. It's club business now," he snapped. He held up a lighter to the white stick in his mouth, and I raised a hand. "Oh, shit. Right. I'll take this outside for the kid's sake. Sorry."

"Beam..." I reached for his leather clad shoulder, feeling a little lightning tingle in my fingers when we touched. "You're a good man. I don't want you getting into trouble."

He smiled. "Trust me, I know how to handle myself. I'm a full patch member here. Not a prospect anymore. The minute that asshole dragged you in here, you went under club protection. Not his. If he fucking roughs you up or makes you cry, you come running to me, baby. I'll make him stop. He doesn't scare me. Everybody who's been around our brother the past few months knows the fucker needs to be taken down a notch."

I blinked, and simply nodded. There was nothing left to say. "Thank you," I mouthed one more time, letting him out.

I went into the bathroom and washed my face. Feeling the cool, refreshing water on my skin helped soften the living nightmare rising up around me.

God, why couldn't I have waited a couple more years before fucking a Grizzlies man?

Beam was just an underdressed gentleman compared to Roman, even if he was playing nice because he wanted in my pants. I understood him. I could talk to him without feeling every muscle in my body tense up, bracing for the unknown.

Unfortunately, wishes didn't mean a damned thing here. I was stuck dealing with the raging bull, and I'd have to ride him until he either set me free or tore me to shreds.

I couldn't let him. I'd play along. I'd bide my time.

I couldn't help cousin Norm or the ranch now. But I'd never stop protecting my son, guard Caleb from Roman's insanity at all costs.

He'd have to kill me before he ever pulled us apart, or God forbid, infected our son with his wicked, moody, outlaw brand of poison. I'd wear the bastard's brand if he forced it on me, but I'd *die* before he ever muscled his way into Caleb's heart, or into mine.

VI: Taking Control (Roman)

She gave me the evil eye every time I stormed into my old room. Sally looked at me like she'd cut my damned throat in my sleep, so I called in favors and crashed at Rabid and Christa's place instead, giving her and the kid some space to settle in.

Christ, *the kid*.

Her dirty little secret upended my life overnight.

A couple days passed, and I still couldn't fucking believe I was a father. I'd missed everything in prison, and then after I was out, months of my boy's life, hidden away forever.

No goddamned way was I *ever* letting that happen again. I didn't know the first thing about being a dad, but I'd learn. My son was worth it. I'd be a man, raise him as I saw fit, and if anybody got in the way of that, I'd tear their fucking head off.

I didn't need nine months of reading books before I took charge. When I saw that baby cooing in his crib, my heart thudded about a hundred times faster. Two emotions shot through my skull.

Love. And I'm talking about heart stopping, kick your ass to pieces love, love so strong it's like having a jet engine blasting in your chest. I didn't even need the bitch to confirm he was mine – I fucking knew it the instant he looked at me.

A man knows his flesh and blood, and I damned well knew mine. Sure, the Prez would force a paternity test at some point, but I didn't have a single shred of doubt. If he wasn't really mine, this primal storm roaring in my head wouldn't have awakened like a bear coming outta hibernation.

Then there was the *hate*. It crept in about the same time that cosmic, thick love stream picked me up and slammed me down at a thousand miles an hour.

I hated while I loved. I fucking raged. I abhorred *her* for what she'd done to me, and then hated her some more for feeding the confusion frenzy rattling my skull.

If Sally were a man, I would've kicked her ass, and wouldn't have thought twice about it for what she did.

Shit, my hands twitched every time she gave me that dirty look. I wanted to rip her pants off, lay her over my lap, and smack that ass until she screamed, bare minimum.

That wasn't the worst of it. She made me feel like a goddamned bastard every time she gave me those big blue doe eyes, and I needed her in my son's life.

Nothing was simple here. Like it or not, Sally reached out and grabbed my dick by the balls, flung me to the moon, and left me throbbing. I wanted to spank her, make her feel my pain, just as bad as I wanted to fuck her.

I couldn't turn my dick off, even though my angry blood threatened to melt me from the inside out whenever I looked at her.

Hell, I wanted to work this shit out the only way I knew how with a woman. I'd grab her throat, press her against the wall, split her legs apart, and smother her tongue with mine. I wanted to ruin every goddamned pair of panties she had, shred 'em 'til she was left with fucking nothing, no barrier to my cock pounding inside her on demand.

I'd fuck her hard. Fuck so deep inside her she'd be too numb with pleasure to even think about escaping.

Fucking fixed what fighting couldn't. I knew it was senseless, I knew it was wrong, but fuck if I didn't want it.

And watching her make evil eyes at me didn't help one iota. She looked at me like I'd just crawled outta the nearest sewer, and I tried my damnedest to control the killer napalm shooting through my veins every time I looked at her.

She was a bitch. I was a bastard. We matched. And crawling in the sack was the only thing in the world threatening to prove otherwise.

Too damned bad it wasn't the time or place for that shit. She'd just have to be wrong, and I'd remind her while I figured out how the hell to handle her.

No, dammit, I wouldn't cut her out like a fucking cancer, even if the temptation to do it burned me up every night before going to sleep, throttled my brain 'til I drowned it out with a few shots of Jack.

We were at a big fucking impasse.

Prisoner and captive. Mama and papa. Soon to be old lady and old man in nothing but name only.

Sally was too big an evil, two timing demon for me to embrace her the way I always imagined making it official with a woman – and the *only* time I'd ever given it two seconds of thought was before everything went to shit with her.

But she was also too sweet with the kid to kick her to the curb. She had a cruel charm, without even knowing it, a venom in her embrace that stopped me in my tracks. She was just sickly sweet enough to make me wish like fuck I wasn't gonna have to drag her to the altar someday, kicking and screaming.

Damn if I wasn't gonna do it anyway. My boy *would* have a ma and a dad one way or another, and it didn't fucking matter if she hated my guts. She'd fume and hiss with my ring on her finger and PROPERTY OF ROMAN stamped in her soft skin forever.

I'd make her learn to love this life, even if she hated my evil ass 'til the end of time. I'd bring up my boy and bring her into line, true love be damned.

Early the third morning, the door to Rabid's place swung wide open and smashed against the wall. I bolted up, reaching for my nine millimeter. I lost the urge to shoot as soon as I saw it was the Veep, but he was heading toward me with a fury like no other.

"You fucking *asshole.*" I got on my feet before he

crashed into me, locking his strong hands around my throat.

He was pretty powerful for a boy several years younger than me, and not as well built, but my neck was still too thick for him. He caught me by surprise and I choked, then began pulling at the vise-like fingers digging into my neck, trying to squeeze me out cold.

"Veep? What the fuck!" I snarled.

Rabid burst into the room, Christa looking nervously behind him, over his shoulder. "Jesus Christ, somebody's gonna get killed. What the hell's he done to deserve this shit?"

"You knew about the kid too, didn't you?" Brass roared, momentarily flipping his hell filled eyes to his best friend. "His goddamned kid, cooped up with the girl in our cocksucking motherfucking clubhouse!"

Rabid's fingers pinched tighter. So rough they really had a chance at choking me out if let him. 'Course, I moved my fists down his wrists, ready to snap his hands and take him outta riding commission for a few weeks if he tried.

Let fucking go, VP. Don't make me do it.

Those two thoughts thundered in my head over and over, and the oxygen deprivation blurred whatever the hell the two men were saying. Then, in one last savage rush, he let me go, shoving me against the wall.

"The Prez warned us about having civilians floating around the clubhouse, and you go and drag your big, dirty secret in while we're in the middle of a war!" Brass' stiff finger shot out like a dagger, aimed at my chest. "I *knew* you were hiding something all these months. It's always the strong, silent types who fuck us over with their drama. Hell, did you walk out on her when she came crying for you at the bar? Is that why you're treating her like she's a fucking dog?"

Fire brushed my veins liked sandpaper. The asshole roaring in my face didn't have a damned clue about anything.

It took every ounce of willpower inside me not to grab the Veep, hold his head in one hand, and bounce my fist off his face 'til he was nothing but a bloody mess.

"I didn't know 'til a couple days ago. She fucking hid it from me the whole time I was in the pen, tried to keep my son under wraps..." I was about to open up on his ass, lay into him for practically accusing me of fucking over the club.

But Christa was still staring outta their bedroom, the scars on her cheeks mirroring the pleading look in her eyes. *Guys, get it together. Don't wreck the house. Please.*

"Whoa, Jesus, guys. Calm the fuck down! One at a time." Rabid took one look at his nervous old lady and stepped between us, spreading his arms wide to keep us separated. "If you start throwing punches, I'm pulling you both outside. This is my house."

"Fine. Here's the way it's gonna happen," Brass said, staring through my soul. "You're gonna get your new baggage moved into a real apartment by the end of the day, and then you're making a decision about how the fuck you're handling this without making it a problem for the club."

"Already did," I growled. "I'm not the fucking idiot you think I am. I'll need a day to talk shit out, get my brand on Sally. The apartment thing'll happen later this week. Not today."

Brass flashed me a wicked smile. Rabid reached around his neck just in time, pulling him back before he could jump me.

Grim satisfaction thudded in my heart. It was weird and twisted watching the two blood brothers fighting over me.

They weren't really related, of course, but Rabid and Brass were tight. Still, the boy who owned this place owed me for backing him over Christa's dust up with the assholes up in the Klamath charter, the same situation that led to her wearing his brand.

Shit, speaking of the chick...it was Christa's turn to get between us. The guys stopped fighting as soon as they saw her in the way, and she shot us all a stone cold glare that could've brought an early winter.

"I'll watch your kid, Roman. Take care of your business. We don't need to fight over this." Rabid looked at her, shook his head, and then shot me an evil look. Probably pissed that his girl was sticking her neck out.

"Baby, you don't gotta get your pretty head in the middle of –"

"Nonsense," the redhead said, a sweet smile vanishing the scars on her cheeks. "I've got plenty of time in my tutoring schedule before the new bar opens up in town. Just tell me where you need me."

I thought for a minute, then nodded. Having Caleb in her hands was second best to Missy or Jackie, and as much as the little prince was growing on me, having him outta the way for a few hours would let me take care of business.

I told her to come by the clubhouse with me in a couple hours. She walked off to the kitchen, humming to herself, while Rabid slumped down in the nearest chair, running a hand over his tired face.

"Fuck. One day, this club'll get a moment's peace…one day."

Not while we're fighting the cartel, and disgruntled charters keep trying to pin our hands behind our backs, I thought. The club's predicaments had shitty odds, but we'd been dealing with those from the very beginning, and no man standing here was stopping now.

"We'll get there someday, Rabid," Brass said, turning his eyes to me. They were a little less pissed than before. "You get your shit together, brother. Looking after an old lady and a kid's no fucking joke. You've got a lot of explaining to do."

"I already told you everything I know. Soon as I found out, I took action, the only thing any of us would do if they found out some bitch was hiding a kid. Excuse me if I've been too fucking busy, running my ass off, to fill everybody in on every damned detail."

"We're cool as far as I'm concerned." Brass paused, an arrogant smile tugging at his lips. "It's the Prez you're gonna have to explain this shit to."

Without another word, the Veep slapped his buddy on the shoulder, then spun around and walked out. A minute later, we heard his motorcycle rumbling to life outside, and then fading away.

Rabid gave me a sympathetic look, and I turned my back.

Fuck it. I didn't need anybody's good karma to protect this fucked up family I didn't know I had 'til I walked into the farmhouse.

I'd find a way to lock shit down and clean up nice, even if it meant I'd have to walk through miles of hell to get there.

Blackjack's face tightened. The old buzzard slicked his long gray hair back the longer I talked in his office, telling him all about how I lost my shit and decided to make a move the second I got upstairs, after I'd thrown Beam off her.

"Christ, son. What's it going to take for you to grow a brain?" Blackjack growled, soon as I was finished.

"Everybody getting outta my way so I can handle my own shit, for starters. I don't need the club's help on this. It's my problem, Prez."

"Bullshit." Blackjack stood, clenching his lip white as the old bullet wound in his leg burned. "We're the only family you've got. Unless maybe you introduced your new woman and boy to your mother before us?"

Fuck. Ma.

I hadn't said shit. I could barely imagine how I'd break the news to her.

Blackjack nodded, satisfied and right. Like he always was.

How the fuck did he do it? Was it just age that gave him some eerie way to read a bastard's mind?

"I'll leave that up to you. What I can't take a hands off approach with is this clubhouse, and every inch of territory we control outside it. I'm disappointed, son. You could've brought this to me right away, before you decided to pack them up in your room."

I threw up my hands. "Fuck, Prez, I told you. I'm working on it. There wasn't time for –"

"Bullshit!" His fist hit the desk so hard I suppressed a jump. "There's always time to do your job and report things you know damned well I need to know about."

Fucker had me by the balls. I looked at him, flexed my fists, and nodded. "You're right."

"It's not about being right. It's about making everything crystal fucking clear while the stakes are higher than ever for this club, including *everyone* who's tied in with a full patch member. Here's what's going to happen."

Shit. Who the fuck had I pissed off to have everybody in the world aiming those words at me?

I blinked. At first, I thought I'd zoned out, missed something the Prez said, but he'd paused. Too deep in thought to continue lecturing my sorry ass.

"No. Giving it to you point by point won't work. Some things, you've got to figure out for yourself, son. It's your turn." He flattened both hands on the desk, using it as leverage to lean over, staring at me like a hungry vulture. "You tell me – how're you going to fix this for the club?"

"I'll have 'em moved out by the end of the day. Rabid's old lady is gonna play babysitter, so that'll help." Fuck, the look on the Prez's face wasn't impressed. "All right, you really wanna know, Blackjack?"

I stood up 'til I towered over him, turning the tables. I respected the Prez, but his question cut deep, and if he really wanted to fucking know, I'd ram those answers straight down his throat.

"I'll sew this shit up tight, same way I would've done years ago if I'd known there was a kid in the picture. I'll claim her. Brand her. Marry her. Move her the fuck in and make her a proper wife, a good old lady. She's *mine*, dammit, and that makes her my damned problem too."

"You think it's going to be easy?" Blackjack whispered.

"Fuck, no. It's gonna be like crawling over broken glass. Shit, I'll be lucky if I'm not going half as gray as you after a year or two. But I'm gonna make it work. I fucking gotta. You know my old man died defending this club."

"That's right," Blackjack said. "Wheeler died defending his family. Both of them."

"And I'd do the same thing in half a fucking heartbeat. I'll die for this club, die for my kid, die for her – even after she's fucked me over hard. I'm a man, Prez, and she's my woman, right or wrong. I don't give a shit if she doesn't love me. I'll make her. I don't know a damned thing about raising kids, but I'll learn. I'm gonna do this right, and nobody's gonna stop me. Not even the club."

He cocked his head, as if my little challenged amused him. "I'm not the enemy, son, and you know it. You've got my support."

He reached for the ashtray across the desk, a huge silver tray with our roaring bear stamped inside it. I started to relax, only a little. Had I actually passed his bullshit test?

"Are we done here?" I asked.

"I wouldn't let you walk if we didn't have an understanding," he said, pulling out a smoke and lighting it. "You won't let this become a bigger issue for the club, and I'll hold you to it. Now, get the hell outta my office and go give that sweet thing a decent place to stay. And if I hear anything about you fucking her up, doing anything that makes her run, you can bet your ass I'll haul you back in here. I'm trusting you to figure this shit out with your words – not your fists. You can't muscle your way out of this one. You've got to use your brains, son. I know you've got 'em, otherwise you wouldn't be wearing the Enforcer patch. Prove me right."

I nodded, and so did he. Yeah, we had an understanding. Now, everything hinged on striking the perfect balance between Sally and my club.

"Let's go, babe. We're leaving."

She didn't wanna come with me after we dropped off Caleb with Christa for a few hours. Too damned bad. I took her by the hand and made her walk, clenching her hot little hand in mine.

Fuck, even when Sally wanted to gouge my eyes out, the chick was hot as fuck. I hated the way she caused my prick to jump every time she shot me those *fuck you* eyes.

Yeah, fuck me.

Fuck me for watching her standing there in short heels and a skirt, a conservative top that couldn't conceal those tits from my eyes if the fabric was made outta stone. Fuck me for trying to keep the hate fires going while she flicked an angry tongue over her lips, trying to hold back from laying into me.

Sooner or later, I knew I'd be laying into her after she got my brand stamped in her flesh. I didn't give a single shit if she hated my guts and then some.

Just like I told the Prez – I'd *make* her love me. I'd make us one big happy family, husband and wife, badass and old lady, or I'd be in a fucking coffin trying. I'd turn her *fuck you* eyes into *fuck me* gemstones and watch her slide down to her knees, my fist in her hair, growling while she begged to suck my cock.

"Let's get this over with," Sally snapped, trotting past me toward the garages.

A few minutes later, she was on my bike, her little fingers digging into my abs hard enough to make me feel it. She held on like a woman grabbing a sharp cliff because it was the only thing that kept her from falling to her doom.

Like it or not, I was saving her, whether she fucking knew it or not.

Holding her up. Making damned sure she never tumbled back to earth with my son in her hands, impaling them both on the cartel's blood red knives.

Fuck.

At the tattoo shop in town, we met this skinny freak covered from head to toe in ink like a goddamned alligator's scales. He did good work on our crew and several of our old ladies, and he had Sally's shirt off in no time, scrawling PROPERTY OF ROMAN on her lower back.

Perfect place to see it when I'd be pounding the fuck outta her in the future. She refused to give me much input on the brand going on her skin, so I chose everything myself.

Thorns around the side. A dark butterfly on one corner, spreading its wings, the only thing she fought me on because I wanted a crow on her skin at the start. We compromised with the bug, and I had to admit, it looked damned good.

When it was all over, she snatched the fabric back over her skin, sat up from the bench, and glared. Ink boy smiled at me, an awkward little sparkle in his eyes.

I nodded, reaching for my wallet, and left it at that. He didn't need to know shit.

Something about watching his hands all over my woman made me fucking pissed. No, it didn't matter that she wasn't mine yet neither.

If it took years for us to break down and fuck, I'd never let another man put his hands on her again. The whole damned world was bound to know what we were soon, and she wouldn't be moving outta my sight without a branded jacket on her shoulders to match the stamp I'd just given her above the ass.

"Take me home," she muttered, as soon as we stepped outside and headed for my bike.

"Cheer the fuck up. It looks awesome, Sally. I got you the best damned ink money can buy here in town. You've gotta be the only girl in the world who gets upset about looking hot."

She shrugged, looking sadly at the sidewalk. Anger and disappointment shot through my chest, as if the shit swirling around inside her somehow escaped and infected my sorry ass.

I wasn't fucking stupid. I got it. I was taking her on a whirlwind ride my way, the *only* way she left open after I blew her cover and walked into my son's life for good.

She'd figure it out in time, or I'd twist her head 'til she did. I wasn't fucking letting up on this girl, or my idea of weaving some kinda real family from this chaos.

We tore down Redding's streets. I couldn't stop wondering just how many drops of blood and tears it'd take to get us to that place I imagined.

"What the hell is this?" she said, stepping off her bike in front of the house tucked back in the 'burbs.

The street was just as quiet as I'd seen this morning, before I hit the clubhouse, and that was a good sign.

"Your only chance to look at this place and let me

know if you wanna settle here or bounce. You'll tell me more about this than you did about the ink, or I'll make this decision for you too." I took her helmet and watched her eyes widen. "I'm giving you *one* chance, babe."

"I already have a home with Caleb and Norm. I don't need a new one."

"You're not setting foot there again 'til this cartel business is case fucking closed, babe. Maybe not even then. I'm gonna be around to protect my family, wherever you end up. Don't make me explain it to you again."

She frowned, sulking. I couldn't hold back. We'd only have a few quiet minutes before the landlord pulled up to show us around, so I had to do everything I could to make her smile before then.

I reached out, cupped her chin with my fingers, and pulled her head up to look at me. "It's gonna be fine. You will be too. I'm not the fucking monster you think I am. You lied to me, babe, and I can kinda see why you did. I fucking hated it. You and the kiddo are coming with me, wherever the fuck I go, whether you like it or not. But I'm gonna make this shit as safe and comfortable for you as I can. Don't you get it?"

For a second, her face softened. Then her cheeks flushed red and her features crinkled. She ripped her chin outta my hands and angrily hopped off the back of my bike.

"Go to hell. You'd better hope this place has a few more bedrooms so you can sleep on the floor."

Sweet. Fiery. Bitch.

She turned her back and started heading for the house, and I sat out there waiting for our man. I fucking hated this shit. Damn if I didn't watch her round ass moving underneath that skirt every step she took, wagging those globes in front of me like candy she wanted to keep to herself.

Damn if I'd let her be that greedy. *Fuck* if I'd let her keep me from busting a hole in her life and taking everything over.

She was mine the instant that brand went on her skin, and once I took hold, I never let go.

The tour went fast. She tried like hell not too look at me. My eyes were all over her as the old landlord with the potbelly prattled on, talking about all the features that were supposed to wow us.

It was a decent place.

Still, the jacuzzi didn't mean shit to me 'til I could pull her in and fuck her senseless. Neither did the remodeled kitchen, unless it meant her smiling at me with honey instead of vinegar, preferably wearing an apron and nothing else.

My dick definitely had an inverse relationship to her pissing me off. The worse it got, the harder I wanted to fuck her, imagining all the ways I'd strip her down and slam into her hot wet cunt in this house.

I'd fuck her in every room 'til she smiled at me with love in her eyes. I'd screw the bitch right outta her, mark every room with our rough scent, watch her convulse all over me in the goddamned grass if I had to.

I'd never had a place this big, even though I could afford it for a long time. Plus there was a nice big yard for my kid to play in, assuming we put our stakes down here for a few years. That had to count for something.

When the man brought us back to the living room, he looked at us both with an easy smile.

"Well, what do you think?"

"We'll take it," I said, fixing my eyes on Sally. I didn't see any reluctance in her bright eyes. "You said over the phone it's move in ready now, right?"

"You can sign the lease today!" he said excitedly, waving us out to his truck for the papers. "Should have the keys for you by tomorrow. I assure you, it's a great place to raise a family."

"Yeah, it is," I said with a smile, looking at Sally again. "Don't you agree, babe?"

"Maybe."

The landlord beamed. My eyes hit her face like a goddamned laser beam, searching for that sass she was giving me before. Her tone was softer, and there wasn't as much tension lining those soft cheeks I couldn't stop thinking about turning bright red as I pounded her to orgasm harder than she'd ever come in her entire life.

I'd already had that pussy a couple dozen times. So why the fuck couldn't I stop my dick from thumping like it knew it was gonna sink into a virgin?

I'd end up between her legs one way or another. If she was really accepting this place, opening herself to *me,* then

I'd be buried balls deep a lot sooner than I thought. I'd pull her into the life I wanted with Caleb.

Day by day. Kiss by kiss. Fuck by fuck. Kicking and screaming.

She became *mine* in more ways than she could even imagine the instant my ink bled into her skin. And once a man in this club claimed anybody, it was damned well forever. We'd never had a fucker kick his old lady to the asphalt since we toppled the old Prez, Fang, and I sure as shit wasn't gonna be the first.

I watched her lean on the hood of the landlord's SUV and sign the lease, before he picked it up and passed it to me. "Here you are, sir."

I ripped it outta his hands and slammed the paper on the metal surface. "Just give me the fucking pen. You know how much extra I'm paying on this place to skip the credit check."

VII: No More Fooling (Sally)

Moving day came with a bright September haze.

Not that I did much moving for the first few hours. I brought Caleb into the house and it took me awhile to calm him down. All this moving around, meeting strangers, passing our days in the strange, noisy clubhouse, had clearly overloaded my poor baby's senses.

I sat in the spare room upstairs, empty except for a rocking chair Roman brought up, staring out the window as he hauled in huge boxes and furniture. Asphalt was the only one there to help, but Roman moved with the strength and energy of a whole moving crew.

Then Norm called. I bit my lip, tensing with my finger on the phone's button. They club hadn't taken it away from me like they did with most of their prisoners. I guess I'd been extra cooperative – and what else could I do except swallow their orders whole?

I tapped the connect button, and Norm unloaded.

"Sally, are you out of your fucking mind? I get maybe going away to that clubhouse for a couple days after the bastard all but dragged you out. But our place is your damned *home*. Not with him. I don't give a shit what they keep saying. I'm not going, and neither should you. That man, Stryker, told me I should've been gone days ago to avoid getting my head chopped. I don't care. I'm not going fucking anywhere, and I can't believe you rolled over for these biker idiots."

"These idiots *are* the only thing between us and a Mexican blade in the middle of the night. Maybe worse." I gathered my breath and sighed. "It's too dangerous, Norm. Don't be a stubborn jackass. You really should get out of there. I know it's hard, I know it's not ideal, but you're going to get yourself killed. This isn't just about me either. I can't have my son living in a place that isn't safe."

Norm laughed, fast and shrill. "Safe? You gotta be kidding! You think you're safe living with that fucking biker? Do you even *know* what those guys do in their spare time?"

"Mostly drink a lot. Sometimes chase skirt."

Or sometimes take a girl prisoner, slap a tattoo on her, and call her 'mine,' I thought.

"Nothing's funny about this shit, Sally. Stop screwing around."

"I know. And I don't want you getting hurt." I paused, listening to the tremor in his breathing. "Norm, we have savings in the business account. We can take the loss this season. There's no need to put yourself in harm's way just to work for money we don't absolutely need."

"You think I don't know that?" He sounded so hurt. "Jesus, Sally. This isn't about taking a loss. These biker assholes obviously can't protect this place like I thought. I'm staying here. I'll have my gun, I'll have my guys, and we'll fill the gaps the MC can't cover. I'm not gonna let some drug dealing bastards roll up and torch my old man's farmhouse. It's been in this family for a hundred years. I won't be the coward watching it burn. We've grown up here for generations, and I owe them better than turning tail and coming home to cinders. My wife's ashes are here."

"Norm…please." Tears filled my eyes.

Jenny died before Uncle Ralph brought me in as a team. It took years for my poor cousin to shake off the loss, to function as a human being again, and now he'd fallen back into his grief. He sounded just as shocked, weak, and stunned as he had after her death.

"Don't. You're welcome to come home when you're ready. If I've got to protect everything this family's ever worked for, everything we've ever had, then I'll do it alone. I don't need you."

The line went dead. I dropped the phone on the floor and walked over to the crib, staring at Caleb. I tried my best not to let my heart stop, blinking away the harsh tears building in my eyes.

Every compromise I could've possibly made was bad. I had to give up something – just like I had to give myself to the bastard pounding his way up the front steps outside.

I watched him through the window. Roman handled the massive coffee table without even breaking a sweat. His muscles were fully flexed, making him look even huger than usual. Hotter too, much as I didn't want to admit it.

Hot, angry, forbidden heat stormed in my veins. The little flashes of fire that told me I *wanted* him were the worst.

It wasn't the first time I'd sensed it. I felt it on his bike, the road purring underneath us, every nerve in my body humming to match the speed of my heart. My body couldn't deny there was an attraction.

There always had been. There always would be.

How long before I let his drinking, whoring, cursing lips touch mine? Even if he agreed to sleep in another room, how long would it be before I gave into my long starved urge for a man's touch?

I shuddered.

A huge crash outside my door brought me back to my senses. I popped the door and looked out into the hallway.

"Cocksucking bastard motherfucker!" The box of toys Asphalt had dropped down the stairs on the landing busted open, strewing its contents out around his boots. He looked like he was about to have a stroke.

"Do you need a hand?" I asked, folding my arms.

He looked up, and the anger in his beady eyes melted into shame. "Nah. Big boy doesn't want you on your feet, throwing out your back going up and down these stairs, carrying all this shit."

"He really said that?"

"He says a lot of shit, and there's no arguing about this. Let us do the work, old lady," he growled, reminding me what I'd become. "That's what brothers are for."

Maybe he had a point, not that I liked being shoved to the side by pure testosterone. Like it or not, I was being forced into the MC's machine now.

I woke up late from a nap, after dark. My heart sputtered as I checked the time, and realized I should've fed Caleb a couple hours ago.

"Shit." The house was quiet.

I walked out of the bedroom and into his room, only to find Roman there, an empty jar of baby food at his side. He sat on the floor, holding the kid – a strange contrast with such a giant, rough man and a tiny baby in his arms.

"Roman?'

He turned around slowly with a finger pressed to his lips, warning me not to wake the sleeping boy in his arms. His gentle movements sent shock and sadness through my veins. I'd never seen him like this before, and it scared me because I didn't know how to react.

Jesus. What was I supposed to think? It was like they were meant to be together, and I'd kept them apart, delayed something beautiful and natural by being the most indecisive bitch in the world.

I wasn't ready to whack myself across the head. But I had to consider the possibility that maybe, just maybe, I was wrong.

Roman might be a drunken cowboy on a steel horse, and a bastard to me, but could he be a good father after all?

Instead of fishing for an answer, I swallowed the lump

on my throat, bridging the distance between us. I kneeled on the floor next to him, running my fingers softly through Caleb's little crop of hair. It was getting darker by the day. He'd *really* look like Roman in a few more years, and I wasn't sure how the hell to feel about that.

Surely, it couldn't be worse than the giant in his leather cut staring right at me.

"You seriously fed him?" I asked.

"Yeah. Went down easy too. It's almost fun when he stops fussing."

"Well, let's put him to bed," I said, reaching for the boy and pulling him out of the biker's arms as gently as I could. Roman stood up and followed me.

We took a moment, staring at the little man we'd created as he turned over. I wasn't sure what the hell we were doing, but I couldn't ignore the fact that it felt like a real family moment. Almost.

If only he hadn't treated me so shitty. If only I hadn't cut him off for almost two years. If only the cartel hadn't come and the MC wasn't so vicious. If only I wasn't born so none of this would've happened.

"Babe, you okay?"

No, goddamn it. I wasn't. I'd been living for about a week with the risk of every word striking my ears triggering tears, and it was starting to get *really* exhausting.

"I'll be fine. It's just a long day."

"Yeah, that's moving for you. Want me to finish putting your bed together, or what?" A sharp glint entered his eyes.

Do you want to bury the hatchet by fucking all night? That was what I heard behind his words, and my whole body flushed accordingly.

"Jesus, no!" It came out way more forcefully than I wanted, and he blinked in surprise. "I mean, I've still got my sleeping bag. I'll be fine. We can get it together tomorrow and start putting things in their places."

"Sounds like a plan."

"What bedroom are you taking tonight?" I asked, genuinely curious, and also a little afraid he was going to demand mine.

"This one. I'm gonna spend the night with my son. I'll crash on the floor. Every fucking minute counts when I've missed so much." He said it softly, but it still hurt like hell.

"Okay. You know where to find me if he causes any trouble, or you need help." I started heading for the door, but before I could get out, he grabbed my wrist.

"Don't worry about that shit. The kid's an angel. You did good, Sally."

I smiled, slowly pulled my hand from his, and slipped outside. I gave the door a gentle pull shut behind me.

When I got back to my room, and nestled into the sleeping bag, the waterworks came like lava. Intense, heartwarming, and suffocating all at once.

I woke up near dawn feeling refreshed for the first time in a million years. I tiptoed toward the bedroom next door, cracked the door, and saw Roman sprawled out on the floor. He snored gently, shirtless and sculpted, laying parallel with Caleb's crib.

Somewhere in another world, maybe father and son shared some dreams.

I never knew something could be so touching and so fucking hot simultaneously. Staring at his chest too long was like gazing at the sun, and my pussy absorbed the heat, tingling with the memory of what his rough body did to me years ago.

It was like my flesh *knew* this was the man who'd knocked me up at some deep, primal level. And as bad as he'd screwed me over and pissed me off, my womb wanted more, wanted to feel his cock thrusting deep inside me.

I imagined him fucking me, biting my lip the entire time. His huge body shadowing mine, flinging me up and down like a ragdoll, burying himself to the hilt and growling in my ear when he unloaded. He'd fill me with what I craved – more of his potent seed – that strange, miraculous chemical cocktail I hadn't felt for years.

God. I had to get away, before I went in, woke him up, and made a huge fucking mistake.

It hadn't been twenty-four hours since I'd hated his guts. I was still his prisoner, after all, his *old lady*, only because he'd forced me out of my house and tagged me like a piece of meat with that tramp stamp.

Downstairs, Asphalt had started stuffing things in cabinets before he left. No surprise, the hotheaded biker didn't have a clue about organizing a kitchen. After about an hour shuffling things around, I wiped my brow, and then walked over to the fridge to see if I could pull anything together from the sparse ingredients he'd picked up on the way to the move.

Nothing but eggs, meat, cream, and peppers. Probably a typical diet for a man as big and built as Roman. Those muscles didn't bulge and work without the right fuel.

Five minutes later, I smiled to myself, cooking up a breakfast for the first time in my brand new house. Sure, it was a rental, but it didn't have the constant morning noise of the ranch I'd shared with Norm for so long.

It was quiet. Peaceful.

Just as I started plating the breakfast, I heard footsteps behind me. Roman's hands wrapped around my waist and jerked my butt dangerously close to him before I could even turn around.

"Didn't know you were a mind reader, babe. Feels like I've been in hibernation and haven't eaten all fucking year. Shit, that smells good." He leaned in close, drawing a sharp breath.

My body tensed, especially when his fingers flexed around my belly, only a few inches from my breasts. *Jesus.*

I reached up and pulled around my collar, trying to hide the way my nipples turned to pebbles. I silently cursed myself for forgetting to put on a bra.

Part of me wanted to believe he was really just hungry for the omelet scramble steaming on the plate next to me. But the way he inhaled, leaning in close, I had a feeling he was smelling *me,* feeding a hunger building in the rock hard length pressed against my ass.

"It's ready when you are!" I chirped, spinning around nervously. "Come on, let's eat."

He barely loosened his grip enough to turn, and locked on tight, holding me against the counter. Of course he still had to be shirtless.

Bare chested and magnificent, the ferocious bear stamped on his chest matching his feral expression.

"You know I want the whole damned package, *right?* You were coming with me and wearing my brand regardless, babe, whether you wanted it or not. I can live with pretending. I can deal with playing this shit up for show."

He licked his lips, pushing his face in, heading for my ear. His stubble brushed across my cheek, and my knees to turned to jelly, melting like hot wax alongside everything else below the waist.

God damn. Was it already too late to back away? I'd forgotten how deliciously electric his touch could be when I didn't want to gouge his eyes out, how easy it was for his skin, his hair, his strength to make every nerve in my skin *sing.*

"I told you I can deal, Sally. You get that?" He paused, stamping his red hot lips on my earlobe. "Thing is, I don't fucking want to. I want this shit to be as real as the Redding sunrise. I want it goddamned terrible, almost as bad as I wanna rip through this gown and fuck you on the counter."

Holy shit. His lips moved lower, grazing my neck. He sucked, nibbled, and then sunk his teeth into my tender flesh, giving me a proper love bite and a swirl of the tongue so unexpected I nearly screamed.

His hands went places. So many places, so smoothly, so possessively, I felt like I'd become a bundle of flames.

Roman's lips moved up, faster and faster, insatiable. The inevitable kiss came, and my panties drenched the second his tongue touched mine.

He growled into my mouth just as I moaned. His hips rocked into mine, pushing me onto the counter, grinding magnificently on my clit through our clothes. Lava stung my veins, bathing my brain in its thick, rampant heat, shutting down every thought except how fucking amazing he felt all over me.

His tongue worked mine harder. Hungrier. *Take this kiss, open your legs, and fuck me,* it seemed to say, telling me exactly what was about to happen without forming any words.

My nipples tensed, became hotter, harder pebbles. They ached like small coals burning beneath my gown. One rough hand brushed up my thigh, heading for my sopping wet slit, and other moved like a fiend, zipping up the silky cotton wrapped around my torso. He found my breast and pussy simultaneously.

Two fingers pushed inside me, just as he pinched my nipple taut. That snapped me back to life.

Too. Fucking. Fast.

No – no! I can't let him do this. Not when he's hurt me so bad.

My eyes snapped open. The humid lust clouding my

senses vanished in an instant, replaced by saner fears.

Christ. I'd completely hated him up until last night, when he showed me he could be more than an irresponsible thug. I couldn't change my mind from *fuck you* to *fuck me* in twenty-four hours, right?

What kind of woman was I? Sure, he'd looked like a good father when I saw him with Caleb, but it was one little footnote in an entire book of crudeness and violence.

My hands flattened against his brutally tempting chest and pushed. Hard.

"Babe? What the fuck's the matter?" he growled, staggering back.

For a second, my eyes caught the raging hard-on tenting his jeans. I knew what that cock could do, and if it came out in this kitchen, no wouldn't even be on the table.

"This is happening too fast, Roman," I panted out. "I'm sorry. I need more time. I still don't know what the hell we're doing here. I don't know if I hate you."

He cracked a smile, tugging on his jeans with his thumbs, probably to relieve the strain of his towering dick against the denim. "I'm told you I'm sorry for the shit that came down before. I'm making it right. I'm gonna build this family into something real, damn it, and I'll spend every waking minute fucking the shit outta you if that's what it takes."

"You can't control me with sex," I snapped. "I don't want anything to do with you like that right now."

But my body does, I thought, pinching my legs together

and feeling the wetness his touch had left behind.

So strange to be annoyed and a little turned on by his brash words. Then again, contrasts were the norm with Roman. The sooner I learned to deal with them without losing my sanity, the better.

"You think I want control? You think I wanna drag you to my cave and fuck you without any say?" He stepped toward me, not stopping until my nipples brushed the hungry bear tattooed on his chest again. "You're flat out wrong, babe. Having you like a dead fish won't do shit for me. I want you to fucking *want* this 'til your heart stops. I want you to *beg* for my come again, Sally. If you're not ready for this shit, fine. I'll put a leash on my dick and keep teasing 'til you are."

Hot sweat beaded on my skin. I ripped myself away from him, ducking to get away, before my body mutinied and I spread my legs wide open for him on the counter like he'd wanted.

"Roman." I looked up, forcing myself to meet his dark brown eyes. "Don't. We can't do this. We can't make another big mistake. Not when I barely even know who the hell you are."

The arrogant smirk on his face melted. "What, you don't have a fucking clue?"

"You know what I mean. We had a few summer weeks of sex and road trips two years ago. We've lived together exactly one day. I don't care if your name's already burned into my skin because you forced it there. You're a walking mystery, and I'm not going to throw myself at you when I don't have a clue if you really mean any of this."

For a second, his jaw tensed up. I thought he'd explode, maybe reach into the cabinets and start shattering the dishes I'd just spent over an hour neatly organizing. Instead, he looked at the floor and headed for the table, jerking out a chair so fast it screeched across the tile.

"Let's just eat some grub. We've got all day to sort this bullshit out before the club bash this weekend. Everybody'll expect to see you acting like an old lady there. Here, right now, I don't give a fuck."

That last part drove deep in my chest like a knife. Whatever he'd said about not caring, the sharp tone in his voice said otherwise. With a sigh, I gathered our plates, pushing his toward him.

"What the hell's that supposed to mean, anyway?" He pointed his fork at me. "You think I'm a 'walking mystery?'"

"I don't even know why you went behind bars. Let's start there," I said, nervously stabbing at my eggs. "And I swear to God, if I hear the words 'club business,' I'm going to –"

"I was covering somebody else's ass, babe. It was a bad run," he said slowly.

I blinked, struggling to shake off my disbelief as I realized he was actually telling me something.

"The club was running arms, special shit we picked up at the start of our beef with the cartel. That bastard Fang, the old Prez, ran the armory too low. He'd spread us thin, fighting other clubs, leaving us in no condition to deal with a threat as big as the Mexicans.

"We were desperate to replenish our shit, get our ducks in a row to fight. The convoy stopped in Redding after pickup north, and I was on escort down to San Diego. We stopped along the way at this biker bar. Some of the other numbnuts got into it with a rival crew there, this club from Texas, passing through our territory.

"They raised a fuck of a commotion, and the local sheriff came roaring in before we could hit the road. Somebody had to stay behind, throw them a fucking bone, make the cops think they hadn't missed half a dozen trucks filled to the gills with illegal guns. I took full responsibility for damaging the bar, fucking up ten guys. Really, I only beat the shit outta five. Some of the boys on that run were bastards, and I'm glad they're gone now, but I did it for the part of the club worth saving. I did it to fight the cartel."

My heart pounded. I could barely remember to eat. Slowly, I reached across the table, grabbing his hand, running my fingers through his.

"They threw the book at me over the fight, and for finding a couple grenades and magnums with their serial numbers filed off in my saddlebag. I did two years for a brotherhood that was fucked up 'til I got out. I wasn't sure about the club then, but I was damned sure the cartel was worse. I couldn't let 'em have an open path to Redding. If they'd gotten up here sooner, they would've fucked up your ranch that much faster, and I wouldn't have been around to help."

He paused, looked up. "I did this to protect the town. I didn't want them fucking with my ma, or anybody who didn't deserve it. The cartels don't have a code. They'll fuck anybody who gets in their way, and I wouldn't let that happen to anybody. Even you, babe, and I didn't even know you were carrying my kid."

"I always knew you had a reason for doing what you did," I whispered, squeezing his hand tight. "Thank you."

"Don't." He shook his head. "I'm no hero. I'm just a man who chose the lesser evil, and by some stroke of luck, it turned out to be the right choice."

He dragged his hand away from mine, tucking into his breakfast. I watched him eat in silence for more than a minute. The story – the *truth* – was so intense he'd left my throat dry as cotton.

Something was missing anyway – my morning caffeine. I got up and walked to the fridge, retrieving an iced latte drink in a carton.

The coffeemaker was still in its box. Roman picked the bottle up and sneered.

"This sugary piss coffee any good, or what?"

I looked at him and smiled. I couldn't help it. "You tell me. It won't take the tattoos off your skin to try something new, you know."

I watched the powerful muscles in his arms bulge as he picked it up and twisted off the lid, sloshing some in a tall glass. "That's all I'm doing lately, babe. I've got a skull as thick as a dinosaur, but I'm smarter than you think. I can learn, and you'll find out just how fucking fast. Just wait."

He pointed at me as he set the bottle down, then tucked into his eggs. We mostly ate in silence. When his food was almost gone, he reached for the drink and took a long pull, slamming the glass back down on the table as he smiled.

"Well?" I said. Keeping the conservation on iced latte drinks seemed safer than everything else.

"It's all right. I still like my shit black, but I can deal."

I returned the sharp smile tugging at his lips. My first breakfast with a badass hadn't turned into the disaster I'd expected as soon as I pulled his hands off me.

"Go get cleaned up and let's get Caleb fed. We'll set his kid seat up in my truck."

"Why? Where are we going?"

"My ma wants to meet her new grandson and the woman I knocked up. We'll pack some snacks and water, make a day of it. There's a park nearby that the kid'll probably love too."

Shit. So much for avoiding disaster.

The short, dark haired woman came out screaming. The screen door attached to the old house whipped open and banged against the wall before we were even out of the truck, and at first I thought her shrill excitement was some kind of strange bird making noise.

Caleb's eyes went wide and he blubbered as the odd woman jumped up and snatched him out of my hands.

"My baby! Oh God! He looks just like you, Travis." Roman's mother beamed at her son as he rounded to our side of the truck to meet us.

Travis, huh? I smiled, amazed it had taken me to years to learn his new name. It was friendlier than the gruff sounding executioner road name he'd adopted in the club. It was also kinda stunning I'd never had it until now.

"Lord – he's precious!" I watched in awe as the sixty-something lady alternated kissing Caleb's cheeks at light speed, as if he she was trying to make up for all the grandma kisses he'd missed his first year at once.

"Come on, ma. Don't suffocate him before we get him in the house." She laughed and grudgingly let go as Roman pulled the boy away from her.

For the first time, she looked at me forcefully, her slim lips signaling a cautious smile. "And you must be the lucky lady," she said.

I nodded. "It's a pleasure to meet you. I'm Sally Jennings."

"Not for long," Roman growled, eyeballing the hand I'd expected to his mom. "This chick's my old lady, ma. Just waiting to get her a proper jacket from the stitch shop in town next week. We'll do something about that fucking last name too."

She looked at me like I'd just stepped off a comet. Then, ignoring the handshake, she leaned on her toes and threw her arms around my neck, covering me in several of the same quick pecks she'd given the baby.

"Welcome to the family. If my son's done *anything* to screw you over, come to me. My friends call me Julie, but you'd better get used to calling me 'ma,' just like him."

Roman showed his teeth. He was half a head shake away from rolling his eyes. "Let's go. We can talk this shit over inside."

There wasn't much to Julie's house. It was a small, simple blue collar place in a little village outside Redding proper, right where the houses tapered off into wild country.

She served us coffee as we sat in the living room. No sooner than I sat down on the soft sofa, Roman took my hand and flattened his in my lap, dangerously close to clenching my thigh through the long dress I'd picked out for the warm autumn day.

"You're a cuter couple than I expected," she mused, barely looking at us as she bounced Caleb on her lap in the huge recliner across from us. "I always figured my son would end up with someone –"

"Trashier?" He finished for her. "Fuck no. You know those sluts at the club were nothing to me, ma. I'd gouge my damned eyes out before I ever had a kid with them."

Except it could've easily happened, I thought sadly. *The only reason I'm sitting her with this bad boy now is because of one wild night and a faulty pill. It could've been anyone besides me.*

"Oh, Trav." She looked up, brushing her fingers through the baby's soft hair. "The playboy days are over, yes? You're going to be a married man. You've got to let some bad habits die."

Jesus. For the second time that day, the M-word came up. I kinda knew it was only one heartbeat away after he'd stamped his name above my ass, but I'd at least expected a proposal, some sort of say.

"We're together now, yes," I said softly. "I hope he's in the mood to settle down."

I looked at Roman. His masculine face tightened so subtly you could've missed it in a blink. The fingers on my thigh were more obvious.

When I said *settle down*, he squeezed, hard and wanting. *Oh, hell.*

"He'd better!" Julie snapped, shooting Roman a sharp look. "And I'm not just talking about the lovin'. Everybody in this house remembers what happened to Dagger."

"Dagger?" I echoed.

Suddenly, Roman's grip on my leg wasn't so tight. Julie stared down sadly at the baby in her arms. Caleb smiled, pawing at her fingertips.

"He would've been an *amazing* grandpa." She looked up. "I can still feel my old man next to me some times, his huge, protective hand on my shoulder. But it's been too long to feel him the way I used to. Roman, you were so young…you can't end up the same way he did and leave this beautiful boy alone."

"Ma! Why don't you get the kid those clothes you told me about on the phone. We'll see how they fit and take him out to the park. It's too damned nice a day to waste it in here all day blabbing about the past."

Julie's face lit up, and she disappeared into the small bedroom with Caleb. "Come on back when you're ready!

These are all hand-me-downs I got from Suzie's grandbaby, but they should fit him fine."

I waited until she was busy rummaging through the closet, cheerfully pipping baby talk back at Caleb every time he laughed. Then I leaned over to Roman and reached for his hand, squeezing it without thinking.

"Was Dagger your father?"

He gave me a stern look. "Babe, you'll know soon enough. Let's just enjoy the sun and watch her play grandma. We'll be back busting our asses unpacking tonight."

I frowned, mostly at the heavy mystery hanging over everything. Caleb giggled in the other room, and I watched her moving a little pair of overalls like a puppet, much to his amusement.

Maybe Roman was right. The darkness in his world left plenty to cry about, and happier times like these just might be the only reprieve from the endless storm sweeping through the Grizzlies MC and everyone in it.

Julie sprinted ahead of us in the park, carrying Caleb all over the place as he laughed, helping him keep his unsteady footsteps way longer than he could've done naturally.

She made a good grandma for sure – not a huge surprise, I guess, given the way her son had taken to his boy. By the end of it, we were all dead tired, resting on a blanket she'd brought along with some snacks.

Afterward, we all drove back to her place, and she tried

to help load the boxes of extra clothes and baby supplies. Roman wouldn't let her, insisting on doing it all himself.

Between what she'd given us and the club's donations, plus the stuff I'd left behind with Norm, we'd have a whole room filled to the brim with nursery and toddler goodies. It was enough for three kids.

"You'd better bring him back soon. Don't make me track you down, son," Julie said before we left, wagging her finger at Roman. "You know I'll send Blackjack after you if I don't get a call. We go way back."

"Yeah, thanks for reminding me like you always do," he growled, not stopping to climb into the truck. "I'm busy as shit, ma, but you'll get more baby time. Don't worry. It's one big happy family now, and that's how I'm gonna keep it."

"Make sure you do," she said, a more serious gleam in her eyes. "Take care of Caleb. Sally too."

I smiled and waved, climbing into the passenger seat and buckling my seat belt. Roman never said anything, he just backed the truck down the long cracked driveway and lifted his hand. Julie watched us the entire time, until we'd driven out of sight.

"I hope I have half as much energy when I'm her age," I said, hoping to smooth things over. "I'm tired just thinking about all the work at home."

"We'll get to it, babe. Piece by piece. We're not heading straight home."

"No?"

"Fuck no. We've got one more stop to make. If you

still don't know who the hell I am, then I'm gonna drill it into your pretty blonde head. You've seen ma – crazy, well meaning, and energy off the charts. That's the light. Now, it's only fair I show you the dark."

I didn't know what the hell he was talking about. My blood pressure spiked, and a strange dread twisted in my stomach, mercilessly building the entire twenty minute drive to the huge, broken down warehouse.

We pulled into a long abandoned parking lot with a rusty, imperfect fence surrounding it.

They say some people are so sensitive they can sense phantoms, especially the sad and angry ones. I wasn't sure about that, but I definitely got an unshakeable, sick certainty in the pit of my soul the instant we drove in.

Something *terrible* had happened here. I knew it before he killed the ignition and ordered me out, pointing toward the corner side of the warehouse.

"Come on. Grab the kid and let's walk," he growled, popping his door as soon as the engine went quiet.

"You're sure it's safe here?"

He snorted. "I wouldn't be bringing my old lady or my son here if it weren't. It's broad daylight. Besides, nobody's been fucking stupid enough to use this place as a rally point since the shit that went down years ago. Not after the media storm and the cops combing it."

I held my breath, stepping out of the truck and reaching for Caleb, unbuckling his safety belt. The baby cooed tiredly in my arms, and put up a little fuss as the cool breeze hit us. He was way more interested in taking a well earned nap after running around with grandma than seeing some grown up drama at this worn down place.

Roman looked behind me, a few steps ahead, waving us forward. I went on, my heart pounding. We approached a small corner with a half-broken down fence, next to a decrepit loading dock.

He stepped a short distance past a wide gap in the rusty brown chain link fence, staring quietly at the pavement. I followed his eyes.

The concrete was broken. Faded graffiti circled a small bronze medallion with the Grizzlies MC logo branded in the middle, pounded into the concrete.

I couldn't make out anything except the choppiest hint of DAGGER in faded, rusty red paint, and a date that looked like it ended in the late nineties.

"This is where my old man met his maker," he said, looking up and locking on my eyes. "Dagger got himself killed for the club. He left behind my poor ma and a really pissed off fourteen year old kid. Me."

He thumped his chest. Lightning caused his face to twitch, like years of rotten memories rushed through him at once.

"I'm sorry," I said, and I meant it. It was also all I could manage with the heavy emotions charging the air.

I'd never seen him like this. The dark, lonely look in his beautiful hazel eyes, his huge shoulders slightly slumped. I saw a man who'd been beaten by one of the few things he'd never control – the past.

I had to know. I swallowed, gathering my words, then

clutched Caleb tight with the other arm as I laid a soft hand on his shoulder. "How did it happen? I mean, if you don't mind –"

"Bad deal went down here. The Nevada Scorps came over to pick up some nasty shit the club played mule to deliver. The Scorps were hot shit back before Reno and Vegas turned into neutral zones no MC could claim. They also liked to flip you the fucking bird and sting your ass raw as soon as you expected cash in hand. The fuckers tried to low ball the club for coke we were selling in the old days at a loss, right as we were getting our hands in other shit."

Pausing, his face tightened, anger threatening to ripple through his features. "They ambushed the MC. Told 'em to take their shitty offer or else, and they had the manpower to back it up. My old man was a total hothead. Like father, like son, I guess.

"He was having trouble at home with ma and hitting the bottle too hard. She loved that man, and was proud to be his old lady, but he stepped in the typical mid-life crisis shit and went crazy. Started fighting with her, drinking like a bastard, probably fucking a few club sluts on the side. Something pushed him over the edge. He fucked up bad, and he lost his life. Right here."

Roman stepped over the red paint, tapped the edge of the memorial with his boot.

I stared at him with wide eyes, and then looked back to the ground. I couldn't believe he was showing me the spot where his father died.

"It happened quick. You don't get second chances in this biz. He punched a Scorp, and they pulled their guns. Knocked his damned teeth out, three blows to the head. Blackjack was there with the old crew, and he found himself up against the wall too, a shotgun pressed against his chest. All the guys watched with rage boiling them alive while the fuckers took the coke, took the money, and kicked the shit out of my old man on the ground 'til he stopped breathing."

Holy shit. Hot tears ravaged my eyes just thinking about it. And he wasn't even done yet.

"They shredded his cut. That's the torn up leather you see framed behind the clubhouse's bar, the same one next to all the pictures of the old guys who weren't complete bastards when they were in their prime. The Scorps' Veep pulled out his hunting knife and flayed a strip of skin off dad's back too while he was dying – up and stole the bear he had on his skin. His blood ran all over the fucking place, swirled around the boots of every brother standing there. That's what Blackjack told me when I was old enough to handle it."

"Sick! Roman, I'm sorry. I get it. Please. I don't need to hear anymore." Caleb squirmed, and I loosened my grip, sorry for practically squeezing him to death while I imagined the nightmarish scene.

"We got back at 'em, of course. A little before my time prospecting, unfortunately. I'd have loved to crack the skull of the motherfucker who skinned him myself. Blackjack took care of that before I could, and the Scorps are just ancient history now."

"Why? Why are you telling me all this?" I stared at his cold, dead face, trying to understand.

"My way of telling you I'm ready to rip my chest open and hand you my fucking heart, babe." He stepped forward, laying a cool, thick hand on my cheek. "I also know how bad my dad fucked up. He snapped and got himself killed because he didn't respect his family enough to keep a lid on his shit, sort it out some other way. I *know* you got your doubts about me."

I bit my lip, shaking off the last of the tears, unable to resist the urge to press my face into his palm. "I can change my mind, you know. Things were pretty fucked up. I was ready to walk away, ready to leave you behind for good –"

"And that's the point, babe. If it wasn't for the cartel, I got a bad feeling I would've missed a whole lot more of my son's life because you couldn't trust me." His hand circled to my back, wrapping around my waist, pulling me and the baby to his chest. "I wanna fucking explode when I think about it. The only reason I don't is because there's no goddamned way I'll ever, *ever* let it happen again."

"Roman…people make mistakes."

Yeah, they did. My head kept spinning, ready to fly off and take the rest of me with it. I couldn't even comprehend right or wrong in this situation. Not anymore. We'd both screwed up bad, but he was *trying* to make amends.

Shouldn't I let him?

Shock and awe didn't begin to describe my reaction. I tucked Caleb carefully between us and craned my head, ready for a kiss.

He pulled away right before my lips touched his, brushing his stubble on my cheek. "Hold the fuck up. You have no idea how bad I want those lips on mine," he growled.

"But I'm not gonna do it 'til it's fucking real. I meant what I said this morning – I wanna hear you *beg,* babe. I took you on a rollercoaster to show you the *real* me. Let it sink in. You can't change your mind in less than a day. You pushed me away this morning, and I'm not gonna fuck you over again by taking something that's only gonna screw this up for the long haul."

"Come on. It's one kiss. I'm not saying I'm ready to fuck you, or anything."

Shit. Was I serious? I couldn't stop feeling his hard cock against my thigh, tense and wanting, making my body shake with need.

Real, genuine, dyed in lipstick and honey *need.* How the hell had we flip-flopped since morning? Suddenly, he was the cautious, conservative one, and it drove me fucking crazy.

"Yeah, you are," he growled, reaching to fist my hair and pulling my lips to his.

We kissed long, hard, and hot. It was almost cathartic, some kinda exorcism written in love, able to banish a little of the evil hanging over this old, abandoned lot.

I moaned into his mouth, truly tasting him. My tongue

whirled against his, led in a steaming, inescapable dance, plucking every nerve in my body to perfection.

Damn! Don't make me beg. He can't be serious about that.

His tongue moved against mine so hard my nipples throbbed. Hot blood rushed through my ears, drowning out everything, making me hear the thumping need in my own heartbeat.

I. Want. To. Fuck.

No, we couldn't, though. It wasn't that easy, and it surely couldn't happen here. I had to stop it there before we went further, especially with the sweet baby still in my arms. I pulled back, struggling to stabilize my knees, following him to the truck. I helped Caleb into his kiddie seat, then climbed in.

"Tasting you makes my dick jerk like a kid who's about to have his first fuck. You know that?" He looked at me in the passenger seat. My cheeks heated. "Still, you keep a lid on that shit 'til you're ready. You give me that tongue again, you'd better expect to get naked, girl."

His hand slid down to my thigh, and his fingers pressed tight, pinching the autumn skirt on my cool skin. Instant fire.

Roman started the engine, but didn't put the truck into drive, looking into my eyes as he leaned over. "Let me make this crystal-fucking-clear – we're gonna do this husband and wife, happy family thing, and I'm excited as hell if you're on board. But when we do the other part – the part that's dirty, hard, and so fucking rough it'll leave you sore for the next week – you let me know. I don't do teasers. I don't do samples. If you wanna fuck me, you spread your legs and wrap 'em tight, because I'm not stopping 'til I've gorged myself on you, woman. I *will* kiss, suck, and fuck everything you've got, babe, and there's no off switch 'til my dick doesn't work."

I wasn't sure what was going to overheat first. My tender thigh, beneath the place where his fingers drilled into my flesh, or my panties just a few inches over. I wouldn't be surprised to find scorch marks on them later. They'd been so thoroughly soaked they forced me to notice every time we were outside and the wind blew just a little bit too hard.

I was drowning, a little at a time, fighting my insane desire to bury the past by twisting our bodies together between the sheets.

"You're mine, babe, and only mine. Every way. All the time. You understand? That's the only word that's ever been as heavy as the ones I spoke when I got my patch. *Mine.*"

I understood him – more than I ever thought he'd let me.

Slowly, I nodded, pawing at his wrist with one shaky hand, pushing him off. I didn't breathe again until both his hands were on the steering wheel, and we were leaving behind the grim memorial for good.

He was right about one thing – this was all happening *way* too fast. Still, I couldn't deny the spark that wouldn't stop flashing through my veins, my heat begging to mingle with his.

My core tightened, and I pushed my tongue against the roof of my mouth. Jesus, my nipples throbbed against my bra, hungry to be sucked, just like my clit. I never knew the need for sex could truly make me *ache* until now.

Sure, we could keep up the safe, sane, careful act as long as I could stand it. But sooner or later, I knew I'd wind up straddling his cock, pulling him deep inside me and letting him take his rightful place there as the only man who'd ever fucked me.

Hell, the only one I ever *wanted* to. Now, it was just a matter of how long until the fire making me sweat and choke on my own breath threw me on my back and spread my legs.

Roman had already taken me over with his brand and the not-so-subtle marriage promise he'd made back at his mother's place. He'd taken me so fast my head was spinning, whirling off the anger and bitterness I'd had when he stormed back into my life.

Soon, he'd take what was his in bed, and I'd give it all over, everything that tensed and exploded when he bit into my ear and growled the word *mine*.

VIII: Bad Blood (Roman)

I woke up in a cold damned sweat two days later. My kid snored in his crib, oblivious to everything, even as I smacked my forehead and sweated out the last Jack in my system for the first time in years.

Goddamn it. Every fucking night in that house was hell when I wasn't waking up next to Sally.

I woke up alone, stretched out on the floor in my sleeping bag, my dick drooling pre-come all over my boxers. It'd been too long since I'd had pussy, and the girl I wanted most was only a wall away.

I'd heard brothers talk about sexual tension over the years 'til they were blue in the face, especially when they get their pricks bent outta shape over some woman they wanted to call their old lady.

Me? I had it worse – way fucking worse.

I'd already claimed her, and she wasn't saying no, but she was off limits 'til she said the magic word.

I had an old lady I couldn't fuck 'til she wanted it as bad as I did, and the chick. I'd done a lot to smooth shit over the last couple days, but nothing compared to getting nasty with her underneath me.

I couldn't fuck her 'til she moaned in my ear, pressed her skin against mine, made me feel her temp rising over a hundred degrees. And I couldn't go back to cockhounds like Twinkie, good for emptying my balls and nothing else.

I wasn't fucking this up.

I'd die before I made the same damned mistakes my old man did. I wasn't gonna say it to her face, but Sally already had my cock pulsing in her hand. I couldn't think about letting that greedy motherfucker have his way with anybody but her, her, *her*.

She must've done some black magic when I wasn't looking. Nothing else made sense.

Shit, women used to come easy, and I had no problem getting hard for a stranger with a rocking body. Now, it was like every other pussy on the planet turned to ash, bronze prizes my balls wouldn't ever accept. I had to go for the gold, and fuck her so hard her hot, tight, golden cunt remembered the shape of my dick 'til we were dead.

Fuck.

I got up and started to dress. Yesterday, I hit the Jennings' place, mostly to check in with the crew and see if they were any closer to moving her asshole cousin to safety before the cartel hacked him to bloody bits.

He was a stubborn bastard. Honorable, but rigid as a goddamned mule.

Brass was there, looking pissed as all hell. He told me Stryker and Asphalt chased a suspicious truck outta the fields after midnight. They would've caught up to the fuckers too, if only Beam hadn't taken a wrong turn, and crashed his damned bike through a ratty old farm fence.

I didn't like that sonofabitch, and not just because he'd tried to muscle in on my girl. He wasn't battle hardened. His whole attitude sucked, and I couldn't tell if him or Stryker were more wet behind the ears, too damned new at this for their own good.

Too bad I had to get used to it. I had to deal with their fuckups, their disrespect, their rookie errors while they shared the patch. I thought of it as practice. Long as Blackjack needed manpower, the club was gonna have a lot more greenhorns patched in who really needed more time to learn the ropes.

Their voting rights bothered me more. The club's charter gave the vote to every full patch member. That might be a problem when these kids had to take the grenade between their teeth, and make a damned decision that would affect the whole club.

I sighed, brushed a hand over my sleeping son's forehead, and headed for the bathroom.

I showered quick, fighting like hell to ignore the raging wood between my legs. My dick was gonna fuck a hole through the wall and take me with it some night if I didn't get between her legs soon.

I walked out shirtless, toweling off. Sally stood on the landing, quirking an eyebrow when I stopped and stared at her.

"You know, this really isn't fair," she said, frustration

in her voice.

"What the hell you talking about?"

"Yesterday. You told me not to tease you unless we're going all the way…well, I want the same thing. You *could* put on your clothes before walking through the house."

I threw my head back and laughed. "No fucking way, babe. There's a difference between teasing and giving up the chase. Long as I've got a pair of balls between my legs, I'll never stop showing off the goods, making you fucking want this."

She threw her hands out and shook her head, trying not to crack a smile. "Whatever, *Travis*. Just bring Caleb down for breakfast."

Before she could turn and get a step away, I ripped off the towel, showing her the mean, throbbing dick that hadn't gone away all morning. "That's what you get for using my real name, babe. Take a good look. I don't wanna hear that shit unless you're moaning it in bed. Preferably later tonight. I'm Roman every second I'm not in you."

She watched me, shock glimmering in her eyes. I wrapped one fist around my dick and gave it a quick pump, smiling as her jaw dropped.

Yeah. You'd better fucking want this, I thought. *I'm turning into a maniac every second I'm not blowing my load inside you, woman.*

Let those worries go. Let's fuck tonight.

Fuck me like my old lady. Ride my dick like you missed it for two goddamned years. Fuck me and don't look back.

I'll bite your little lip 'til you come on my cock. We'll fuck it all out 'til you can't remember how to breathe.

Her hand trembled a little as she hit the staircase and started down, desperate to get away.

"I'll have the kid downstairs as soon as I'm dressed!" I growled after her, reluctantly throwing the towel back around my waist. Fuck, this sexual tension shit was killing me, minute by minute.

Probably for the best she beat a retreat. I would've come like a young buck getting his first taste of a woman's touch if her hand wrapped around my cock just then – let alone anything else.

I had to eat and get the day started. Blackjack wanted me at the clubhouse to debrief with some Prairie Devils dudes coming down from Montana. They were covering our northern flank, making sure the cartel assholes didn't slip past and start fucking up supplies.

They'd always be Prairie Pussies to me, but I guess the bastards hadn't been half bad since we buried the hatchet between the clubs to fight the Mexicans. They'd helped us take down that destructive fucking psycho, Fang, and put Blackjack in as President with me as Enforcer.

A man couldn't argue with results.

It was just four of us in the meeting room. The Prez, the Veep, me, and the Devils' own giant, a big boy almost as tall and wide as me named Tank.

"You sure you can trust all your guys to collect the heavy arms?" Tank asked, staring at the Prez and then looking down at Brass and me.

"What's that supposed to mean?" Blackjack stubbed out his smoke in the ash tray and flattened his hands on the table, giving our guest the evil eye.

"Lotta rumors about rats in your club. Don't know how the hell the cartel could embed any fuckers in an MC. That's what Blaze thinks, and the Prez knows the lay of the land better than I do here."

"It's bullshit." Blackjack waved a hand, dashing the concerns away. "Tell your Prez to stop second guessing. There's no clause in our little treaty about telling another MC how to do its job, and you know it. You handle the supply run, and we'll handle pickup on our end. Simple as that."

Blackjack looked to me and Brass. The VP quietly nodded, and I did the same – except with a lot less confidence.

For an outsider, Tank knew an awful lot.

"Prez is right," Brass said coolly. "Your job's to make sure the deliveries go smoothly. We're happy to have you in this clubhouse, Tank, but you can go home and tell my brother-in-law everything's cool here. We're kicking their asses back across the border a little more every day. Soon, we'll be talking new deals with Canada and abroad. All this shit'll be behind us."

The Veep's voice rumbled whenever he mentioned Blaze. He'd been forced to accept his sis marrying the Devils' Prez awhile ago, but it still wasn't one big happy family. Just an understanding.

"That's not what I hear," the big man said, leaning back in his chair. The tough line in his jaw was an obvious challenge.

I slammed my palms down on the table, leaning toward him. "What? More rumors? You'd better spit 'em out before we all get the wrong idea about what's going on down here, *friend.*"

Tank's eyes narrowed. "We know the cartel's been sniffing around your own turf here in Redding. Boys come back from runs through Idaho and Washington, delivering our shit to Vancouver. They hear things from your boys up north. Word on the street says mother charter's about to get fucked six ways from Sunday. Everybody knows there'll be another civil war in your club if that happens."

"It won't," Blackjack snapped. Just in time, before I fucking exploded. "Frankly, I'm disappointed. I'm *pissed.* Blaze shouldn't be putting so much stock in hearsay, and he definitely shouldn't be passing it along to his boys."

"Prez doesn't pass along shit," Tank said. "We hear it firsthand and bring it home to him. You've done a good job locking things down here in NorCal, guys, but your brothers up north in Washington are waiting to pounce if this charter gets its skull split by some Mexican's machete."

Brass looked like he was about to flip the table over. Tank's words pissed me off too, but the bastard was telling us the truth, and that was always something Blackjack prized above everything else.

That was the new way. Running the club off bullshit

was done and buried with Fang, even if we'd been one united club under him, ruled by fear instead of the new path the Prez forged.

"Then they'll have to keep waiting. We're not going anywhere, goddamn it, much less dying on some cartel bastard's bullets." The Prez stood up, clenching his jaw tight as the old leg wound peppered his brain with pain. "We'll do the usual pickup tomorrow. Same time, same place. If Blaze has a problem with that, he's welcome to call me. Roman, show him out, and make sure he's set up somewhere for the night."

Tank looked at the Prez and nodded, then got up to follow me. I walked him down the long corridor. The guest rooms were already filled by several guys who'd come up from SoCal, so I had to put him in my old room instead.

"You need anything, just say it. You're welcome to join the bash tonight out back. Booze, smokes, and girls if you're interested."

The big man smiled and shook his head. "Girls? Fuck no. Maybe a couple drinks. My old lady would kill me if I even touched another chick. I've had one too many fucked up brushes with the reaper for that shit. Besides, we're working on our first kid soon, right after we're officially hitched. Here."

I watched him fish out his phone and tap a few keys. He shoved the screen toward me, showing off a pretty blonde girl in scrubs who had her hands on their clubhouse bar top, grinning at the camera.

"She's hot," I said. "I gotta thing for blondes too."

Yeah, a thing. More like a fucking stick of dynamite in my balls that's gonna blow my guts out my head if I don't fuck my girl's blonde pussy soon.

Tank nodded thoughtfully. "I'm gonna crash for a couple hours. I'll be out for some whiskey later. Shit, I barely get fucked up anymore since she walked into my life. Can't wait to get home from this run. Just between you and me, I'll keep the shit I hear to myself unless Blaze really needs to know."

"Good. There's no goddamned threat. We've got this shit under control, Tank. You guys can worry about your own biz up in Missoula. We'll finish off the cartel by Christmas."

"Hope you're right. Watching your war's about all we do when we're not taking care of our own biz. It's been too quiet the last few months." He frowned, and then shrugged his huge shoulders. "Can't say I miss the bullshit. Long as my old lady's happy and my brothers are safe, life's good."

I gave him one more nod and then stepped away, closing the door behind me. Most of my shit was cleared out now that I'd officially moved in with Sally.

The Devils were always a softer club than the Grizzlies. But something in his tone told me he wasn't bullshitting when he talked about peace.

I didn't know what the fuck that was since the time I was patched in. I'd fought, killed, and served time behind bars for this club. I was ready at a moment's notice to shred any asshole who fucked with us.

Shit, my fists lived to beat, lived to shoot, lived to kill. But ever since she walked back into my life with our kid, all that was changing. The same crazy fucking tingle wasn't there anymore – not even when the whole damned world was collapsing on my head.

Maybe peace didn't sound so fucking bland. Hell, once I started fucking her, I'd need it just to make up for all the lost time. I wouldn't be able to focus on shit once I started owning her pussy good and proper.

And if a day finally came when the club didn't have to fight the wolves so hard, then so be it. I'd welcome it with open fucking arms.

Sally looked hot. My dick almost burst through my pants and shot to the moon.

She came waltzing down the stairs in this tight country girl top, a short skirt hugging her thighs, and cowgirl boots to complete the fuckable trio. More important, she was wearing her old lady jacket for the first time. I caught a flash of the back – PROPERTY OF ROMAN.

Everything – and I mean *fucking everything* – about seeing that shit made my balls dump fire in my blood. I grabbed her as soon as she was in reach, whipped her into my chest, and smashed my lips down tight on hers.

She moaned with surprise, savored me for a second, and then pushed me off. It didn't take much to heat her sweet cheeks. Thank fuck, because that meant my odds were damned good ending up in her bed tonight.

"Holy shit," she muttered, wiping at the lipstick I'd just smeared. "Calm down, big boy. We've got a long night ahead of us."

Fuck, did I love the sound of that. Lightning hummed in my cock.

"Is the kiddo okay, or what?" I asked.

"He's fine. Jackie's got him tucked in for a nap. She'll wake him up in a little bit if he's hungry."

I nodded. Missy dropped by a few minutes ago to drop the teenager off, on her way to the party with Brass herself. Her kid sis had suddenly become everybody's favorite babysitter, and it was getting harder to pencil her in now that school was in full swing.

"Good. That's our cue to bounce." Without another word, I grabbed her by the wrist, and led her out to my bike, relishing the heat in her hand.

Christ, what the fuck was she doing to me? Just touching her fingers sent pure lightning ripping through my skin, energy invading my brain 'til I couldn't think about anything about her soft hand wrapped around every inch of me later.

No, dammit. Not now. I had to focus on the road.

"Hold on tight, babe," I told her, passing her the spare helmet. I fixed mine and waited 'til hers was on, then we took off.

My cock pounded in my jeans the entire time her hands were on me. When we were just a few miles from the clubhouse, she pushed her hands against my abs like they were some special stones. Damn if it didn't set me off.

All I wanted to do was pull over, throw her down in the grass, and fuck her brains out. I'd jerk those hands over my neck and slam my hips into hers, fucking and rutting and coming 'til we were both spent.

Shit, the way this night was going, I wasn't sure if I'd survive without a straitjacket.

The clubhouse was booming by the time we got in. A couple new prospects nodded respectfully and opened the door for us.

I held onto Sally tight, pushing through the tight crowd of men in Grizzlies cuts, prospects, locals, whores, plus one Prairie Devil. Tank raised his glass when we passed him at the bar, and I nodded back.

We squeezed in next to Rabid and Christa, waiting our turn as the poor bartender worked frantically to keep the booze flowing to all the rowdy brothers and their women. Rabid's hand landed on my back just as I caught the bartender's eye, pointing to the huge bottles of Jack behind him.

"Goddamn it's good to blow off some steam, isn't it?" he said with a grin.

I nodded, and even cracked a small smile. Being strong and silent all the damned time was the best way to keep this club in line as Enforcer, and I'd never loosen up too much, even among my own brothers.

Still, I beamed on the inside, especially when I heard Sally laugh.

"Jesus Christ, girl! Now we match. Yours is so nice and

shiny!" Christa beamed at my old lady, the scars on her face fading in her happiness.

She'd been tortured by our old fuck of a President, Fang, before we managed to kill the dead weight. Then she'd been through the wringer again a couple months ago, caught in the middle of our clashes with the Klamath charter up north. It was a fucking mess 'til Rabid and the rest of the crew cleaned shit up.

I grabbed a beer and mixed it with several big splashes of Jack, passing one to Sally as she yammered away with Christa.

"So, is this the norm when you're a taken man? Just sitting here all night drinking?"

Rabid laughed and shook his head. "Nah, bro. You gotta get some grub too, and take your girl out back to dance after everybody else starts to pass out or fuck around here."

"Dance?"

"Yeah. Christa loves it." His smile faded a little and leaned in close. "Only thing is, I think I've created a fucking monster. She's so into it she wants to set up dance nights once we get the new bar running in town. She wants us to take tango lessons and shit come winter so we can be the ringleaders."

I laughed and took a long pull of my drink. "You're fucked."

"Nah, I'm man enough to deal, Roman. I'd do anything for that chick, even if she is a little fucking crazy sometimes." His hand slapped my shoulder again. "Believe me, that's the way I like it. You'll find out soon enough."

"Yeah." For once, my hyperactive brother wasn't just bullshitting and looking on the sunny side.

I had a feeling he was right. Sally pulled on my cut 'til I turned toward her.

Fuck, that top. It got me every time. Her cleavage peeked out perfectly – just like the damned thing had been designed to get my cock going turbo.

"Where's the food? I'm *starving.*" She jokingly grabbed her belly.

Fuck, something about the motion made me wonder how hot she looked knocked up. I'd missed that.

Well, no fucking way would I be missing it again. My dick jerked, thinking about pumping another load inside her, giving her another kid I'd get to see from the very start this time around.

Someday, I thought with a growl, helping her up and leading her into the small kitchen behind the bar.

Missy was back there with Brass, busting some cook's balls over the hot wings. The Veep looked at us with a shit eating grin on his face, thoroughly amused.

Hell, he had good reason to be. Putting on the brand does something to a woman, gives her spice and spunk. Not much different than the way a man changes as soon as he earns his bottom rocker.

"It's all open on the carousel over there. Meat galore. Don't be shy about stuffing yourself, babe, there's plenty more where that came from. They keep grilling all night at these bashes. The crazy shit that starts up after the families drop off always leaves the boys hungry."

She cocked her head, and then a knowing smile spread across her face. I followed her to the buffet line, mercifully empty, and started loading up my plate.

"So much for eating healthy today. It's a miracle some of your older guys haven't had coronaries."

I laughed. "You fucking with me? Red meat and hot sauce is practically rocket fuel in this club. Shit, same goes for any MC headquarters worth its salt that I've ever been in. Stop worrying about those hips. They'll still get me hard as fuck, even if they get a few inches thicker."

Her jaw dropped. At first, I thought she'd taken it the wrong way. Then, the little minx stopped in front of me, giving her ass a solid push into my dick.

Fucking shit, I almost dropped my plate. I'd stuff myself with snacks and lay off the booze. The night was going better than expected, and I didn't wanna drink too much so we could get home sooner.

Hell, I'd pay Jackie her full dues for a couple hours babysitting if I had to. A small price to pay for hauling her into the new bed and getting my dick wet.

"Let's go," I said, leading her back into the big bar area.

We found an empty table and devoured our dinner. Wasn't sure what Brass' old lady was digging her claws in about because it was pretty damned perfect to me. Still, no matter much it pleased my tongue, nothing would taste better than having her lips on mine tonight, this time as a prelude to making every perfect curve on her ripple.

I couldn't wait to eat her. I'd tongue-fuck her cunt so

long, so deep, I'd be tasting her for days.

A couple sluts walked by, both hanging on Asphalt's shoulders. One of 'em was Twinkie. She saw me and gave me a wink. I gave that bitch the coldest, deadliest stare ever, the same one I used during the interrogations.

There was no easing away from sluts once a brother decided to stop fucking 'em. It had to be a clean, harsh break, and it took me a few seconds to meet Sally's gaze, knowing she'd probably seen the fucking sideshow that just went down.

She had her arms folded, giving me a cautious look. "Are you still into her?"

"Get the fuck outta here!" I growled. "Babe, you've got two pretty blue eyes in your head, so I know you're not blind."

I shoved my plate aside and pushed my chair over to her, slapping one hand on her thigh. I squeezed her 'til her skin rippled, leaning into her ear, pouring my hot breath out in a whisper.

"Ask me again. Does this look like I'm into that skank?" I swallowed, trying to hold the lust in, keep it from throttling my whole damned system just a little while longer. "Does *this* feel like I'm fucking into her?"

She shuddered as my hand slid up her thigh, brushing the skirt aside. I touched her panties near the center.

Soaked. My dick pounded, pulsed like it was surrounded by a bed of needles.

God fucking dammit. I needed to fuck this chick, and if she really couldn't see it, then I was gonna show her in the worst ways.

"Better answer me quick, babe," I whispered in her ear. "We've got a lotta people here, and not a lotta space. Some of 'em are bound to see my fingers going in your cunt. I'll flick your clit 'til you come right here in front of everybody if you don't tell me the fucking truth. You think I'm into that slut, or you? *Tell me.*"

I meant it too. Hell, I meant more than I'd threatened. I'd shove the table aside and bury my face between her legs if she didn't spit it out. She needed to tell me I'd broken through her icy wall *now*, or else I'd smother her sweet cunt with my tongue 'til she creamed all over me.

"Me!" Her voice hitched, trying to hold back the pleasure as my fingers toyed with ripping her panties down. "I'm sorry, Roman. I shouldn't have doubted you. It's me you want…isn't it?"

"Damned straight. This is the last warning, babe. You give me those jealous puppy eyes again, and I *will* throw you on my lap and smack your ass. Then I'll bring you off so fucking hard you forget there's even another pussy on this planet to get upset about. My dick, my mouth, my hands only wanna go in *you* from now on, and I'm gonna get real fucking rough if they don't get there soon."

Panting, she threw her hand on mine, just as I slid my fingers through her folds, finding her clit. I pulled my hand off hers, all at once, feeling my blood churn like magma, pooling in the steel pipe between my legs.

My hand was gone and she jerked up, straightening her skirt. The jealousy vanished by the time she looked at me again, and I gave her a satisfied nod.

Yeah, that's what I fucking thought.

I noticed our near empty plates and grabbed them, stacking hers on mine. "You want some more, or what? Another drink? We'd might as well enjoy this shit while we're here – unless you wanna get home earlier?"

Unless you wanna get home and feel a thousand times better than I just made you feel with two fingers on your bud, I thought with a grin. *Unless you wanna find out how good this dick feels balls deep in your cunt.*

She pursed her lips and ran a hand over her face, wiping away the sweat beading on her brow. "No, we'll hang out a little longer. Not that I'd mind turning in early. Let's go find your friends and their old ladies. But first, I need to run to the lady's room."

I pointed her toward the big open one down the hall. My eyes followed her round ass as she disappeared into the crowd.

Shit. My cock wouldn't stop hammering, especially when I realized this chick was built to breed. She had the kinda wide swagger that makes a man drool like a goddamned maniac. Hell, I practically had to wipe my mouth, remembering how I gripped her ass while she rode my cock two summers ago.

How had I survived without that perfect ass for this long?

She'd filled out a little more since our last romps. She'd gone from fuckable to damned near perfect. Needless to say, I wanted a piece of that the same way a starving wolf wants fresh meat.

I couldn't wait to sink down deep in her cunt, reminding her she was always made for me, and only me. With her, there was something different, and it wasn't just the son she'd already given me.

I knew I'd never need to fuck another hole again as soon as I got her under me, owning her the way I should, taking over all I'd ever need for my greedy fucking dick.

I sat so long in la la land, thinking about all the nasty ways I'd fuck her tonight, that I lost track of time. All minutes we'd lost didn't hit me in the face 'til an earsplitting scream rang out.

The first screech was so shrill and sudden, I thought it was some slut, or maybe just a high note in the half-muffled rock pouring through the speakers.

Then it happened again, an octave up, high and loud and unmistakably hers.

I threw the plates on the ground and took off, shoving fuckers aside like they were cardboard cutouts. When I saw what had her upset, I nearly went through the goddamned roof.

A couple brothers and their old ladies gawked at the scene, their fists trembling, unsure what the fuck they should do. Beam had Sally up against the wall, pinning her down tight, anger lining his face – way too fucking close to hers.

Instinct kicked in. I shoved two guys to the floor in my mad rush over. He spun around right before I reached for his shoulders. The dumb bastard flattened his fist in my chest. I had so much muscle there his best hit wouldn't even leave a bruise. His hand bounced off like a rock, and I grabbed him.

Clutching at his cut, I swung him around, threw the bastard at the wall like a shitty piece of furniture. Something cracked, but it didn't knock him out like I'd hoped. He yelled, tried to charge me, right as the rest of the clubhouse realized hell was coming down.

Everything exploded around us.

Asshole Beam crashed into my chest. He was a lean motherfucker, but he'd gotten enough leverage to knock me down flat.

We both hit the floor, fists swinging, snarling like feral animals, a death match surrounded in screams.

I grabbed his face and shoved it, hard enough to rip him off me, assuming I didn't crack his fucking skull first. Then his fingers connected with my jaw.

Blood flooded my teeth. I instantly knew the asshole smashed me in the face with brass knuckles – there was no fucking way any other bastard would bust my jaw this hard with his naked fist.

My arms wrapped around his back and felt for his spine. He wasn't just out to fight. He was going to fucking kill me if I slipped up. I had to fight, had to kill him first.

Asshole threw another punch, and I rolled my head just in time. His brass knuckles slapped the floor with a deafening bang, like a grenade exploding next to my ear, and I dug my fist into his goddamned vertebrae, pounding the same weak bone like a jackhammer.

Die. Die, you cheating, worthless sonofabitch.

I fucking wanted him to. But of course, I wanted to make him suffer first. Suffer good, hard, and long for putting his filthy paws all over my woman.

Too bad the brothers had other ideas. Before I could crack his spine, the asshole pulled away from me, like he was lifted up into the air by strings. Then it was like nine hundred pounds of bricks collapsed on top of me, knocking the air outta my lungs.

The bastards intervened, right when I had him where I wanted him.

"Let me the fuck up!" I growled, screaming with all my might. The pressure piled on top of me caused it to slip out like a whisper.

"No, goddamn it. Hold him tighter. Pin him the fuck down."

"He's gonna kill somebody!"

I couldn't even make out who the hell was shouting. The voices all blurred together, Rabid, Brass, Asphalt, and Southpaw. All aligned against me to prevent me from snapping Beam in half.

They scrambled, directionless, forced to control the Enforcer who was supposed to be keeping their asses in line.

It took four mean bastards at full strength to keep my hands behind my back. Slowly, the pressure eased, and I got on my feet.

"Jesus, let him go!" Sally yelped, soon as she saw me. "He's bleeding!"

It was true. I'd been goddamned lucky not to lose a few teeth from Beam's punch. The blood kept coming, mixing with my spit, so fast and heavy I couldn't swallow it without getting sick.

I craned my head and spat on the ground. When I looked up, I saw Beam across from me, being held by several burly prospects. Hate blazed in the asshole's wounded eyes. I sent two blistering fireballs back at him outta mine.

"Piece of shit. You lost. Keep your goddamned dirty hands *off* my old lady, or I'll kill you next time for sure."

"There isn't a ring on her finger yet, asshole," Beam growled back.

The other guys stared at him like he'd flipped his shit. A couple seconds later, all eyes were on something else. Blackjack marched up the hall with his tough old fists at his sides.

"What the hell's going on here, boys? I've never heard a bash so quiet you could hear a glass shatter, and I've been to hundreds."

"Caught these two brothers fighting over Sally, Prez," Brass said, jerking my arm. "We stopped 'em just in time. They were gonna kill each other."

"And I would've snapped his goddamned neck like a twig!" I shouted, spitting another bloody mess on the floor. "He tried to fuck with my old lady, Prez. Caught the bastard throwing her against the wall, and she was fighting him too."

Blackjack swiveled to face Beam, a volcanic storm

building in his features. "Is this true?"

Beam clenched his jaw, refused to say shit, even as the Prez got in his face.

After a minute, he cracked his lips and whispered. "The bitch wanted me before this asshole took her prisoner. I was only trying to make things right, Prez, find out how she really felt."

"I didn't ask for any of it, you bastard!" Sally screamed. "I told you to keep your hands to yourself. You wouldn't listen. I didn't get two words out before you pinned me down, tried to cover my mouth. You tried to pull me into your room, alone."

Blackjack's teeth flashed. He shook his head for about a second, and then his fist darted out, crashing against Beam's mouth so hard I heard bone crunch.

"You're a goddamned idiot, son," he growled. "Are you seriously so new to this patch you don't realize another man's old lady is untouchable? Let's be clear – Sally's *Off. Fucking. Limits.*"

Beam shook his head, drooling more blood than I did. "It's not like that. We had something. I fucking swear it."

He looked at Sally. Anger and sadness filled her eyes, and her head rolled from side to say. *Not a chance.*

"Get him out of my sight! And make sure you keep the brass away from him." Blackjack's face twisted with disgust, and then he turned to face me. "You're right to be upset, son, but we'll resolve this like the club charter says we will. Go home. Take your girl with you. We'll settle this in the morning. As for the rest of you – get the drinks flowing again, dammit! Crank the music up. This is our night, and the entire club won't have its fun ruined by two brothers locking horns."

Blackjack turned and passed through the cheering crowd. An instant later, the boys released me, and I stumbled outta their grip. Took all my strength not to follow Beam, being led away by the other guys, out to the lockers where he couldn't do more damage.

I fisted Sally by the wrist and started heading for the garages. A little ways later, she ran ahead of me, flattening her palms on my chest. I stopped.

"Jesus, Roman, I'm so sorry. You know I fought him all the way, don't you?"

I wiped stray blood off the corner of my mouth and smiled. "Yeah, babe. I do. You proved something to me tonight. This loyalty thing goes both ways."

She nodded. Her touch softened, became more delicate, slower as her hand glided down my abs, dangerously close to my cock. Before I could take another step, she let one hand fall below the belt line. That raging hard-on the fight killed sprang back to life with a vengeance.

"Save that shit for later. You tease me for another second, I'll blow the roof off this goddamned place." Slowly, she drew her hand away, mumbling an apology.

I shut her up with a rough kiss, pulling at her bottom lip with my teeth before I broke away. "You got nothing to be sorry for. Now, let's get the fuck home."

We tore down the road. Sally never held onto me so tight. She kept asking me if I was really all right every time we hit a stop light.

I told her I'd never been better, and I fucking meant it too.

I'd have hellfire shooting through my jaw tomorrow, and it didn't matter one damned bit. Long as I got her alone, naked, and moaning underneath me, I'd suffer a hundred blows from bitter cocksuckers like Beam.

Christ. My dick sapped badly needed blood from my damaged face. Lust pounded in my veins, so harsh and tight and explosive I couldn't even think.

Never knew how the hell I managed to pull the bike into the garage and drag my ass inside. Jackie came walking down the stairs. The teenager's eyes lit up when she saw my screwed up face.

"Holy shit, is he okay?"

Sally looked up, and her face held a sexy prediction only I could read. "He'll be fine. Here, a hundred dollars, just like we agreed, plus a little extra for cab fare."

She stuffed the bills into her purse and beamed. Whatever concerns she had about me getting fucked up were smoothed over instantly by money.

"I'll be upstairs, babe." I walked up and took a quick look at Caleb, sleeping like an angel in his crib.

Then I went into the bathroom and started cleaning up. The hot water felt good, but it didn't do shit to suppress the hard-on becoming a damned missile in my pants. Every time I remembered the way her ass rubbed on my cock, fire crashed through my veins, lust incarnate.

I had to fuck this chick tonight. I absolutely *had* to.

The sexual tension tore me up inside a thousand times worse the way I'd gotten my teeth rattled.

I wiped blood off my face and gargled to get the metallic taste outta my mouth. My jaw resonated fire, but it was nothing some horizontal acrobatics wouldn't fix.

I heard the taxi pull into the driveway to pick up Jackie and take her home, then growl its way out again. That shit was like a signal to my dick, telling it we were *finally* alone, all except our sleeping son.

Fresh lightning sparked in my brain and spread through every nerve. *Fuck her, fuck her, fuck her.*

It kept hissing through my vein like a damned mantra. I toweled off and walked out shirtless. Found her standing in Caleb's room, admiring our kid, looking intense as all hell.

"She did a good job putting him to bed," I growled softly, coming up behind her. I wrapped my hands around her waist, nuzzling her neck, trying to resist sinking my teeth into her soft, sweet flesh for a few seconds longer.

"Yeah, she did. You feeling better?" she asked, spinning toward me.

I didn't answer with words. I took her by the hand and led her back into the hall, gently pushing the door shut behind me with my boot. Then my greedy hands hugged her closer, tighter, winding straight down to her ass.

I captured two big handfuls of the curves I'd been admiring all night, and lost it. "You tell me, babe. I'll be better after I fuck you so hard I wipe away every last trace of that asshole's fingers on you. Hell, I'll be better when you're screaming my name tonight, begging me to work this dick in deeper."

"Roman," she purred my name, wrapping her hands around my back and pulling me tight.

It was all I needed to lean into her, making sure she got a nice hard brush from my cock, still raging like a warhead in my pants. I must've caught her clit in the thrust because she arched her back and moaned, shriller than before.

"I've missed this hot, sweet pussy wrapped around me for two years. Two fucking years too long. Come on, babe. Let's catch up, talk skin-to-skin again."

IX: Rampage (Sally)

His eyes were full and dark. He'd fought like hell for me. I wasn't sure how he was even standing after the savage blow from Beam's fist, but he was, and the rigid cock brushing against my pussy said lust was a much bigger problem than his pain.

"Come on, babe. Let's catch up, talk skin-to-skin again."

He lowered his head, growling as his lips met mine. My mouth tensed up, opening for his tongue, and I moaned into his kiss as every muscle below the waist unraveled.

We kissed for more than a minute, hot and rough and wanting. Then he snatched me up, pulling me into his arms, speeding toward the bedroom.

I hit the bed and bounced as he shoved me down. Roman pressed me into the sheets, covering me completely, moving his mouth over mine. He kissed meaner than before, trying to get his tongue deeper, deeper, *so* deliciously deep.

It was like he'd forgotten how good I tasted, and he

never wanted to again.

His hands slid beneath me, cupping my ass, and squeezed. My legs instinctively wrapped around him, and I moaned when he broke the kiss, bringing his marvelous mouth to the nook of my neck.

Teeth. Fireworks. A molten heat like nothing I'd felt for two years exploded in my core.

His huge cock rubbed me through his jeans. I didn't know whether to shred our clothes this instant, or just let him keep going, forcing me to come right through my panties and skirt.

"Fuck, babe," he growled, breaking the love bite near my throat. "You know how bad I've been starving for this? I'm *dying*, ever since I got my brand on you."

"Not half as bad as me," I whimpered, fixing my eyes on his. Then the bad girl took over. "Fuck me, Roman. I want you inside me so fast and hard it wipes away the last two years. I want you to fuck the bitterness right out of my heart, fuck away the pain, fuck me blind until I can't see anything except the future."

His lips peeled back and he growled. He leaned up, throwing his cut off, before peeling off the Grizzlies MC shirt underneath. The roaring bear emblazoned on his chest showed itself, and so did half a dozen other rough MC symbols, swords and skulls and thorns inked on his beautiful skin.

"God, I've missed this. You've added to the canvass, I see." I ran my fingers over the new additions near his abs, a 1% sign in a diamond patch, dripping like black blood.

I'd noticed them before, of course, all the other times he'd been walking around shirtless. But for the first time since he'd moved in, since we'd reconciled, they were all *mine*. I could study his incredible body in all the detail I wanted – at least until I couldn't do anything except beg for his cock.

"Bring those hands lower, babe. There's another surprise."

He grabbed my hand and guided it down to the ridge tenting his jeans. His fingers squeezed over mine, making me feel his cock. I shuddered, and then jerked up when I felt something small and unnatural near the tip of his cock.

"What the hell?" I swallowed and grinned. "Jesus, is that what I think it is?"

His hands ripped at his belt and he shoved his jeans down, then worked off his boxers, the smile on his face growing. "You tell me, woman. Put your hot little tongue on my dick. Think about how the new improvement's gonna feel inside you."

Orders, orders. And I couldn't help but comply. He leaned on the bed, helping me up with his hands, then running one hand through my hair, balling several thick blonde strands in his fist.

I rubbed my thumb over his swollen, angry head, finding that little stud. Jesus, it was real after all.

A small, cool, very metallic bead planted dead in the center of his tip. Just imagining all the ways it would feel inside me made my clit burn. I looked up at him as I loosened my lips, stroking his massive length, opening wide to draw him into my mouth.

Roman groaned and lifted his hips when I swallowed him. Pure, rich, masculine heat bathed my tongue. I started to work him slow and steady, circling underneath his head, taking as much as I could.

I hadn't sucked cock for years, and all I knew about sucking it was exactly what he'd taught me. But my brain tingled as the memories came back. I remembered the two tender spots around his crown that always drove him crazy, and I aimed for them with my tongue, swirling and moving my head rhythmically.

"Oh, fuck. Keep going, baby girl. I tried to forget how good you sucked all those nights in prison." He pushed my head into him, increasing his pressure. "My cock never did. Putting a piercing through this mean motherfucker doesn't change shit. It remembers, babe, and it wants every goddamned inch of you."

I moaned. I seriously wondered if my panties had completely disintegrated in the hot, wet mess steaming underneath my skirt. No man's filthy words turned me on like his.

Even when I'd kissed Beam that fateful day, it wasn't the same. His lips were hollow, weak, meaningless.

I didn't want to admit it then, but now I knew for sure – Roman *owned* me. He took me over the minute he knocked me up, magnetizing me to his flesh, making me respond at some wicked, primal level no man could ever match.

My nipples hurt like they had clothespins pinching them underneath my shirt. I tried to focus on sucking them, but I lifted one hand up, working off my bra for dear relief.

No sooner than I popped the clasp, Roman reached for my fist, tugging my hand back to his thigh. "Keep your hands on my cock, girl. I'll do the rest when I'm good and ready."

I sucked him for a couple more minutes. He closed his eyes, the growls in his throat rumbling like a nascent avalanche, building toward the inevitable crescendo.

His hands fell behind my head, holding me there, tight and perfect for fucking my mouth. His hips picked up speed. I couldn't help but think about how hard he'd stroke me later with that little bead mounted on his tip.

Could sex actually be dangerous? I worried how my body would react, how good he'd feel deep inside me. But it couldn't be worse than delaying the sweet release any longer, right?

I wasn't sure, but I was going to find out. If he killed me with pleasure tonight, then at least I'd die happy.

"Fuck, babe, the way you move your lips…" His fist jerked on my hair and his hips slammed to a stop, deep in my mouth. I thought he was going to come, but he pulled my lips off him instead, inhaling so hard his huge chest ballooned.

"Good?" I asked, wiping my mouth.

"Just half as good as your pussy's gonna feel wrapped around it. Get that shit off now." His hands fell all over me, ripping at my shirt, throwing my bra behind him.

One rough hand tugged at my skirt, and I rolled on the bed to help him. When it was halfway down, his opposite hand felt the soaked lace between my legs, and his satisfied thunder rolled into my ear.

"You're wet as fuck, aren't you?"

"Isn't that a given?" I bit my lip, all I could do to stop myself from coming as his hand cupped my mound, feeling my heat, my wetness.

He laughed, low and throaty, sending a fresh sensual chill up my spine. "Careful playing smartass, babe. My cock's so riled up I'll fuck that sass right outta you if it keeps up. The only lip I wanna hear right now is how loud you scream when I fuck you right through the floor."

God! I quaked when his fingers wrapped around my waistband. In one fluid jerk, they tore down my thighs, so quick I felt air rush over my pussy.

I was totally exposed, but not for long.

A new heat smothered the firestorm building in my pussy. His fingers rubbed my folds and pushed deep inside me, all in one stroke, just as his thumb found my clit. He had his finger on the trigger now, and I was thoroughly *fucked* in all the best ways.

Well, maybe all of them except one.

"You're not getting this dick 'til I'm good and ready, babe. I'm gonna savor you. It's been two years. Two fucked up years straight from the pit of hell. You know how often I jacked off to this in the slammer? How many times I thought about pinching these tits, how hard I'd make your sweet cunt gush when I got the fuck out? I wanna taste you everywhere. Fingers, lips, teeth, tongue. Give it the fuck up."

Holy shit.

My hips began grinding into his hand as he fucked me with his fingers. Oh, fuck. I didn't have a clue, but judging by the insane edge in his voice, it must've been hundreds.

His other hand reached around and covered one breast. He tightened his hold, pinching one nipple between his fingers, never letting up on my pussy for a second.

Heat rushed into my head like lava. I wasn't going to last long at all like this, especially if he didn't –

Stop. What the hell?

My thighs were shaking as they gripped his hand, too low now to tease my pussy. A minute must've passed. His free hand moved to my other breast, plumping the lonely nipple there soft again, making me tingle in all the right ways and teasing me in the worst.

"Come back, baby. Come back, Travis," I murmured, knowing I was playing with fire using his real name. Hey, he'd said it was fair game in the bedroom, right? "Please. You're *killing* me."

"That begging's hot, babe, but I've had my fill. Roll over and spread your legs. I'll decide how and when to fuck you. Right now, I'm thinking my hands aren't going anywhere near your clit again 'til you come on my mouth."

Oh, God.

Before I could even think about protesting, he flipped me over, shifted between my legs, and ran his rough stubble up my right thigh.

The wild sensation should've prepared me for his tongue sliding through my slit a second later, but of course it didn't. Two years untouched by a man – especially *this* man – left me a near virgin mess, trembling from the shock.

His lips *consumed* me, hot and overwhelming, hellbent on making me lose control. And it didn't take much.

He shook his head between my legs like a wild animal. The earthquake spread to my thighs.

Too intense. Too fucking good. It was everything I'd missed, and so much more.

My legs tried to quiver shut from the insane shock, and his hands caught my thighs, shoving them apart. Nothing was stopping him from owning me the way he wanted, forcing me to come all over his mouth.

Not that I needed much encouragement. Several more rough licks focused around my clit did me in. In one wet flesh, my muscles tensed, winding up like a spring deep inside me, ready to give it up.

"*Travis.* Roman! God!" My fingers grabbed for the sheets and balled them as tight as I could.

I couldn't think. Couldn't resist. Couldn't even remember to breathe.

The white hot ball inside me exploded, pulsing through my nerves in one go, making me convulse from head to toe. Yes, especially the toes, which curled over his shoulders. Roman's fingers dug into my legs and pulled me tighter, pushing his tongue deep, all the better to fuck me while I gushed into his mouth.

I came with lightning crisscrossing every inch of my body, shearing me with the pleasure I'd been deprived of for two whole fucking years. Maybe I came harder because I thought it was going to be denied forever.

He'd taken me back, and this time, he wasn't letting go.

I twitched and writhed and came for him, twisting my head from side to side, tearing at the sheets. Slowly, his licks softened, and I started to come down from the stormy heavens.

My lungs sucked in badly needed air. My muscles squirmed with sorely needed relief, but there was still a strange tingle behind everything, a background static in my body that wouldn't be switched off until I had his cock, his come, his everything buried inside me again.

I blinked and looked down at him, reaching one hand toward his face. He raised himself up when I grazed his cheek, admiring the masculine sandpaper on his hard face.

"You come just as hard as I remember. It's fucking beautiful. I could watch you lose it for a thousand years and I'd still want more. No bullshit."

I smiled, slid my legs along his muscular sides, opening wide for him. "Hmm. Better watch me again. I want you inside me, baby."

A savage flicker lit his handsome dark eyes. He lifted my legs high, grabbed my ankles in his massive hands, tilting me back, open and achingly ready.

"I'm not gonna stop after one round," he growled. "Fair warning. You got any idea what two years of blue balls for the best pussy in the world does to a man?"

The look on his face was almost scary. I shook my head. It didn't stop me from reaching for the huge hard-on jutting out between his legs, wrapping my fingers around it, and squeezing my desire.

No, I didn't have a clue. But I absolutely wanted to find out.

"Fuck me," I whispered. "Let it all out. Claim me like your old lady, Roman. I want it all, inside and out."

He looked at me for another breathless second. Then his hips rolled forward, and he shoved my hand off his cock, replacing it with his own fist. He guided the pierced head of his angry length to my entrance, snapping his hips forward when he found the right angle.

He filled me in one fluid thrust. My pussy tightened around him, fit him just as well as it had before. Having Caleb hadn't ruined anything.

Hell, I had to bite my lip and push back to take every inch, easing him into me. My wet pussy needed time and practice to hold him just right, and his first few strokes were almost painful as they glided through me. Deep, hard, hissing with desire.

I moaned, stretching to spread my thighs, opening wider. His thrusts quickened amazingly fast, plowing into me, like a hurricane picking up speed.

His movements matched his words. He fucked me like

a man who'd been starving, a man who hadn't known a woman's touch for years. Yes, he'd had at least one stinking skank in between, but they weren't what he wanted.

It was me.

I couldn't imagine him moving this way with them. He fucked me like he wanted it with every fiber of his being, rearing up and slamming into me, charging his hips into me. The new bed slapped underneath us, lifting my ass up and crashing it into the mattress again.

Jesus. Don't stop, Roman. Keep fucking me.

It felt too good to say the words. I couldn't do anything but moan, clenching him tight, wondering how may seconds I'd last before I screamed.

About twenty. Roughly the same number of thrusts he leveled into me, each one harder than the last, growling a little more every time he drove to my depths.

His pierced tip scratched an itch I didn't know I had. It glided through me, seamless as the rest of him, teasing my walls like nothing ever had.

No vibrator, no dildo, *nothing* matched this freak of a dick inside me, and I freaking *loved it.*

His balls slapped my ass harder as he hit full force. I was coming apart each time he drove it home, and then in one last fiery collision, I lost it. My moans became howls. My legs pinched around him like a vise, digging into his granite muscle, desperate to hold on for the grand finale.

"Come the fuck all over my dick, babe," he growled, reaching one hand behind my head and fisting my hair.

"Let it all out. Make your pussy milk my balls dry."

The dirty talk slayed me. I thought I'd come myself blind when his tongue was lapping at my clit, but now his cock taught me different each time he drove deep, stroking my little bud with his pubic bone. One more stroke sent me straight to ecstasy.

I couldn't dream of holding out. I tightened up, locked onto him as hard as I could, and screamed bloody murder.

Holy fucking hellfire!

The convulsions hit like a tsunami. My pussy gushed, pinched, and sucked at his cock. He fucked me faster through the climax, fucked me until the entire world rocked and churned around me. I threw my head back as he jerked my hair in my hands, loving the burn, feeling the fire roasting me from all directions.

This orgasm ripped into shrapnel, searing every distant nerve, kissing my blood with hot lava.

And just when I thought it peaked, his manic thrusts stopped, but he wasn't done. He roared, holding me against the bed with all the power in his hips, burying himself to the hilt.

His massive cock swelled impossibly bigger. Then he pulsed, jerked inside me, and I felt the first molten pump, the seed flowing into me in one magma jet after another.

Oh, fuck! *Save me.*

But nothing could do that now except spiraling face first into another orgy of release. I rocked, grunted, came, and shrieked like a mad woman as his cock exploded inside me. Our animal voices meshed just like our bodies, two energies colliding into one, creating something so hot and unbelievable I could barely comprehend it.

No, I couldn't even try.

Not while he was still pumping his seed in my womb, flooding me, spilling his essence into my raw pleasure.

I knew the risk. He'd fucked his way through my protection before, I prayed it would work this time.

But I didn't pray for the pills to do their job this time until it was all over. For just one second, locked in our flaming release, I *wanted* him to knock me up again.

My body knew damned well what it wanted, and this insane thrill tore me apart. I needed his come inside me, and my greedy pussy milked him just like he commanded me to.

He stayed hard inside me long after the spasms stopped. Roman leaned down, buried my lips in his, plunging his tongue in and out of my mouth. Coming hadn't slowed him down one bit.

He led my tongue in a mouth-to-mouth fuck with the same hot vigor his cock used inside me just minutes ago.

"I fucking love your body, babe. It's goddamned crack."

And I fucking love you.

I almost said it. Something made me bite my tongue.

It wasn't time for that yet, and – Jesus! – was he really still hard? The man was a fuck machine, and it wasn't an exaggeration.

His hips shifted into me in small, shallow strokes, beginning to thrust all over again. He kissed me again.

This time I bit his lip, the roughest tease I could manage.

"Up on your hands and knees, Sally," he growled.

"You really don't need a break?"

"I had my break behind bars. I already told you – we're fucking all night, every night, as long as you're wearing my brand. We both know I've missed too many nights already. We're fucking double to make up for all the lost time."

Smiling, I rolled as he reluctantly pulled out, and his strong hands helped me into line. I hoped he'd at least let me have a few solid hours of sleep in between this long night of frenzied sex and feeding Caleb at the crack of dawn.

No luck. Unless you call lucky being fucked by a badass half a dozen times before he even let up – and maybe I did.

Roman fucked me with every molecule of the full dizzying force his massive body had to offer. My breasts swung wild beneath me as he thrust, slamming into me, slapping my clit with his heavy balls each time he went deep.

I'd heard plenty about the G-spot, but I never knew where mine was until that little silver bead in his cock stroked me at just the right angle. Everything between my legs billowed up in a hot, tense mess. He ripped my head up by the hair in his fist, just in time to scream.

"Holy. Fucking. Christ!"

A new sensation tore through my pussy. Hot lightning shattered me whole, made me lose control. Roman fucked faster, hurling me off the cliff into the pleasure zone. My clit sang, and I felt myself losing something hot and wet all over him and the sheets.

It kept coming as he power fucked me too. Just when I thought I was about to blackout, he pounded deep, held his swelling cock there, joining me in the greatest climax ever.

Roman's opposite hand pinched my ass, puling me tight. We sank down and hit the bed together. His cock pumped more searing come into me, filling me to overflowing. Our cream spilled out and stained the bed, and we weren't even finished.

We came like there was no tomorrow. Hell, locked in his embrace, I wondered if that old cliché might be right. A few more romps like this, and I might not wake up alive.

He brought me back to life with a gentle slap on the ass. "Fuck, babe. I always knew you could squirt."

"Is *that* what you did to me?" I whispered, feeling him pull out and turning around to face him on the bed.

"You tell me." He pointed to the wet spot between my legs. "You did that for me, woman, and you'd better get used to it. Start bringing a fucking canteen to bed. If your pussy doesn't do fireworks when you clench this cock, I haven't done my damned job."

Growling, he leaned down, caressing my cheek with his soft lips and rough stubble. "And I *always* work like hell 'til it's done. Don't ever doubt that shit for a second."

I shuddered. My whole world folded into him,

collapsed into that big, strong vastness in his powerful arms. Twisting my head, we kissed for several minutes.

I wondered how my body kept going when the new tingle started in my pussy. It came slow, a rising wave of need. Roman must've felt it too. He cupped my folds in one hand and squeezed, possessive and seductive.

"Don't die on me now, woman. This is only the first night. It's a week long fuckfest I'm after. We're only stepping outta this room to see our kid and get some grub. You've been mine since the moment I knocked you up, babe, and we're making up for two years of lost sex in the next week, even if I've gotta rub my dick raw."

His thumb sank deeper, sliding through my wetness. He sounded insane, but he felt so *good*, especially when he covered my clit, stroking new circles that opened my legs again. It was like he'd figured out the password to my body, and I burned every time he opened me.

He wasn't really going to keep me locked in bed for an entire week – was he? His tone said he wasn't joking. Hell, did he *ever* joke around?

I saw my fate, rolling out like new shadows in the dark room. I was in bed with a ferocious, possibly crazy, badass. Totally at his mercy, and that wasn't even the worst part.

Each time I looked into dark brown eyes through my narrowed lids, my heart hummed three times faster.

Say all you want about Stockholm Syndrome. Whatever was happening to my brain and body cut deep, and it was *real*.

I was falling in love, and it scared me to death.

X: Paradise Rocked (Roman)

For the next three days, I did everything I promised, and then some.

I fucked my woman horizontal, diagonal, up, down, hot and cold, sideways, and fucking zigzag. I burned her scent and taste into my brain so deep I'd remember it as a senile old fart on my deathbed – if I avoided dad's fate like I intended.

And damn if I wasn't gonna try. I'd fight like hell for this new family.

But shit, it was hard to imagine battling anything at all laid out here, with her wrapped around me.

The cartel war's violence and danger seemed like a distant world in bed. We ordered in and put on our robes in between nonstop fucking.

Watching our kid toddle around the living room and tug on my feet for attention was almost as satisfying as having Sally underneath me. I'd become an honest-to-God, no shit family man, and it made me pretty fucking happy too.

A man could get used to this. Now, all I needed to do

was shove a ring on her finger and make all this official. My son wasn't growing up wondering why the hell his folks weren't hitched.

On the third night, we put him to bed, and turned in early. Sally came trotting into the master bedroom from her bath, wearing this lacy red stuff with pantyhose and bitch heels that instantly made me wanna feel them digging into my ass while I hammered into her.

Shit!

"Get the fuck over here," I growled, grabbing her as she climbed onto the bed.

Kissing this woman became a dangerous addiction. I'd never been a druggie like the Veep, but I imagined every time my lips hit hers, I got a taste of that bliss he'd pumped into his veins before he sorted out his shit.

Drug or not, this chick was dangerous. She'd rewired my brain, and I'd do fucking anything to keep her from slipping away ever again.

Christ, she tasted divine. My hands tore off her bra. Lingerie looked pretty, yeah, but my fingers burned every minute they weren't on her tits or pussy, and my tongue ached to be wrapped around her too.

"Travis!" she gasped, moving her long nails around the back of my head, tightening the hold my teeth had on her nipple.

I sucked it deep into my mouth, lashing it with my tongue again and again. My cock jerked each time I did, hounding me like a relentless motherfucker to get between her legs.

Patience. Teasing her sweet ass always made it better for both of us. When we finally joined, it was like a goddamned warhead went off every time, blowing our brains out our ears each time our bodies pulsed.

"Roll over, babe," I ordered, grabbing at her hot red panties. They looked like they'd been made by the devil himself to hide her perfect pussy, and I wasn't gonna tolerate that shit for long.

She smiled and hissed hot breath when I smacked her ass, making her twist over me faster. She straddled me, putting her sopping wet cunt against my dick.

I aimed my pierced cock right at her clit and rubbed, coating myself in her juices, thinking about the hot wet heat I'd soon be buried in, all the way to my balls.

She pinched her eyes shut and let out a loud, low moan, drawing her hands down to my chest. Her nails raked long and slow, making me *itch* to impale her that second.

I had it bad. The only relief was fucking this chick 'til she screamed even louder than the time before.

"Damn!" Sally groaned. "You don't get to tease me like this, Travis."

I thrust my cock over her clit again, toying with her entrance, grabbing her wrists with both hands. "Keep using my real name like that and I will."

Her eyelids drooped again while I thrust harder. Then she pushed back at my dick, so hard and good and unexpected I saw red stars. The hell with this dry humping shit.

"Fucking shit. Get on top of this cock and ride, babe. You've made your point. We'll both leave a damned crater in this room if we don't fuck. *Now.*"

I dropped the grip on her wrists, placing my hands on her ass, tugging her forward. She shifted, drawing her slick pussy away from my cock.

What the hell?

"Not until you tell me why they call you Roman. You've never explained it. Is it the way you fuck?" She smiled, curious and teasing at once.

Was she goddamned serious? Sally expected me to tell her about my road name while our lust threatened to burn this bed to cinders?

"Because I'll crucify any asshole who gets in my way. I've done it, and I'll do it again," I growled, yanking her against me harder, squeezing my cock against her cunt so she couldn't wrestle away. "That includes you, babe, if you don't drop the Q and A and take me deep now. I'm doing you a favor. Your clit wants friction, Sally – not some gory fucking details about how I nailed some fuckers arms and legs to the nearest post and watched 'em bleed out in front of me and the guys."

Her lips quivered. Fear flashed in her eyes, but her skin got a couple degrees hotter. Okay, I liked a chick with some freak in her, and Sally was the perfect mix.

I knew what turned her on, and I obliged. She wanted rough? She wanted bad?

Fine. I'd give it to her in spades.

Remembering she was with a bad boy, an outlaw, a

fucking *killer* got her hot – at least when she'd swapped her goody farm girl boots for those hot red bitch heels. And if she wanted to fuck Roman the outlaw biker instead of Travis Forker, father and future husband, then I'd let her.

I'd be whatever the hell she wanted to get her cunt exploding on my dick.

I bared my teeth. Reaching up, I grabbed her by the throat, jerking her head close 'til she stared right into my eyes. "Drag your pussy down on this cock. Fuck me hard and fast. Fuck me like you gotta impress me to stay alive, babe. I'm not asking again."

For a second, she looked at me like I'd lost my goddamned mind. Then, her legs parted, and I felt every slick inch of velvet engulf me.

I pushed deep like I always did. Hard. Didn't fucking stop 'til I felt my balls snug against her ass.

I hissed like I always did when I got my first taste of her pussy on my dick for the night. My hips slammed up to meet hers. Our flesh crashed, and she threw her head back, squirming from the pleasure bomb I unleashed in her belly.

My hand swept around her neck, fisted her hair, and held it while I slapped her ass with my other hand, forcing her to pick up the pace.

The bed creaked like a motherfucker while our hips pounded together. We thrust, quaked, and slammed against each other like maniacs. Her heels caught the sides of my thighs and dug in.

It only made me fuck her faster.

She scratched my chest, clawing at the bear, probably drawing blood outta the GRIZZLIES MC, CALIFORNIA rocker around it. I grabbed her ass with both hands and jerked her up and down on my cock.

Faster, faster, faster – I'd go so rough she turned into fucking splinters on top of me. I rattled her bones hard enough to hurt, and she loved it.

A few more strokes, and her pussy convulsed, sucking me deep as her fingernails lost their tension.

Her blonde hair whipped back and her sweaty face tensed. She came beautiful, belting out curses that gave me a good run every time her body spasmed. I couldn't hold the fuck back.

I slammed into her harder, letting my hands do all the work, pounding her hips into mine and bringing it home.

"Fuck! Take it deep, baby girl. Take every goddamned drop of my come. I want you *full* of me."

She whimpered, begging for it, just like I'd trained her. Sally's greedy cunt sucked me hard when my cock swelled and burst, drawing out every thick rope I shot from my tip.

We lost ourselves in the hot, wet heat. Nothing else mattered in this paradise, this glorious friction fusing our bodies and syncing our heartbeats. I could've mounted this woman forever and pumped my fire inside her, if nature would've allowed it.

Instead, I did the next best thing.

Soon as she stopped thrashing and stabbing me with

those heels, I drew outta her, reawakened her from her sex coma with a kiss, and slowly turned her over.

My cock barely needed a moment's rest with this girl. Maybe I'd overload and blow the fuck up someday. Maybe I'd fuck so hard I gave myself a stroke.

Whatever, at least I'd have good reason to get *he died fucking happy* etched on my tombstone.

She panted as I spread her legs apart and slid into her, feeling my slick seed mixed with her cream, running down her thighs.

"Again?" she whimpered. "God, you're crazy."

"Keep fucking me, babe, and you'll be too. I'm an animal when your naked skin's against mine."

"You say that now," she moaned, arching her back as I did a full thrust. "What about next month? Next year? Will we still fuck so much then?"

I threw my head back and laughed. Then I answered her by slamming in so hard her tits bounced, feeling my balls touch her clit, holding it there against her womb. The friction almost murdered her.

"You think I'll get tired of emptying my balls inside you? You gotta be shitting me. You *really* believe that? Come on, babe. I know you're not stupid."

She opened her mouth, but nothing except another shrill moan came out. I reached for her hair, yanked her close, and brought my mouth down to her ear.

"Let's make this crystal-fucking-clear, in case it already isn't. I *own* you, Sally. I *need* you. You're the only chick on this planet I ever wanted to put my brand on. You're the only woman I'll kill for, die for, bury my dick inside 'til the day I die. You're the only one who's given me a son, and you're gonna give me a whole lot more before I lay off pounding your cunt seven days a week."

She whimpered, and her cheeks flushed hot against my stubble. I made shallow strokes inside her, making her feel every inch of me, stroking myself all over her walls.

Except it wasn't just hers anymore.

My walls. *My* pussy. *My* everything, now.

I owned this woman, and I'd never, ever let the fuck up. *Never.*

"Tell me you understand, babe, or I'll forget about taking shit slow and easy." I paused, listening to her murmur nonsense, pleading as my cock slid through her. "I'll pull out, march the fuck over to your purse, and throw every packet of those pills out the window. I'll knock you up tomorrow without a second thought if you've still got doubts about *any* of this."

"Oh, God. Roman...please."

"Please, what?" I growled, nipping at her earlobe. Her pussy kept getting hotter and hotter around my cock. "Fucking say it. Say you understand!"

My rough palm slapped her ass. Then she said the words that almost sucked all the wind outta my sails.

"I'm sorry, I don't know what it is. I don't know what I'm thinking anymore. I love you!"

The L-word left me too stunned to speak. I did the only thing I could – I grabbed her round ass and fucked her as hard as I could, showing her the shit I couldn't bring myself to say in every thrust of my hips.

I'd never been much for words, especially when all this raw emotion swept me up like a damned wave, pouring its energy into my hips.

She came lightning on my dick, and I emptied myself in her for the second time of many that night.

Much later, after we'd fucked ourselves sore, I watched her drifting off to sleep. I pulled her closer, settling her soft cheek on my chest, brushing the golden locks outta her face.

"You think some crazy shit, girl. All these fucked up misunderstandings between us…they're over. We're starting over." I paused, filling her ear with hot, eager breath. "I love you too, babe. Don't you ever doubt it again."

Day four of my attempt to jam two lost years of fucking into one week started like gold. I sucked her sweet cunt 'til she came, then took her again in the shower, watching her ass bounce as the cool water washed away last night's sweat.

We cleaned up and went down to get breakfast with Caleb. She started cooking eggs and bacon on the stove while I fed the kid, making those rocket sounds that made him laugh every time I spooned food into his hungry little lips.

Then my phone lit up next to me, buzzing on the table. I swore, picked it up, and cursed a second time when I saw Brass' number.

"What's going on, brother?"

"Get your ass down to the Jennings' place now. There's been an incident."

"Fuck." I stood up, shoved the chair away, hoping Sally hadn't heard her family name dropped. "What the hell happened? Cartel?"

"Two guys down. One of ours. They got that stubborn bastard, Norm, too. He's fucked up real bad. The ambulance just picked him up, and the Prez'll be by shortly to deal with our contacts in the Redding PD to keep this shit quiet."

"Sonofabitch. I'm on my way." I was about to hang up when I thought about my girl. She deserved to know about her cousin. "Wait, is it safe to bring my old lady?"

Brass paused. "It's daytime. They won't have the balls to show their faces here for a repeat, especially while the cops are swarming in. Come on, brother, move your ass."

The line went dead. Sally stopped cooking and she was at my side, her face creased up with fear.

"We gotta go, babe. I'll talk to Christa or Missy to see about somebody watching Caleb. Your cousin's hurt."

"What?! Norman?" Hot tears exploded in her eyes. "*Idiot. I told him to get out while the going was good! I tried.*"

The anger melted, and she clutched at my arm. "Is it bad?"

"Dunno. Come on. We gotta fucking move."

Stryker sat next to Asphalt on the farmhouse porch, a torn shirt wrapped around his bicep. The blood seeped through it like dark crimson paint, and I saw equal fucking red every time I looked around the small war zone around us.

Glass blown out all through the kitchen, spilling into the garden out back. Some fucker had taken out the windows, blasted an automatic straight up the side of the house. I wasn't sure where the hell Sally used to keep our son, but thinking it could've been *him* in there, waiting to get cut to pieces by some asshole's fire, filled me with a special rage.

"Spit it out. What the hell did you guys see?"

"I just got back from making the rounds," Asphalt said, tensing up. "Stryker and Beam were supposed to be watching the house. No sooner than I stepped off my bike, parking it out back by the barn, the truck tore in and lit the place up. I hit the ground and drew. Started firing at the windshield. I put a couple holes through their glass, but I don't think I hit any of the motherfuckers. They whipped the truck around and screamed outta there before anybody could blow their tires."

"And that's how you ended up with a bullet in your arm?" I looked at Stryker.

He nodded. His eyes were wide, as if he was still processing the shock. The boy looked too damned nervous for my liking, but sometimes new brothers were like this when they saw their own blood hit the floor for the first time.

"They got inside. Don't know how, maybe some sneaky fucks on foot, maybe another vehicle. I heard Norm screaming downstairs, went running to back him up. Next thing I know, the windows exploded. Some cartel SOB kicked the back door open and sent hell my way. If I hadn't moved fast enough, I would've caught this shit in the chest." He pounded himself on the heart with his fist.

Lucky man. Too fucking lucky for my liking. I folded my arms, staring them both down.

Asphalt would never screw us over. As for our new additions – and where the fuck was Beam, anyway? – I wasn't so sure.

"Rest up, brother. I'm going in to survey the scene." I walked in and found Sally already inside.

She stood in the kitchen, staring at the mess, two bloody streaks on the floor left behind by Stryker catching lead on his way to the basement. Her big blue eyes looked up at me, and then she turned, heading for the downstairs door.

I caught up and grabbed her wrist, spinning her against my chest. "Don't. I'm going down first to make sure it's all clear. It's my job. Prez said it's fucking gruesome. Stay the hell up here unless you wanna see your cousin's dried blood too."

I didn't mention the busted teeth scattered on the ground. Men had definitely gotten into the house, and they'd surprised the stubborn farmer, pistol whipping him into a coma, or maybe using something bigger and heavier than a gun.

"You're right," she snapped. "I need to be with him. How much longer?"

"I'll take a quick peek downstairs, and then we'll head to the hospital."

I ripped open the door and pounded down the narrow stone steps, ducking as I made my way into the hole in the ground that doubled as a laundry room and storm shelter. Scattered light poured through the crack in the storm door to the side. The basement's lone light bulb was smashed in the commotion.

I saw something move against the wall, and my hand instantly drew. Beam's ugly face appeared in the shadows. Anger tangled up his bitter mug when he saw me with a nine millimeter aimed at his head.

"You gonna finish what we started at the clubhouse by blowing my brains out my skull?"

"Depends on what the fuck you're doing down here. Why aren't you upstairs?"

"Same reason you're down here, brother. I'm taking it all in. Trying to figure out what the fuck happened. Prez thinks we've got a rat in our ranks. Looks like it's Stryker to me."

Fuck. I goddamned despised being on the same page as this asshole. I lowered my gun, kicked aside some broken glass left by the light bulb. A few tiny pellets bounced behind the washer – probably the poor bastard's teeth.

"The storm door was locked up tight. They busted the window, undid the lock, and fucked him up before he could get off a shot." Beam pointed to the bloody shotgun laying in the corner. "It's like somebody knew exactly how to get inside. Only thing I'm not sure about is what the fuck drew him down here in the first place."

"Leave that shit to me," I growled, trying to keep the hot gun in my hand aimed at the ground.

"Whatever you want. Listen, I'm sorry we got into it the other night. I was a fucking idiot to keep going after Sally after you'd claimed her. I know that now."

"Stay the fuck away from my woman, and we won't have any more problems."

The bastard managed a thin, awkward smile. I didn't trust him – especially not with that punk rock haircut looking like he'd just walked outta the nearest pet shop. He'd get his ass whipped hard in prison for that.

Too bad I wasn't sure if Stryker was an even bigger bastard. Neither of these boys sat right with me, and my rat senses droned every time I looked at both of 'em. If only we'd waited a couple weeks before handing them the patch.

Fuck. I'd have never voted yea.

"Shake on it." Beam stuck his hand out. "The Prez doesn't want any bad blood in the club. I'm man enough to admit I fucked up bad, brother, and I hope some day you'll forgive me."

It took me several seconds to finally take it. I squeezed him so hard his fingers flinched in mine. Then I broke away, stuffing my gun back in my holster.

"Just get outta here and take the other door. I can forgive you, but my old lady's not ready for that shit after what you did."

He nodded, and I watched him undo the storm door's

lock. It banged behind him as he headed out, going up the small stone steps leading to the garden behind the house.

I looked shit over again. None of it made sense. I also realized I'd forgotten to ask the bastard where he'd been all night, and I'd need to remedy that as soon as we all calmed the fuck down.

When I got upstairs, Sally sat at the kitchen table, her face resting delicately in one hand. She stood up when she saw me.

"Well?"

"Let's get outta here. We'd better go see your cousin before the Prez rides my ass to debrief on this shit. I've got a few hours, if we're lucky."

She followed me back to the truck. The whole drive out to the hospital, she clung to my hand, as if I'd single-handedly swept down from the sky and carried her away from all this.

That was only half the battle when I marched in and took control. We'd gotten lucky that I'd gotten her and the kid out before things went to shit.

Lady Luck winked at my sorry ass this time, but I wasn't gonna rely on her help again. I had to find the rat and make sure the Mexicans were chased outta NorCal forever. Anything less put my old lady and son at risk, and I'd fucking die before it was their blood on the ground instead of Norm and Stryker's.

The man in the hospital bed had the hellfire sucked right outta him.

Norm's arms and legs were shattered. They'd busted his jaw too, fractured it with such skull-cracking force the poor bastard would be lucky to operate a good pair of dentures or some implants one day.

I watched my girl kneel at his side, her hand tightly clutching his. "Why did you have to be this stupid? This stubborn? *Why?*"

She kept shaking her head. I stepped up, put my hand on her shoulder, and squeezed.

"Just let him rest, babe. He did a dumb thing, digging in his heels when he knew he didn't have the support. But he stood up for your place like a man, and I can respect that. He's a tough motherfucker. I gotta feeling he'll be on his feet again sooner than you think."

So I hoped. I wasn't just hoping my woman's cousin would bounce back for her sake neither. He just might be the only man there that night who could tell us what happened, without feeding the club a line of bullshit.

I barely trusted letting Stryker and Beam outta my sight. Their wounds and tough words didn't prove shit. Somebody ratted to let the cartel slip through for this kinda attack, and there'd be absolute hell to pay when we found out who.

Sally stood up, blotting at the angry tears slicing down her cheeks. "Maybe you're right. I just didn't think it'd come to this. I knew the cartel was horrible, but seeing their brutality like this, up close and personal…"

I didn't let her say another word. Just pulled her in tight and smashed her face to my chest. I held her for a long time, eyeing the beat up shell of a man in that bed.

He'd fought the bastards hard and lost, stumbling into disaster without realizing how shitty his odds were. Maybe mine weren't much better, the same as the rest of the club, but damn if I'd get my ass kicked so easily.

These fucking invaders would *never* put my old lady or my kid in a bed like this. I'd be in my own grave before they did.

"Don't ever do this to me," Sally hissed, fire lighting up her bright blue eyes. "I won't survive seeing you torn up like this. I'll lose it, Roman, I'll –"

"That's enough." I dug my fingers into her chin, tilting her small face to mine, giving her the most reassuring look in the whole damned world. "We're gonna beat them, babe. I don't give a shit what it costs, or how long it takes. You're gonna help this old boy back onto the farm when we're done, and he'll live to pick up where he left off."

She bit her lip and tried to break the lock my eyes had on her, but I wouldn't let her. I didn't release her head 'til she stopped looking so panicked, sinking into my arms with a heavy sigh.

"Now, stop worrying. I'm gonna get you home and I'll hash this shit out with the club. All you gotta worry about is keeping the kid fed and happy. Nothing else."

Later that night, I sat on the edge of the bed, long after she'd slumped into a melancholy sleep. My dick ached.

That thing between my legs was an emotionless demon. It had no goddamned context for tragedy, and didn't give a shit about anything except the fact that our week long fuckfest had been rudely interrupted.

Just watching her sleep made me want her so fucking bad. I stood up, stretched my legs, and crept into the closet for my clothes.

I was pulling on my cut when I walked into Caleb's room to check on him. The baby rolled over in his crib, awakening just enough to catch a glimpse of me. He grabbed at the wooden posts on the side, reaching one small hand through the gap.

I stepped up and took it. "Be good for mama, little man. You and her are the only fucking thing I've got. Rest up."

Caleb cooed. I stood up and swept my hand gently over his head, then walked out and quietly shut the door behind me.

There was something nasty in the air tonight. Some dark, evil shit breathing down my neck like an invisible dragon, threatening to take away everything in this house forever.

Maybe it was Lady Karma, checking in on me for all the assholes I'd killed and maimed. Wasn't like they hadn't deserved it.

They were all cruel, outlaw sons of bitches. Rapists, druggies, and killers who'd crawled onto their bikes as an outlet for the blackness inside them. Not for freedom or honor or any of the shit that was supposed to make life in a one-percent motorcycle club worth living.

I'd been their executioner. I'd blown their brains out

with quick, fiery shots, or nailed them to wooden posts and slowly smashed their bones with the nearest blunt object, listening to them beg and plead, scream by scream, never letting up 'til Blackjack told me.

Usually, I didn't let up 'til they were dead men.

That shit had to catch up with a man sooner or later, didn't it?

Before Sally and Caleb, I knew the answer was *yes.* Now, that invisible dragon shadowing me like a goddamned pitbull reminded me nothing had changed just because I'd decided to take off my patch and play family man.

I was due for an ass kicking of one sort or another, sooner or later. Someday, I was due for death.

Whatever, the reaper would have to wait. I didn't give a single fuck how much blood I owed the universe, or how fast that greedy motherfucker with the scythe wanted my mortal soul.

I'd never leave her and my kid willingly. I'd kill a thousand more motherfuckers with my own bare hands before I left 'em high and dry the way my old man had with ma.

Sally couldn't understand the big picture, and neither could the kid. Someday, maybe they would, and I was deadly determined to explain everything in the flesh.

I went downstairs and brewed coffee, something thick and hot to pry my eyes open and wipe away these monstrous thoughts.

My phone buzzed. I ripped it out and answered on the

first drone. Blackjack normally didn't call church 'til later in the morning, but I'd been expecting the call all night.

"Yeah?" I growled into the mic.

"We need you at the clubhouse. *Now.*" Brass rumbled into my ear. "I'm having Missy give your girl a wakeup call in a couple hours. I want all the old ladies and the kids at your place, seeing as it's the only one big enough."

"I'll make sure she knows," I said, but there was no one on the line.

He'd hung up before I could say shit. Some real serious fuckery was about to go down.

I stood in the doorway and pounded out a couple quick texts, telling her to listen to anything Brass' old lady said. Missy and Christa had both been through the drill a couple times, and I trusted them to help my family keep their heads down during crisis.

It was hard as hell to roll outta that house. The autumn sun wasn't even up, and the air had an almost wintry chill, biting at my skin, icy and uncaring.

The wind didn't care about the shit I had rolling around in my head, and neither did the club. Not now. I fired up my Harley and tore outta the driveway, wondering if I'd given her a wake up call after all.

The room was packed, all except one brother missing.

Stryker.

I took my seat next to Blackjack's empty spot. Nobody said a word, waiting for the Prez. The door popped open and he came strolling in a couple minutes later, wearing a shadow of the same pain stricken expression he'd worn when his leg was acting up.

"Beam, get up here," Blackjack said, picking up the bear claw and slamming it down on the table to bring us to session.

I held my growl inside, watching the punk rock asshole swagger up to the head of the table, and dump a thick folder out in front of us. Blackjack yanked it open and began pulling out pages, photos, and what looked like a couple maps torn from an old atlas, shoving the evidence over to us and the rest of the brothers.

"What you're looking at is the same thing that was brought to me last night. It's damning. The rat gnawing away at this club is a man we were glad to call brother." He paused, looking at Beam. "Thank God both our newest additions aren't traitors. Tell them what they're looking at. The same thing you've shown me."

"The man in the photos you're seeing, besides Stryker, is Manuel Ruz Gonzalez, or 'Uncle Manny' to our missing brother. He's retired and lives in Florida, pretty fucking well off in my book. I did some digging, found out Manny was a chef, traveling between the States, Mexico, and Nicaragua all the time. Thing is, Uncle Manny didn't get rich by cooking for the high and mighty down there. He was toting more than just gourmet ingredients back and forth between the borders."

Further down the line, Asphalt slammed a page down on the table, running a stiff hand over his face. "Jesus Christ."

It looked like an old shipping manifest. Beam looked directly at me, smiled, and it took everything in my power not to let my guts twist.

"Keep it moving, brothers. The Veep's got what I personally consider the best bit of evidence. You see that man at the table with Uncle Manny?"

Brass looked up, and I reached across the table, snatching the photo to see for myself. It had the grainy look of a shitty camera from the eighties or early nineties. A small group of men in suits sat at a table, drinks in their hands, smiling gratefully at the chef standing over some huge platter on a tray.

"There's two cartel dons getting their grub from Manny. One of 'ems still hot shit in Mexico City, spearheading their operations in the States."

Fuck. He was right.

The huge crest on the wall behind them gave it away. I'd recognize that eagle swooping down on the serpent in the desert anywhere. Some of the assholes we'd interrogated and killed wore it, and Blackjack kept a couple similar patches locked up in a drawer in his office. They were gray, not nearly as vibrant as the colorful icon in this picture, stained with the blood of the underlings we'd slaughtered.

"He's right," I said, shaking my damned head. "There's no denying it. Where the fuck is Stryker?"

"Prez put him on leave to heal up a couple days," Brass said. "We were gonna send him around on patrol with some prospects before this shit broke, probably to watch the old ladies and the kids."

Fucking shit. My heart sank. If this motherfucker really was the rat – and it looked goddamned likely – then we'd practically given him the keys to the kingdom.

I had a vision of trucks surrounding my place. Rough, stone faced bastards beating down the doors, knocking out the girls, binding their arms and legs and taping their mouths shut. As for the teenager, Jackie, and my poor son…

My fists swept up and slammed the table. "We gotta fucking find him. Learn for ourselves whether or not this shit's true."

"Son, you know it is," Blackjack said coldly. "Stryker's the only man invited into this club whose background wasn't an open book. I overlooked the holes in his record. I'm also man enough to admit when I fucked up."

"What're you talking about?" Rage tore through my veins, hot and angry, confusing everything in my head.

"I'm apologizing to you, brother, and everyone else in this room. You warned us about all this fresh, impure blood flowing into the club. We let our desperation turn a blind eye to common sense. Hell, I did it too. My drive to wreck the cartel, to save this club, to make sure no good brother ever has to suffer again in this hellish contest."

I shook my head. Seeing the sadness and anger flashing at the same time in the Prez's eyes gutted me.

"Don't deny it, son. I want everyone at this table to take as much time as they need to digest what Beam has brought us. Then we'll vote on introducing our poisoned brother to the bear's jaws." He paused. "And after that, if you'd like, we'll vote on whether or not I'm still fit to lead this club."

The room erupted. Men began screaming, begging him to stay. Half the paper being passed around the table flew off and hit the floor as men swung their fists, hit the wood, roared.

Blackjack grabbed the makeshift gavel, slamming the bear's paw on the wood like a mallet, over and over again. I flexed my fists sadly, ready to back him up as Enforcer if everything went to shit.

We had to keep order. Even if it might eat the whole fucking club alive this time.

I shoved my chair back so hard it slammed the wall, getting on my feet. The clatter caused the room to go quiet.

"You're staying, Prez. Everybody in here's screaming for it. As far as I'm concerned, we've already voted."

Men nodded. Everybody except Beam, who stared down at the almost empty folder in his hands, clenching his jaw.

The bastard was a weirdo, but he'd just saved our asses. As for Stryker, once we hauled him in, he faced the harshest fate anybody in this club had since the bad old days under Fang.

He'd fucked us over royal. Nobody knew what the hell the cartel had, and he'd tried to cover his tracks with that fake ass shot to the arm. The fuck probably fired the bullet himself.

We'd make him fucking scream before we tore the skin off his back, stripping our symbols off his flesh, everything the bastard wasn't fit to wear to hell, before we shoved him into his grave.

"Let's do this thing, brothers. We need to find our man, haul him in, and find out what he knows. The Prez wants us to vote on it, and that's what we're gonna do."

Blackjack nodded, darkness filling his eyes. "Sit down, son. You've said your part, and you're exactly right. Rat or not, Stryker deserves the same vote any man wearing this patch does, and he'll get another one before we make his heart stop too."

Men nodded glumly. Brass looked at me from across the table, his temples throbbing, chewing on the same wicked tension all of us had caught between our teeth.

"Everyone in favor of bringing our brother Stryker in to face judgment, say aye." The Prez picked up the bear claw gavel and looked at Brass, beginning to go down the line.

One by one, we voted. By the time it circled back to me, the last man standing, it was unanimous.

When the Prez's gavel hit the wood, it sounded like a bullet cracking past my ear. "That's it, then. The only thing left for us to do at this table is to decide how to bring our brother in with the least resistance."

Me, Brass, and Asphalt waited at my kitchen table. The women laughed upstairs, probably playing with the kid, taking their minds off the dark, heavy shit facing the club.

'Course, none of them knew shit. It was club business, and we'd told them to stay the hell away from Stryker if he showed up, without any further explanation.

The fear in Sally's beautiful eyes matched the same spark shining in Christa's and Missy's.

"Shit. You really think he's coming – here?" Asphalt grabbed his coffee cup and took a long pull, snorting when he saw there was nothing but a few cold dregs left.

"With any luck, he'll go straight to the clubhouse," I said. "That's where the Veep ordered him. Who the fuck knows if our new prospects got loose lips too. If they do, and he decides to swing by our safe place here, we'll be ready."

"He'll listen," Brass growled. "Fucker's been dazed and confused since he got shot. Not too many guys think clearly when they're nursing a kiss of lead."

I hoped to fuck he was right. Something in my gut shook, pumping angry dread through the rest of my system. My hands ached to draw blood, almost as bad as my dick hounded me to march upstairs, pull Sally into the bedroom, and fuck the stress right out.

"Roman?" I heard her voice and spun.

"What the fuck? I told you to stay upstairs with everybody, babe. It's too fucking risky down here." I stood up, walking over to her.

She had the kid in one hand, and an empty tote bag in the other. "Caleb threw his spoon on the floor and got it dirty. Besides, the girls could use some more coffee, and I thought I'd come down and brew up a fresh –"

I raised my hand, cutting her off.

Outside, a motorcycle rumbled. Not one of ours. Brass and Asphalt were up with their hands on their pieces before I could blink.

"Stay put, dammit. Go upstairs. We've got shit to take care of." I didn't wait to see if she listened.

I pounded out behind the boys, feeling adrenaline hit me like a shot to the heart as soon as I got in the open garage. Stryker killed his bike and ripped off his helmet, wincing as he flexed his fucked up bicep, still wrapped in a dirty looking tourniquet.

"What's going on, brothers?"

"I told you we're supposed to meet at the clubhouse," Brass said coldly, stopping at the edge of my garage. Asphalt and I were right behind him.

"Yeah, I already talked to Wisp. He said you were all gathering here, and the crew was light, keeping an eye on the girls. Just came by to see if you could use a hand trading shifts, or whatever."

We were close to him now. Stryker swallowed. I watched his hand carefully, making sure he wasn't going for anything dangerous strapped to his body, waiting for the Veep to make the first move.

"We've got ourselves a problem, brother," Brass said, only inches from his face.

"Yeah, the cartel –"

"Bullshit. I'm talking about your failure to follow a direct order, besides the shit you've been keeping to yourself, playing dumb."

The lean kid blinked, anger and confusion crossing his face. "Dumb? What the fuck are you –"

Brass grabbed him by the shoulders and shoved him down. I helped, smashing his face into his bike's seat, so fucking hard I could've shattered his nose right there.

"You fucking asshole! Did you really think we wouldn't figure it out? Did you really think you could rat on this club and get away with it, cartel piece of shit?" The Veep exploded, snarling as he twisted Stryker's wrists back, just short of snapping.

Behind me, I heard Caleb wail in Sally's arms, and a new kinda anger flared in my gut.

XI: Blinders Off (Sally)

I should've listened to him. I never should've wandered outside, even when Stryker started screaming, and the men circled him like sharks, knocking the wind out of him with savage blows to his stomach.

I wasn't the only old lady who came running to see the commotion. Missy and Christa stepped in front of me, the better to cover Caleb, urging me inside. But they were also there to sneak a peek firsthand at the chaos.

I stopped in the doorway and watched as two men dragged Stryker up, blood trickling through his teeth.

"Get in the fucking truck, asshole," Brass growled. "We're going for a ride. You know the club likes things neat, but we *will* slit your throat right here and mop up the mess if you make one wrong move. You try to fuck with them, and we'll do a lot worse than that."

The VP pointed a furious finger our way. Then his brow furrowed deeper, rage throbbing in his temple, and he must've realized we'd defied a direct order.

"Goddamn it! What the fuck are they doing out here? Roman!" Brass ripped the injured man around by the shoulder, nodding to Asphalt holding the other side of him, and they pushed him toward Roman's truck.

My man spun around, took one look, and started coming toward us. "Shit! Get the fuck back inside – all of you!"

The two old ladies in front of me jumped in from the garage, brushing past me and Caleb. I waited for the inevitable punishment.

My heart raced like a freight train. The last time I'd been reminded what Roman really was, we were in bed, tangled together as he sent me straight to ecstasy. It was fantasy then, a heatwave rippling up my spine every time I brushed his chiseled body.

Fucking an outlaw made me shamefully wet. But seeing what they did to Stryker in the driveway – what wasn't even finished – reminded me there was *nothing* sexy about the harsh reality of their bloodletting.

"I told you to stay inside," he said, his voice like ice. "Next time, you fucking listen, babe. This isn't social hour. These boys didn't drop by and sit with me all morning because we wanted to play cards. We're taking care of business, and there's no way we're letting any of our women get in the way."

"Business," I repeated, studying his stark mad face. "What kind of business involves beating a man with your own patch to a bloody pulp? Are you going to kill him, Roman?"

I wasn't sure why I asked the question. Did I really *want* to know?

"Club business," he snapped.

God, I hated that phrase a little more every time I heard it. Each time it came out, it curdled the air, as if somebody took a sledgehammer and knocked a gaping hole into our happy life.

"Get upstairs. Don't come down 'til you hear from me or one of the boys. We'll send a few prospects around to check up on you later. I gotta deal with this, and I can't stand here all day waiting for you to listen."

As if to underscore it, the truck's horn began blasting outside, and didn't let up. The roof was about to come off with the incredible rage blasting out of these men, but his was the only hellfire I really cared about.

Caleb stirred in my arms, irritated by the sound. I pushed his face into my chest, trying to cover his poor little ears.

"Don't go if it isn't safe, Roman. Please." I looked at him, feeling my heart drop. "I've got a terrible feeling about this. You guys are about to get in over your heads. I warned you once before, begged you not to go…"

Snarling, Roman twisted away from me, ripped the door open, and screamed. "One fucking minute!"

The horn stopped. Brass gave him a stern look that said *not a second more.*

"Stop worrying, babe. I know what I'm doing, and so do the guys. We're doing this shit for you and every other chick holed up in this house. You can dig me up and kill me again if I don't come back. Now, shut up and give me a kiss."

The tears came hot and cruel as he grabbed my face, held it tight, and smashed his lips to mine. I kissed him anyway, even though I was losing control, thinking about all the awful ways he could die. The crap I'd seen them do to Stryker was just the beginning of a thousand horrors.

Like it or not, I'd handed my heart to a man forged in violence, and now it was going to pieces.

"Don't. Fucking. Go." I couldn't resist whimpering it one more time as he broke away and turned to the door.

He looked at me one last time, the light in his eyes darkening. "Go upstairs, babe. We'll talk about how much you doubting me's complete bullshit when I get home."

Anger shot through my veins. I sucked in a breath and was about to curse him, but the door whipped open and slammed shut. Half a minute later, Asphalt's bike fired up, and peeled out ahead of the truck.

"Bastard!" I screamed it anyway, if only to blow off the steam he'd left behind, burning me up inside.

I was back to hating him, but my love wouldn't die so easy. This stupid, proud man was going to get himself killed and repeat his family curse, if he didn't kill me first with heartbreak.

Upstairs, later, Caleb dozed on Christa's lap. My phone blew up for the tenth time in the last two hours. I grabbed it, hoping it was Roman, but I saw the mysterious number instead.

Every time I answered, it was nothing but muffled static. The last time, I Googled it, and found out it was coming from the hospital.

Norm was awake, and trying to contact me, apparently. I wanted to take off, leave my son with the girls, and find out what the hell was going on.

But it wasn't so easy with Rabid and the prospects downstairs. He'd only poked his head in a few times. The kind, reasonable biker I'd talked to before had hardened into the same emotionless superman as the rest of them, and he only had one thing to tell us.

You're staying put. Club's orders. Don't even fucking think about going anywhere without our permission.

Maybe I should've been used to it by now with the way Roman bossed me around. But hearing it from another hard man with the bear patch…I quietly seethed.

Raged and worried too. The mystery that crept into my phone each time it chirped was killing me.

Missy touched my shoulder as the line went dead, and I lowered it back into my lap. "It'll be okay. I'm sure we'll hear from the guys soon. They never keep us in the dark for long when there's serious crap going down."

"Easy for you to say." I looked at her and frowned. "Your kid sister doesn't know how lucky she is, missing all this shit at a friend's house. What if Norm has something useful for the club? Roman intended to grill him, ask him what happened that night he got torn up on the farm."

"It's not my call," she said softly.

Christa looked up, shifting Caleb in her arms. "I'll talk to him. He's my old man. I've got nothing but mad respect, but I don't understand it either. There's no danger taking a ride to the hospital. Even the crazy cartel assholes wouldn't be insane enough to try something there."

I pursed my lips. I wasn't so sure about anything now. I'd brushed up against a world I really didn't understand, didn't *want* to understand, except for whatever it took to bring him home safe.

My boy needed his dad. I needed a man, and I wasn't ready to lose him when I'd finally gotten him back.

"Let me take him." I stood up and walked over, pulling Caleb into my arms.

I felt my son's soft warmth before I laid him down in his crib. His eyes cracked open, bathing me in the same dark eyes that matched Roman's a little more everyday.

Jesus. If he didn't come home safe...

The door opened and closed. That got the guys' notice downstairs.

"What the fuck?" I heard a gruff voice say.

Missy and I leaned against it, straining our ears to listen.

"You're not supposed to be down here, baby. What the hell are you doing?"

"Trying to talk some sense into you," Christa said coolly. "Her cousin keeps calling, you know. He was there when the ranch got attacked and Stryker was shot up."

"Don't mention that fucking rat's name again!" Rabid spat.

Hearing how he said *rat* caused my heart to skip a beat. I had a feeling it was something like that, but knowing it...God. The young man was as good as dead if he'd truly done something to fuck over the club.

Maybe he'd be crucified, just like the other men Roman talked about killing. Or maybe there'd be something worse. I cringed every time I thought about the way the same rough, strong hands that roamed my body might be used to destroy another human being.

I had to be honest – I loved a killer. A thug. An utter bastard who wasn't afraid to wreck and ruin with the worst pain he could think up.

And I couldn't stop loving him, even though the rational part of my brain was screaming, telling me how deep I'd gone down this rabbit hole.

"Rabid, stop. I'm doing this for a friend and the club. She deserves to find out what's going on, and it might help the rest of you too."

"You're wading goddamned deep into club biz, and you know it's not my call, Christa." There was a long pause, and then a loud, masculine sigh. "Fuck it. Just for you, I'll call the Prez."

My heart sputtered. Missy and I shared a long, excited look, trying to listen anxiously as Rabid presumably turned away and hit the phone.

"Fuck," he grunted, a few minutes later.

"What is it?" Christa asked.

"No answer. Look, I'm sorry, baby, but I can't do shit as long as I can't get in touch with Blackjack. I've got my orders, and I'm holding you here. All of you. The Veep'll have my fucking head on a pike if I let you chicks out and shit happens."

"And you don't think something might be happening to the club – something we could prevent?"

"Ah, come the fuck on! Don't pout. Don't give me some shit about magic solutions either. You don't have a clue what we're dealing with, and that's the way it outta be."

For some reason, I cracked a smile through the thick of it. Missy exhaled a sharp breath, shaking her head.

"I thought you were supposed to take matters into your own hands when there's an emergency? Aren't you man enough to decide what's best?"

I could practically see him wagging a finger in her face. "Don't. Now, you're stepping on my damned toes, and it's not gonna get you anywhere."

"I'm not trying to get anywhere. I'm trying to save some fucking lives!" Christa's voice cracked, high and strained. "I know you'd never let anyone put new scars on me again. I *know* what it's like to be tortured. Don't you think I've had all the dangers that come with wearing your brand burned into me for life? Don't you think that *maybe* I understand what I'm dealing with?"

"Baby, I know you do. It's not like that –"

She cut him off. "Exactly. It's about wasting precious time. What if Blackjack doesn't call you back until it's too late? What if men die because Norm could've told you something critical?"

Another long silence. Then, at last, I watched him throw his hands up.

"Ah, *fuck!* Get your shit together right now. We'll go to

the damned hospital, but I'm escorting you the whole way with two prospects. Missy stays here with the kid. I'll give you girls an hour before we're back at this house. Not one second more, understand?"

She answered him with a wet, happy smack of lips, and then I heard her feet pounding up the stairs. I grabbed my purse and flung the door open before she'd caught up to us.

"You sure you're okay to do this alone?" Christa asked in the waiting room outside the ICU, bathing me in soft, concerned eyes.

"I have to. We've got – what? – forty minutes? I need to make the most of this."

I swallowed, letting her wrap her arms around my neck one more time before I followed the nurse waiting for me outside the huge steel doors.

Walking in there felt like going into a tomb. The ward was freakishly quiet, so dark and silent and severe I imagined a person could hear death's footsteps if they listened closely enough.

Norm sat up in his bed, his jaws wired shut with some massive apparatus around his head. His arms and legs were both in slings.

When he saw me, his eyes lit up. Surprising, especially when his system must've been pumped full of pain meds.

"Oh my God. How did you even pick up the phone?"

He made a sound, halfway between a grunt and a sigh. My heart sank.

It must've been a nurse who'd made the calls, tried to get me over here.

Whatever he wanted, I didn't have a clue how the hell he was going to tell me anything.

Not like this.

"Norman." I reached for his hand, wondering if he could even feel mine. "You're going to beat this, I fucking promise. The guys are working to make our place safe again right as we speak."

Our eyes locked, and then he blinked. One time, slow and deliberate.

"Is that a no?" I asked softly.

He blinked two more times. *Yes.*

A bitter lump formed in my throat. Uncle Ralph did the same thing after his first stroke, before the second fatal one took him away forever. It was hell reliving it, except Norm found his strength, forcing out his words in a way I'd actually recognize.

I paused for a moment, looking at the bland gray clock on the wall. A little under forty minutes.

Shit. Whatever he wanted to tell me, I'd be lucky to get it out of him in time if we had to patiently play question and answer.

I decided to start with an easy one. "How did you call me? Did you use a nurse?"

Two blinks. Faster than before. *Yes. Of course.*

I swallowed, forcing back fresh tears. There'd been a lot of those earlier, and this was definitely no time to cry.

"What happened that night? Who did this to you? You

got ambushed…"

He stared blankly. *Slow down, girl. He's not telling you a damned thing unless it's got a yes or no.*

All right. Think.

"Did the cartel surprise you?" It couldn't get much easier than that.

Two blinks. *Yes.*

"Were you able to fight back? Did you hit anyone?" One blink. "It happened too fast?"

Yes.

I swallowed, licked my lips, and slowly gathered my words. My heart pounded, threatening to explode in my chest. "It was someone in the house, wasn't it? Did Stryker do this to you?"

His eyelids moved. Once.

Jesus Christ. I leaned in. I had to double-check.

"Norm, I'm asking you again…did Stryker hurt you?"

No.

"Was it Asphalt?" I knew I was stalling, saving my brain from going down that pitch black alley all logic pointed to.

No.

"Did Beam do this? Is he the traitor?"

One. Two. *Yes.*

I swerved, grabbing onto the wall a couple feet away for support. My palms hit the cool glass, and it was the only thing that kept me from passing out.

The bastard who'd tried to force himself on me, who'd almost tempted me with his lips, his touch…he was the rat.

He was the bastard.

He was the one threatening to steal Roman away from me forever, and rip our family to smithereens.

"Jesus Christ…" I fought the urge to bolt out the door and go running back to Christa and Rabid. "Thank you, Norm. I'll be back as soon as I can. I've just…I've got to go. You'll beat this."

He gave me two more blinks, and I saw the faintest hint of a smile in his eyes. *Damned right.*

I gave his arm one last squeeze. Too rough. He winced. Then I tore out of the room and pounded toward the doors, leaving the nurse on duty at the tiny computer desk inside yelling after me.

Outside, I crashed into Rabid, who got up with Christa when he saw me coming, holding out his arms. I was a shaking, adrenaline fueled mess. It took me a few seconds to speak while they shouted.

"What is it? What's going on?"

"Is your cousin okay? Talk to us!" Christa's voice blasted through my other ear.

"I know who the rat was. It's not who you think. It was Beam all along." Rabid's eyes went wide, and then filled with a dark, inky anger. "You've got to call Blackjack right now, get your President on the line, tell him everything. Hurry, before they –"

He pushed me away, probably a little more roughly than he intended, and I went spinning into Christa's arms. She caught me, shot Rabid a dirty look, and then walked me into the waiting seat.

"Stay the fuck there. Both of you. I'm already on it."

I wiped my eyes while Christa shoved tissues and a water bottle into my hands. I needed it too. My throat felt like it'd caught on fire, and then froze over, choking me alive.

"It's like a fucking nightmare," she said sadly. Her eyes were glued to the door, waiting for Rabid to come back.

We both inwardly prayed he'd get in touch with the others this time. Jesus, they might be tearing Stryker to pieces that second, and all for nothing.

I didn't know how Beam had framed him, but he did. Worse, I doubted it was just to cover his own ass. The men might be in real fucking danger while we sat here waiting, and there was nothing we could do about it.

"You can wake up from nightmares," I told her. "This just might be permanent."

XII: Better Mousetrap (Roman)

The torch felt like a block of ice in my hand. It was amazing that the shit inside could ignite, hot enough to sear human flesh in a heartbeat.

Stryker wouldn't live to let the black eyes we'd given him show. The fucker was tough, and really good at playing stupid, far better than I'd given him credit for.

We'd whaled on him and pulled all the usual mind tricks for more than an hour, and it hadn't yielded a damned thing. The bastard kept his lips sealed, telling us to go to hell, warning us we were making a big fucking mistake.

All the usual stone cold denials of a guilty man.

I grabbed the torch after Blackjack backed away from him, clawing at the rat's shoulder. He'd asked him about Uncle Manny again, and the asshole admitted to it, except he claimed the grinning chef in the pictures wasn't *his* Manny.

He told us the pictures were off, manipulated. Someone had taken his pics and changed them, lifting Manny the chef into the middle of a cartel don's dinner.

Bullshit.

Guess he didn't know the Prez had a guy into digital shit connected to the club comb over everything. The verdict was in, and there were no doubts.

Over against the wall, Asphalt, Brass, and a couple other guys shook their heads every time he hacked out more lies. They'd both had their chances to loosen his tongue, digging their knuckles into his wiry body so fucking hard they were lucky their hands didn't break. And the look they were giving me now was begging for another chance at making this asshole squeal, or else put him outta his goddamned misery.

"You want me to repo our colors now? Maybe that'll open up this asshole up." I looked at the Prez. We shared the same dark fire, boiling in our eyes, a little hotter every second, watching our boy twitch in his restraints like a cornered rat.

Blackjack paused, straightened his long gray hair, and reached into his pocket for a fresh smoke. The Prez was still a man, and puffing on that endless supply of cigs calmed his nerves. It also made him meaner, righteous in his ruthlessness, confident in his justice.

"Do it, son. Our lost brother isn't even trying to soften the dagger he's shoved into our backs. As far as I'm concerned, he's no longer fit to wear the bear on his skin a second longer."

Adrenaline shot through my veins. I lit the torch, and watched the hot blue flame dance, holding it up in front of my face. Stryker squinted at me through his narrowed, beat up eyes. For the first time since we'd started, I saw a flash of mortal fear on his ugly mug.

Smiling, I stepped forward, taking my sweet time. We'd already wasted more than a damned hour – what were a few more minutes? When you wanted to break a man, more than half the equation's psychological.

The pain comes secondary, but once this flame touched Stryker's inks, he'd be in a world of nothing but searing, brain ripping agony.

"No, no, no!" he snarled, thrashing in the chair we'd bound his arms and legs to. "You can't fucking do this, brother. Not for the love of Christ! I didn't do it. It was some other asshole, somebody set me up, somebody who really wants to see this club killed!"

I cocked my head, bringing the flame so close to his face the fucker flinched. "Really, now? You're telling me there's somebody else with Mexican cartel connections who got off with a little blood wound the night the cartel came calling? I saw what you did to my girl's cousin, asshole. You'd better believe we're all gonna fuck you up twice as bad before you're buried in concrete."

His eyes opened wide as I started to move the flame close, first to that filthy tourniquet wrapped around his arm. The fucker's tongue must've went numb. I'd seen it happen with other dudes, right before they realize imminent death's around the corner, ready to snatch his soul in a blink, or at else make him wish he was getting off that lightly.

For this jackass, the end was coming slowly and

painfully. I watched his eyes widening, lighting up with a thousand pleas for mercy.

No. NO. NO!

I ripped the flame away, right before it lit the bandage. Fucking shit. The sudden noise bleeting through the empty warehouse interrupted me.

My phone droned for about the fifth time in my pocket, reminding me there were darker things to think about than the worst ways to ship this rat sonofabitch off to meet his maker.

The torch sputtered out as I released the button. Growling, I reached into my pocket, hauled out my phone, and stared at the missed call. Another one from Sally.

What the fuck was happening? Rabid tried to call the Prez a couple times too, but he wouldn't take it, too wrapped up in his frustration over cracking Stryker's armor to worry about anything outside this old warehouse.

"What the hell's the hold up, son?" He said, never taking his smoke outta his mouth. "Move your ass. He's not going to tell us anything until he's let off a few screams first. We don't have all evening to shake his tongue free."

"I'm sorry, Prez. I keep getting these calls…fuck. Just give me a second. Please."

Blackjack bared his teeth, practically biting his smoke in two. I told myself it would only be a minute, maybe two, no more.

Something tightened up in my gut. The calls shouldn't have kept coming after we ignored them, persistent and mysterious.

I walked over to the opposite corner by the exit out back, right where Beam had been standing a couple minutes ago. I was too busy staring at my phone to wonder whether he'd stepped outside for some fresh air or a piss or what.

Several voicemails blew up my inbox. Whatever, I had to make this quick, so I skipped over them and hit the reconnect button for Sally's phone instead.

She answered on the second ring.

"Jesus, where the fuck were you? Please tell me you haven't gotten to Stryker yet."

I gritted my teeth. "What's this about, babe? Start talking. You've got thirty seconds."

"I went to see Norm –"

"Norm? Fuck me, where's Rabid at? He was under direct orders not to let *anybody* step foot outside that house."

"Roman! Just calm down – listen! Give me one fucking second!" I'd never heard her so wound up, screaming 'til my goddamned ear was left ringing. "It was Beam all along. You've got the wrong man. Norm told me face-to-face he's the rat, the one who ambushed him, broke his bones. Well, sort of..."

"Sorta?"

"He could only blink to communicate. I asked him the questions. But I triple checked everything. I know he was telling me the truth. I already told Rabid, baby, but he couldn't get to you guys either. He's on his way to –"

"Babe, come the fuck on," I growled, shaking my head. "You really expect me to believe all the dirt the club's got on Stryker's nothing but complete shit? And all this from a dude who's so fucked up he's probably got more pain killers than blood in his veins?"

I really regretted answering this fucking call now. The shame of the Prez and the boys overhearing everything was all that kept me from exploding, hurling the phone against the wall, smashing it into a million pieces.

Yeah, she was my woman. But right now, she was fucking disrespecting me, feeding me this crazy bullshit, sticking her damned nose where it didn't belong.

Where the fuck was Rabid? I wondered again. *And why the fuck wast he boy so gullible?*

There was a long pause. Just as well, because we were about done. I had to get back to work.

Now, my hands really ached to do some damage to that fuck in the chair. They'd have to hold me back before I went deeper than his ink, burning him to a goddamned crisp, roasting his bones.

"What?" Fear chilled Sally's voice, and so did disbelief. "Oh, no. No, no, no. You've got to believe me, Roman. I'm not making this up. I swear!"

"Didn't say you were. Seems to me we've got the facts screwed up. Fact is, your cousin's fucked up, and I'm gonna need a lot more than a damaged dude's word when he's not even in his right mind. Too bad we're outta time to wait for this to go to trial."

"Roman – no! Don't do this. You can come to the

hospital with me, talk to him yourself. You'll see. If you'd seen the look in his eyes, how coherent he was, there's no fucking way –"

"Goodbye, babe." I thumbed the phone and ended the call, once again resisting the urge to rush over and destroy that motherfucker. This time, I completely shut it down before I made my way back.

Stryker was halfway outta it by the time I got back underneath the beam of sunlight filtering through the busted window. My girl had bought his evil ass a few more seconds to accept his fate.

Fucking wonderful. I'd have to make him suffer twice as hard, invest a little more energy to make this place echo with his screams.

I picked up the torch. My eyes flicked to the Prez, and he nodded his approval, an anxious spark in his eyes telling me to finish what I'd started.

There was a deafening rumble as the flame sparked to life. Way too deep to be a fiery hiss, and too damned close to be thunder. It was clear overhead.

Engines. Lots of them. Vehicles that sounded much bigger and more numerous than bikes.

All the guys in the room perked up, even Stryker, lifting his miserable head and giving me a surprised look. My heart got such a heavy shot of adrenaline I nearly forgot to kill the torch and slam it back down on the old crate holding our implements.

"Who the fuck's out there?" Blackjack growled, clenching his fists and marching toward the narrow slit of dirty glass next to the back exit.

"Sally said something about Rabid showing up." I sounded like a fucking ghost. There's no way Rabid and a couple prospects would've made that much noise with their bikes.

One by one, the boys went to the glass, and stopped dead in their tracks. I knew it wasn't good – whatever the fuck was waiting for us out there was a disaster. Didn't stop me from snatching my gun off my hip and walking up to join my crew.

"Grizzlies motorcycle club! We know you're in there. Come on out, or we shoot our way in!" A tanned man in an ivory white suit leaned outta a sunroof on an SUV, his gold teeth gleaming in the evening light every time he moved his mouth. "You have exactly one minute."

Other men stepped out of the six or so huge trucks lined up around the broken down courtyard, the place we'd always used as a graveyard for traitors and enemies. They were all Mexicans, packing automatics and shotguns, and they looked pissed.

I looked at the three guys next to me, one by one. Brass had no fear. Asphalt looked pissed. Blackjack wore the same freakish calm he always showed in situations like this.

I had to hand it to him – his guts never wavered one bit. Even when we were about to walk out into an ambush, outgunned and underprepared, vulnerable to every fucking double cross in the book if the cartel wanted to end this war right here.

As for me, I had faith. The bear owned our fates now, and we were already dead men, or else the biggest goddamned underdogs who'd ever worn this patch.

Blackjack looked at us and nodded. "Lets go."

"Right behind you, Prez," I growled, stepping in front of him and pounding the door open.

More than a dozen cartel bastards waited, their weapons drawn. Blackjack walked out, holding out an arm to keep us back. When the fucker with the gold teeth saw him, staring through his oversized shades, he ducked down into the SUV and slid out the passenger door a couple seconds later, smoothing his suit as he stood up.

He looked like a fucking lounge lizard, but the large silver crest on his lapel told us exactly what we were looking at. His emblem had the same eagle swooping down on the desert snake I'd seen before. But the only dudes who got these fancy medals were cartel bosses, and now there was one in front of us, a general on a mission.

"Ah, Blackjack," the Mexican said with a grin, his thick accent more noticeable out here. "You're even older than I've been told. If you hadn't killed legions of my men, I'd shake your hand."

"Shut the fuck up and get on with it," the Prez snapped. "What're your terms? I know when my balls are in a vise."

The cartel boss' grin melted. "I believe in fighting fair. I'll offer you the same thing you've given my soldiers – a quick, clean, easy death like men."

Asphalt snorted. He reached for his nine millimeter,

and suddenly a dozen men jerked like one machine, readying their guns and aiming them in our direction.

"Don't. I know you're a smart man, and a reasonable man. You have lost, old man." The don's gold teeth reappeared, this time like a vicious wolf. "It's completely up to you whether you want your MC to die in agony. Perhaps we'll spare your life for a few hours to talk big picture after every last one of your brothers here is dead. Step out of the way."

"No," the Prez growled, digging his boots into the concrete. His old wound must've scorched like fuck. "You want to talk terms, then you'll do it with the rest of my boys, and you'll kill me first. Go, collect your rat inside, and get on with it."

The boss looked at one of his guys, muttered something in Spanish, and sent him behind us, into the warehouse. The grunt returned a couple seconds later, marching out Stryker, his hands still bound behind his back.

When I saw the big Mexican return to his leader, leaving Stryker behind with the rest of us, my fucking heart sank. They were either enormous bastards who'd butcher their own informants…or Sally was right.

"There's nothing to collect except your bodies," Gold Teeth said. "We've already got our insider, and he's going to be rewarded quite handsomely."

Shit. She *was* right.

Stryker couldn't be our rat, unless this was all a sick joke. Not out of the question for these fucking demons from across the border.

But I knew it wasn't that easy. I knew we'd just spent our last couple hours on earth torturing a fellow brother, an innocent man. That shit alone made me want to walk right into the gorilla holding the shotgun, and feel the hellfire cut through my chest.

Fuck, fuck, fuck. Is this how my old man felt before he lost his mind and got himself killed?

The whole world condensed into a tight black ball. The Prez's mouth was moving, but my ears wouldn't work, and I had to grip my gun tight to keep from passing out.

An SUV's door slamming brought me back to life. I saw the devil himself walking toward us, through the cartel ranks, Beam, complete with his fucked up hair.

"You sick, fucked up sonofabitch," I growled, getting in front of Blackjack.

All the guns were trained on me. The asshole kept coming, slithering past the evil bastard who'd offered him his pieces of silver.

"Easy, big boy. Your old lady wouldn't like you going out in a hail of rage and bullets – not that she's got much choice at this point. I'd *love* a shot at giving you the same treatment I gave Norm. Go ahead and give me a good reason."

My fists had never been so damned hungry in my whole life. It took every ounce of strength I had to fight the urge to pop this fucker's brains out his skull.

As long as I controlled my rage, I wouldn't end up like

my old man. At least not by one careless, explosive instant.

It wasn't looking good for us, but every second we delayed and kept ourselves alive evened the odds against these bastards. I couldn't let the caveman urge to tear his fucking head off steal my whole fucking future with Sally and Caleb. I had to let him swing his dick without trying to hack it off until the time was right.

"Carlos!" The cartel boss barked, and Beam whipped his head around. "Get back in line. Now."

Gold Teeth stepped forward, shoved his way past me, and got in the Prez's face. "Well? You going to take the deal I offered, or not? It's the best one you'll get, old man. And you're all out of leverage."

"No. You'll take my counter-offer, or you'll kill us all, and get no terms with the club. No treaty means you'll have to destroy every other Grizzlies charter, all the way to Seattle. They'll never give up unless you've got a piece of paper with my name on it. Don't think you'll get anybody to flip. We've already cleaned house in every charter that would even think about cutting you a deal, *capo.*"

The Mexican clenched his jaw when the Prez called out the cartel captain. "A pity you didn't do such a good job keeping your own charter clean. Believe me, I'd love to spill your blood where you stand."

"Here I am," Blackjack growled, stepping away from the cartel boss and spreading his arms. "Do it. Firing squad style. What're you afraid of?"

Several men aimed their guns, locked and loaded on the Prez. *Fuck!*

The rest of the boys stirred, ready to jump in front of him and take every bullet if they needed to. Shit, shit, we were gonna die together anyway, but I sure as fuck wouldn't before I watched Beam and the cartel boss bleed out on the cold pavement underneath our boots.

"Afraid? No, old man, the only one who ought to be afraid here is *you*." The boss stared at us, snarled out something in rapid fire Spanish, and all but two of the men lowered their guns. "I'll give you a few minutes. Think about what you're doing. Enjoy one last puff on your tobacco. Then, we'll see if you come to your senses. The only reason I haven't cut you and your men to pieces is because I'd *really* like to see your signature in blood on a new treaty. You do that for me, and anything can happen here today. There's still time to save lives all across your club, Blackjack."

"Go to hell." Blackjack reached into his pocket, plucked out a smoke, and lit it up.

For the first time since I quit that shit ten years ago, I wished I hadn't. It would've been fucking sweet to enjoy one last smoke.

But not half as sweet as tasting my woman's lips one more time, or hearing my kid laugh at my feet. The fucking assholes a couple feet away were taking it away, one second at a time. Thinking about our shit odds was like watching grains of sand running through a goddamned hour glass.

Can a man feel like a ghost before he's even dead?

I tried to think, straining my eyes, looking for any

weakness. Asphalt, Brass, and even Stryker did the same. I didn't look too much at the last name – every time I did, it made me fucking sick.

I'd almost torched his skin off, for fuck's sake.

Maybe I deserved the dark, bloody end that was coming. Maybe today was the day karma would bitch slap me, force me to pay the brutal debts I'd stacked up over the years. Maybe my family could manage without me. I hoped to God they would.

Sally was strong. Caleb was bound to grow up a badass. This family had it in the blood.

No, I wasn't gonna see it – I wasn't gonna *fucking see it.*

My heart froze over, and so did the hellfire in my blood, every time I took a good look at those rifles trained on us.

The last thing I'd ever do in front of my killers was weep like a little bitch, but it was raining black sleet in my soul. I watched the Prez puff, in between sneaking looks at the smug, almost bored looks on the Mexican's faces.

When Blackjack's cig was down to a stump and Gold Teeth's back was turned, quietly talking to one of his men by the SUV in the center, Beam made his move. He came toward me again, wearing the smirk that made me want to knock his fucking teeth out.

"You're a dead man, you know." He gave me a cold look and spat at the ground.

I didn't flinch. "Better dead than a fucking rat. The cartels have their codes too, as fucked up as they are. How long before these bastards decide to chop your head off too, Carlos?"

I used the name Gold Teeth yelled. He gave me a nasty look, and then his face twisted.

He laughed, higher pitched than I'd heard before, betraying his anxiety. My ears pricked up at another noise coming through his shit – something lower, roaring, droning.

I squinted, looking past him toward the very edges of the old complex. I saw the faintest puffs of dust behind the old fuel tanks. Bikes were on their way, coming up the route we always used to get back here, right through a break in the rusted gate.

Fuck. Just in time.

Beam stopped laughing and drew his wicked black eyes back on me. "You think you're hot shit, don't you? You walk around thinking you're a good man, a strong man, now that you've got your wife and kid. Let me tell you something, asshole."

He pushed against my chest, as hard as he could. The lean little fuck was too weak to move me an inch, even with anger spiking his blood.

I cast a quick look at Blackjack. The Prez's face didn't show shit, but his eyes were fixed on the tiny smoke coiling in the distance too. He knew what was coming.

Beam kept talking, slinging the best shit talk he had. "You'll want to listen to this, fuckface. Listen good. I'm going to track down your hot blonde princess when we're through here. I'll find her, take her, and fuck her all I want. I'll take her in every hole, all fucking night, make her forget every last trace of you while she's howling on my cock. Then, when I've had my fill, I'll drive her well stretched ass to Mexico to be sold. She'll survive a year, maybe two in the game. But I'll give her a fighting chance, just for you, by fucking her 'til she hurts. I'll turn her into my whore, Roman. It's good practice once some of the cartel's friends get a hold of her."

I snorted. "You done yet, Carlos?"

He shook his head. His jaw tightened, stretching his skin tight across his fucked up face. For a second, that shitty punk rock broomstick on his head looked like it was sitting on a skull.

"I'll do it all, you bastard. I swear I will. Every. Fucking. Word." His head snapped back, and he flew forward, hurling spit in my face.

Slowly, I raised one hand, wiping my eye. "You're gonna have a hard time with my girl," I said, sliding my other hand to my hip.

"Why's that, asshole?"

"She doesn't like dudes with ruptured balls and broken dicks."

Two seconds. That was all I needed to make my move.

My knee shot up and smashed Beam's junk so hard I wasn't sure if he ever felt his nuts split like rotten eggs. My gun's barrel hit his temple too fast, and I pulled the trigger.

The Mexicans started screaming before he even hit the ground. I went down, holding onto his corpse like a shield, listening to my boys behind me start shooting.

My whole universe became screaming lead, kicking at the dusty pavement and flesh around me, each hot flash threatening to snuff out my life just as quickly as I'd done to the rat.

Brass roared, firing over my head. I angled my gun up as soon as I hit the ground, firing at every dark moving shape I could see. Several cartel boys ran forward, and their chests exploded outward, death blossoming in bloody vines.

Rabid and the prospects were here. The cavalry hit them from the back, slaughtering those motherfuckers like hogs.

Gold Teeth ducked between two vehicles, dropped his fancy looking magnum, clutching a bleeding wound on his leg. Bright red gore poured through his lily white trousers.

I emptied my clip and burst two more heads. It was too fucking dangerous to reload, especially with a bastard holding an automatic coming toward me, spraying down suppression fire.

The hellfire advanced, coming on like a line of advancing rain.

Inevitable. Outrageous. Fatal.

I thought about Sally's hot lips on mine as she was wrapped around me, thrusting like my life depended on it between her legs, snarling as I pushed her over the cliff into ecstasy.

I remembered Caleb's laugh, smiling as the bullets

came closer, sparking on the cracked cement like firecrackers. It was like somebody slowed down time, just enough to let the things that mattered flash before my eyes.

I couldn't get my boy's cherub laugh outta my skull, even if it might as well have been on fucking Jupiter with death racing toward me here. I'd never hear it again. Not for real.

I thought about ma. She'd looked happier than she had for years holding my kid, bouncing him on one knee. Probably amazed that Sally and me created such a perfect miracle. She'd still have that after I was gone.

My brothers' faces flashed in my head, one by one, locked in perfect rhythm to the tracers coming toward me.

Blackjack. Brass. Rabid. Asphalt. Southpaw. Stryker.

So many fucking more. Too many faces, and not enough time. Never enough –

Fuck. Fire ripped through my side, and I felt like a goddamned water balloon losing its contents.

Two seconds later, the shooting stopped, but it didn't really matter. I saw myself sprawled out on the ground, passed the fuck out, my eyes dead and vacant.

I floated away from everything, and there were no brakes. I was already a ghost, even as some brother caught up to me and started shaking me, screaming in my ear. His words were like listening to a man screaming down a long tunnel.

They blurred into nonsense. I heard someone else talking, a voice I hadn't heard for nearly twenty years. The last words my old man ever said to me surged in the blackness like a giant tidal wave, pulling me deeper, crashing across my soul.

Live the life I couldn't, son. Live like a good man 'til the day you die. Don't forsake your family.

XIII: Under the Gun (Sally)

I'd never had so many emotions flickering through me at once, tearing me to pieces like twisted currents.

Hatred. Bitterness. Sadness. Love.

Each time Roman's face flashed in my mind, I didn't know whether I wanted to kiss him or rake him across the cheek with my nails. Mostly, I just wanted him to come home so I could make up my mind, preferably before my intestines tangled up in a permanent knot.

It was so fucking dark out. Almost midnight.

There hadn't been a word all evening, not since we got home from the hospital, and Rabid took off with his guys, leaving a two man skeleton crew of prospects watching over us.

Caleb stirred in my arms. He kept crying no matter how often I tried to feed him, fusing every time I rocked him or smoothed his brow the way he liked. The kid could sense the tension on some scary primal level.

"Damn it!" Missy whispered for the third time in an hour, tearing the phone away from her ear. "Still no answer. I tried all of them. I really *don't* understand this.

Somebody should pick up. Even Rabid isn't talking."

Christa's shoulders slouched. I watched her bring a hand up to the scars on her cheeks, touching them and then snatching her fingers away, like they burned her hand.

"Something's wrong. They've never kept the line dead this long, and never all of them at once. We can't just sit here all night."

"What's your plan? Lower a rope made out of our skirts and jeans down the window? Rabid said we're not going anywhere. I'm scared too, but there's no way we'll get past the prospects down there. You sweet talked your old man, but those boys only care about following orders, whatever it takes to earn their bottom rockers."

She narrowed her eyes. "You think they're not sweating rivers down there too? Hope you've got a mop, Sally. Their orders only go so far. They'll be just as confused as us the longer they wait with no word from the rest of the brothers."

"We have to try something!" Missy exploded, stood up, and reached for the door before I could say another word.

Maybe she was right. My heart throbbed pure adrenaline, a cold, harsh fuel for the pessimism grinding my heart to ashes.

I wanted to believe he was okay. He had to come home. But this world had no guarantees, and the damning silence gave a good idea about what happened without the specifics.

I looked at Caleb and clutched him tight, carrying him

out as the other two old ladies ambled down the stairs. My mind had already gone to that dark pit, wondering how I'd afford this place if Roman was really gone.

Jesus, and it wouldn't get any easier as the years went on. I couldn't lie to my son, not when he'd barely met his father.

One day, I'd have to look him in the eyes, and tell him his dad did – what? Defended his family? Or went down the same as his grandfather, pulled into a world of savage violence he never should've embraced?

I'd say anything to stop it from becoming a family tradition. Caleb would never end up like Dagger and…Roman?

My heart turned to cold, dead rock just considering the possibility he was gone.

I shook my head, following the girls downstairs. Missy and Christa did most of the talking. The two prospects eyed us glumly, sharing nervous looks.

"Can't do that, ladies," a prospect named Thorn said. "The brothers'll have our asses if anything happens to you. Shit, we don't even know what's going on at the clubhouse. It could be compromised too."

"Oh, please." I rolled my eyes and stepped forward. "The whores still sleep there. They'd be the first to come screaming if anything happened."

"Yeah, assuming they could. You know these invasions can happen so fucking fast it'll make your head spin, right?" Thorn gave me a sharp look, his goatee twitching.

I cocked my head. "You sound like you're talking with

experience. Jeez, at the rate the club's bringing in new blood, you've been wearing that prospect patch for like a month, maybe two? Hard to believe you're a battle-hardened biker badass in just a few weeks."

His face tightened. Christa and Missy laughed. Brass' old lady pushed through us and got in his face.

"Come the fuck on. We'll drive carefully, take my car the whole way there. We'll pull over a couple miles away. You boys can go on and make sure the coast is clear. I'm sure the Prez and VP will appreciate somebody looking over home base."

"She's right. What? You're not scared, are you, boys? I hear the ones who show some initiative get their bottom rockers a whole lot faster." Christa smiled, and we all suppressed a laugh, watching them eyeball each other like nervous owls.

"Whatever, you bitches are crazy, you know that?" Thorn growled at last. "We'll ride in front and rear 'til the very end, and then we'll go on ahead to scope it out. Soon as we're in, you're getting guns and going in the back. I'm not letting anybody out in the bar 'til I hear something from higher up."

"Sounds like a plan!" Missy said. "Very thoughtful. Very original. Totally not mine."

She reached up and slapped Thorn on the shoulder, then turned around and led us out. The prospects scrambled to get their bikes going before we pulled out of the driveway. I sat in the back, holding Caleb, trying to let the light humor wash over me.

The girls made me laugh, even with the uncertain hell waiting up ahead. But I couldn't hold onto the comic relief.

Not until I knew what happened to Roman. *Please, God, let him be okay.*

I'd closed my eyes the whole way there. Not far from the clubhouse, Missy pulled over and waited. It took the prospects about ten minutes to ride in, comb through the place, and then give us a call to come through the gate.

We parked and made our way to the back. They shoved several guns into everybody's hands. I'd learned to shoot with Norm and Uncle Ralph. I wasn't afraid of guns, but there was something strange about having one in my purse on the floor while Caleb sat on my lap.

I prayed I wouldn't have to use it, but I would in a heartbeat to defend my baby, or any of these girls here. We headed for the storage room in the back.

It was the only place with a thick metal door. Missy and Christa both suffered here, back when the club was run by Fang. He'd used it as a torture chamber, and I could feel the black pain dripping off the walls, cold and unsettling. I cuddled Caleb close, if only to guard him from the same dark energy.

We huddled together, waiting for what felt like half the night, though it was only another hour. Caleb finally dozed off. I was afraid Christa would wake him when she jumped up, pressing her ear to the wall.

"You hear that? Motorcycles."

Missy and I stood, following her to the thick wall. It wasn't easy to hear through it, but the longer I strained my ears, the more I could make out the distinct guttural roar of Harleys. Lots of them, swarming like bees.

A couple minutes later, Thorn pounded on the door. "Coast is clear, girls."

"We're ready! Let us out!" I yelled, covering my son's ears.

The door creaked open. The same two prospects blocked our paths, and Thorn muttered something about guns.

We all reached into our purses. I was relieved to get rid of mine, and hopeful because it meant *maybe* things were going to be okay after all.

But at the last second, something stopped me. No, I didn't want the gun around, especially with Caleb. But what if I needed it someday to keep him safe?

I looked at the empty hand Thorn held out for mine. "Let me keep this for a little while."

He squinted. "Can't let you do that. Club property."

I rolled my eyes. "Oh, come on. I know you guys have tons of these things. The serial numbers are all filed off too, aren't they? I know how to shoot. My Uncle took me out to blow up bottles in my teens. He sent me to a safety class. I know how to handle these things."

"Christ. You gonna give me anything but trouble today?"

"Maybe. But I guess that depends whether or not you want me to explain to Roman how you yanked away the only thing making me feel safe…"

He let out a long sigh. "Fuck it. You win. Keep the gun. But if something happens, you didn't get that thing from me. Promise?"

I nodded, smiling to myself. I didn't want to carry it around anymore as soon as we got home, but something made me feel better about having a spare at home.

Even if this all blew over, Roman couldn't always be there. One day, I might have to depend on myself.

The men were filing in through the garage door when we got into the bar. Blackjack stepped through first, motioning to Asphalt and a prospect. They were carrying a strange, sweaty man in a dirty white suit. When I saw the deep, dark blood stain all the way up his leg, I covered my mouth.

"Keep moving, boys," Blackjack growled, following his men. "Get this piece of shit in the back. We'll get something on the bastard's bum leg after everybody's done playing doctor. Then he's *ours.*"

They disappeared down the hall we'd just left My heart pounded like a war drum, and I counted all the familiar faces filing in.

Brass and Rabid appeared together, their faces solemn. Christa and Missy bolted out of their seats. They hit their guys hard, locking their hands over their huge necks, smothering them in kisses and questions.

More prospects came. Southpaw was next. Then a gigantic man wearing Prairie Devils MC colors, the Grizzlies old rival-turned-ally. He was almost as big as

Roman, and he carried a black bag, marching straight toward the back where the others had gone.

No sign of Roman.

Missy and Christa were still chattering away when I walked up. Rabid saw me, and his gaze darkened.

"Where's Roman?"

"They're working on him now, Sally."

Oh, God. If it wasn't for holding onto Caleb, my knees certainly would've dropped out. "Working on him?"

"He's gonna be okay. He took a hit in the shoulder, lost a lot of blood. We've got the crew patching him up, disinfecting his shit. Tank's here from the Devils too, and he's got his girl on the line. She's a nurse. He's learned a thing or two about dealing with this kinda shit, or so he says."

"Girl, wait!" Missy called after me, tried to stop me from spinning around, but I wasn't having it.

I stroked Caleb's head and moved forward, heading for the back, looking for the spare room the club used as a makeshift infirmary before these bloody battles. My heart threatened to give out, drop me to the floor with every step I took.

The door was cracked. Men yelled inside, and so was a woman, cutting through the static. I shoved it open with my foot.

My jaw practically hit the floor. Roman was slumped in the bed, looking ghost white, a tube running into his arm from a blood bag suspended overhead. A shallow metal bowl sat next to him, a rusty looking bullet in the center. The big man in the Devils cut had his phone propped up on the small nightstand next to him.

He looked down at Roman's bloody shoulder, a needle balanced in one hand, thread dangling all over the place. "Say it again, babe," he growled toward the phone.

"You've got to pull the skin *tight,* Tank. Stitch by stitch. Hurry, before it's left open too long! There's germs in the air, all over the place, really. That disinfectant only works so long!" the woman barked over the phone.

The prospect on the opposite side of Roman saw me, looked up, and waved his arm. He pointed to a chair in the corner. "Get the fuck in, or don't."

Holding Caleb tight, I stepped forward. I stuffed back tears, watching in horrid fascination, wishing for nothing more than being able to walk up and grab his hand while they worked on him.

Tank's thick hands moved fast. They seemed to do the job, but he also moved like he wasn't sure, and that made me nervous as hell.

"Don't fucking know about this, Em," he whispered into the phone. "This shit's a lot bigger than the ones you taught me how to patch at home. He's still bleeding, slower and darker."

"It's clotting, Tank. Keep going. Seal him up quick. He's plenty disinfected by now."

Tank sighed, working his hands, swearing when he stubbed his finger on the needle. Roman's eyes twitched, and he kicked his legs slowly.

"Hold him the fuck down," Tank told the prospect.

"This is gonna be ten times harder if he starts flopping like a goddamned fish. Guess we should've given him more of that ether shit after all…"

The prospect made a face, and walked to the end of the bed, flattening Roman's feet. I stood up, saw my in, and took it.

"Let me. He knows my touch. Here, hold the baby for a second." I didn't wait, pushing Caleb into the bewildered prospect's arms.

Tank gave me a sharp look, but he didn't order me away. Roman's movements beneath my hands were so weak, so fevered. His chest rose erratically, somewhere in between sleep and pain and rage.

"Rest up, baby," I whispered to him. "He's trying to help you. Just let him patch you up. Caleb's here. So am I. You're going to be fine."

Up here, I had a scary view of the wound. Whatever tore through his shoulder, it wasn't small. It looked almost like a dog bite, if dogs had teeth more like sharks.

"Last one, babe," Tank said sternly into the phone.

"Now do the seal. Just like I taught you. Wrap it up, clean and neat."

My stomach did a sickly flip as I watched Roman's torn flesh mesh together. Tank formed what looked like a knot before he shifted the clamps on Roman's shoulder, holding the skin together. He didn't stop until he cut the last thread with the small silvery scissors.

The tools slammed down on the nightstand, and he grabbed the phone. His hands were a bloody mess.

"It's done. I gotta hang up so I can talk to their Prez. I think he's gonna live, hopefully without any fucked up complications."

"Make sure somebody's with him for the next twenty-four hours. Don't let him sleep alone. You need to tell them to refresh the fluids too. Don't just assume they're going to know –"

"Babe, I've got this. Believe me, some of these boys'll put my ass on the line if he dies. I'm doing everything by the book as fast as I can so I'll be coming home soon. Love you, Em, I gotta go."

He hung up. We shared a brief, tense look, and he nodded to me.

"Shit. Looks like we do have the same tastes after all…"

"Huh?" I didn't understand what he was getting at.

"Nothing. Stay with him. I'll fill you in later on what to do. I gotta find Brass or Blackjack." Tank stepped quickly out of the room, opening up the narrow space on the chair next to the bed.

I pulled it close and gripped Roman's hand. He was cold, freakishly heavy between my hands.

For the first time since he'd stormed off with his crew, my emotions aligned. Everything faded away. All the hate, all the confusion, all the anger.

It all evaporated into a great yawning nothing, void of everything except the slow, steady thud of my heartbeat, feeling for his pulse. I wanted to make his match mine, anything to bring him back to life.

Don't die on me. You can't fucking die.

Not now. Not ever.

For the next four hours, I prayed and fought my tears.

Caleb woke me up crying. I'd fallen asleep shortly after Blackjack came through, eyeing his man and whispering a few things I couldn't really understand. He told me to get some sleep before he stepped out.

Christa and Rabid came by to keep me company too. She was still up with a cup of coffee in her hands, keeping watch while I napped. She must've taken the baby as I went to sleep because when I woke up he was bouncing on her knee and smiling.

"Sorry," she whispered. "I think the little guy needs a change. Want me to take care of it?"

Before I could answer, Roman's fingers wrapped around mine. "Babe."

"Holy shit." Both my hands flew to his and squeezed him tight. "Christa, go ahead. I just need a moment with him…tell them he's awake too."

They'd said he wouldn't come out of it before noon tomorrow. The old clock hanging on the wall said it wasn't even seven A.M.

His color looked better, and he was warmer too. I leaned in, spilling my tears, dragging his heavy, strong hand up to my lips and giving it a kiss.

"We gotta talk," he said, his voice low.

"Roman, we can do all that later. You're hurt real bad. You just need to rest."

"Bullshit." He tried to move, but his body instantly

OUTLAW'S BRIDE

turned against him. "Fuck."

I felt him tense up and then slump down on the mattress about five seconds later. "Baby, just rest. Don't strain yourself. You'll only make it worse."

"My shoulder's burning like a motherfucker," he growled.

"Let me talk to them. I'll tell them you need something stronger for the pain."

His strength surged, and I gasped when he grabbed my wrist. "No. I don't give a shit about that. There's something else bothering me. Come closer."

I leaned down, wiping away another tear as his stubble grazed my cheek. It made me think about the better times when we were so close, feeling his naked body against mine, rough and hot and powerful.

"I'm sorry I doubted you, babe. You were right about everything, and it's fucking gutting me. We walked into an ambush, and I nearly got my ass killed, just like my old man."

Talk about slayed. I felt my heart ripping in half when I looked him in the eyes, saw the sorrow, the regret, the shame.

Jesus. Yeah, I'd been mad at him before I found out he'd be lucky to ever say another word to me, but I never asked for *this*.

And he wasn't done yet. Oh, no.

"Roman…" I shook my head.

"Quiet, babe. I'm telling you the honest truth, and I gotta lay everything out there, in case I can't later. I'm supporting you and staying in Caleb's life no matter fucking what. Still, this shit's taught me I can't make you a prisoner to this if you don't wanna be. I can't leave my brothers, just like I can't leave you. But I'll be an even bigger bastard if I don't offer you an out."

"What?" His words were barely making sense. I couldn't even comprehend leaving this incredible bastard, even if he'd torn his way across my life like a storm.

"I'm not gonna force you to do a damned thing except keep your pretty head safe. You see the shit I get into. There's no guarantees it won't happen again, and maybe next time, I won't be so lucky. If you wanna scrub the brand and walk the fuck outta my life, I won't blame you. I won't chase you. I want you to be happy, babe, and something tells me you might be if you're not my old lady."

I looked at him for about ten long seconds. Two futures flashed in my head like lightning.

There'd always be drama, passion, and sometimes as little taste of hell as long as he was around. But the alternative was a thousand times worse, dark and dead and gray.

Empty. Void. Meaningless.

"Think about it," he growled. "You don't have to tell me a damned thing right –"

I had to be careful touching him, but just then, I wasn't even thinking. I stood up, leaned over, and pressed my lips to his so hard I almost bruised myself.

We kissed long and hard, and I didn't let up until he

understood. I'd make him feel the message, through all his pain and regret, straight through whatever the hell they'd given him for meds.

"Babe…what the fuck was that?" he said, his eyes wide and more alive than they'd been a minute ago.

"That's me telling you love doesn't back down. I don't care what the future holds, Roman. The only one I want is with you, and I'll get your name inked in three more places before we're married."

"Fuck." The kiss must've breathed more fire into him. He grabbed my hand with only a little less ferocity than when he was well. "That's happening as soon as I can walk. It has to."

"What?"

"The wedding. I'll get a proper ring on your finger as soon as I'm outta this place. Right now, all I can do is grab your fist and pull it tight. I'm asking you one more time – you wanna make this official for more than just the club? You really want to be my old lady and my wife?"

I laughed and threw my arms around his neck, shoving my lips to his again. "You know I do. Come on, Roman. Don't tell me the shot to your shoulder's blinded you."

Smiling, he grabbed my hand, and pulled it tight. His lips steamed across my fingers, kissing me with a hunger so intense it made me imagine his face between my legs, growling and tonguing me to perfect chaos.

"Babe, my eyes are wide a-fucking-wake. I'm gonna shove my ring right where I just kissed you before Halloween hits, and then I'm gonna fuck you 'til you're seeing stars."

Laughing, we kissed some more. I didn't blush until I turned around and saw half the guys standing in the room, complete with Missy, Christa, and Caleb next to them.

"Finally some good news," Brass said, throwing an arm around Missy and tugging her tight. "I'll tell the Prez. Soon as we finish the sick fuck we've got in the back, we'll throw this club a party it'll never forget."

"Shit," Rabid growled. "Never thought you'd beat us to the punch, brother. Now this club's gonna be hearing wedding bells for a whole damned year."

"You know I don't fuck around," Roman said, his eyes still locked on mine. "This thing was a given the second I hauled her back here and met my son. Long as I'm still breathing, this woman's *mine*."

XIV: Clean Cut (Roman)

My shoulder still ached every time I twisted my damned arm, but at least it didn't look like a bad butcher's cut anymore.

I was back on my feet and riding for the first time in days. I'd finally gotten out of the infirmary the day before, and fuck if it didn't feel good to sleep with my girl that night, in my own house.

Sally laid on my bare chest, careful to avoid the patch covering the stitches in my shoulder. Her fingers gliding over my chest soothed the crazy animal stamped on my skin. Too bad they didn't do shit for the beast inside.

My dick jerked hard, coming back to the life for the first time since I'd lost my blood on the pavement. Shoving my fingers through her hair, I pulled it tight, moving her face to mine.

"What's up?" she purred.

"Nothing. Just thinking about how many days I've gone without tasting these lips." And I sure as shit wasn't content to just think.

Without another word, I smashed my lips on hers,

driving my tongue into her mouth. Sally opened like a good girl, coupling her tongue with mine. I slid mine in and out of her mouth, unable to resist the insane momentum building through my body, the need to fuck her the same way we kissed.

Growling, I ignored the hellfire in my arm, and rolled on top of her. My cock hummed like dynamite on a short fuse. I didn't want to explode anywhere except inside her.

After the wedding, we'd be talking family again. Coming close enough to feel the reaper's bony hands on my head forced to look at my mortality. There was no goddamned way I meant to leave this world without a few more kids.

I'd be fucking her constantly soon, dumping her pills in the trash with a grin, and spilling every drop of come inside her 'til she was knocked up again. Just thinking about her swelling up with my seed, giving me the greatest gift a man could get, caused my hips to shake. I thrust my dick hard against her panties through my boxers, feeling her moan sex and sugar into my mouth.

"Oh, fuck. Baby," she whispered, snatching her lips away from mine. "You need to be careful. We really shouldn't be doing this. The guys and that nurse said –"

"I don't give a fuck about doctor's orders, babe. You're the only medicine I care about right now. I've lost too many nights feeling your nails on my back, hearing you whimper my name." I reared up, leaned on my knees, and pulled her up with me. "I'll feel that gunshot all over again if that's what it takes to fuck you. Or you can get on top and ride me like there's no tomorrow. Your choice."

The concern in her eyes faded as I reached between her legs, found her clit, and swept my thumb over it in slow, smoldering jerks. Her lips pursed mischievously before turning into an O-ring of pleasure.

She pushed my hand away and rolled. I fell down flat on my back, ripping off my boxers. My dick sprang out, hot and slick and ready, twitching between my legs every time I thought about her hot pussy clenched around every inch of me.

Sally moved, but not fast enough. Soon as she straddled me and lifted up her thin nightgown, I went for her panties, tearing them down her creamy thighs. She shuddered from the motion, barely remembered to move her legs so I could push them the rest of the way off.

"Get on this cock, babe. No more playing around. I've missed your heat like a fucking eagle misses the sky."

I knew I wasn't the only one jonesing for flesh. Her eyes narrowed and she bit her lip while she curled her little fingers around my big dick, aiming at her entrance, dripping cream against the sheets.

Fuck. The look she gave me was so goddamned hot I almost shot my load then and there.

Then I thought about the other looks she'd give me when my dick throttled her. I wasn't gonna come 'til she clawed at the pillows and screamed my fucking name through our house, snapping those long blonde locks in my hand like lightning cracking on the horizon.

My hands clapped her ass and squeezed tight. I helped

lower her onto my cock, giving her ten seconds to sink down and adjust to my size.

Our hips rocked simultaneously. It didn't take long to pick up some speed. I watched her hot, pink nipples bobbing as she fought to keep up with me, grinding her swollen clit on my base every time I sank deep.

"Don't you fucking stop, woman. Not for anything. Show me how much you missed me." I picked my hands up and slapped her ass hard again.

She gasped pleasure, and her hips picked up, riding me harder. We fucked hard, bouncing her curves and rocking our bed. Fire bit my shoulder, reminding me to slow the fuck down, but I wouldn't listen to that shit for anything.

When her face tensed up and I knew she was on the verge, I doubled my thrusts, stroking her pussy in such quick, rough thrusts I put her damned vibrator to shame. She'd never need that fucking thing again as long as I was on the job.

Her warm cunt clenched a second later, and her knees began to shake. "Roman! Travis! Fuck!"

Her hot tits swung down in my face as she collapsed over me, her whole body shaking, everything around my pistoning length tightening like a hot, wet sleeve. I made it halfway through her orgasm, fucking her at turbo, before my balls couldn't take anymore.

"Fuck, babe, don't you goddamned stop. I'm coming. This pussy's *mine*."

My fingers dug into her ass so hard, hot flesh bloomed between my fingers. I held her down as my dick swelled, bathed my brain in fire, and unloaded the lava seething in my balls.

My cock plunged in to the hilt. Something wicked and primal took over, the overwhelming desire to fill her the fuck up, shooting every drop I could in her womb.

She moaned and panted each time my cock hurled thick ropes into her depths. My hips slid against hers like a man possessed, locked into place, fused 'til my balls were done pumping.

We fucked, came, and writhed forever. Satisfaction swirled in my heart. This woman was *mine,* damn it, and I'd keep owning her like this every night of our lives as a reminder.

Only thing hotter would be fucking her when she had that ring on her hand. Fuck, my dick throbbed again at the thought, ready for a second round before I'd even pulled outta her.

The urge to rest was too fucking much – especially when it felt like I had a pitbull chewing through my shoulder. The pain caught up to me, the brutal reminder that I'd almost lost all this for good.

I could've easily bled out on the cold pavement that day. By some miracle, I hadn't.

"Roman? You okay?" she whispered, rolling off and laying next to me.

"Yeah, and okay's all we need for now. Give it a couple weeks, babe. We'll be sitting pretty fucking nice in a matter of months. Just gotta tie up a few loose ends this week, while you plan the best wedding ever in a two week time crunch."

"Shit. The wedding!" Her eyes went big, but she was wearing a smile. "It's really happening, isn't it?"

"You'd better believe it. Call up Christa and Missy for some help. It'll be tight to swing it like this, but it's gonna be good. Don't have a single doubt about it, and you don't need to either."

"Oh, you know I like a challenge. Keeps things interesting." Her nails touched my skin and slowly slid down my side, angling dangerously close to my cock when she got lower.

"Fuck yeah, you do. We wouldn't be sharing a bed if you were the kind to flip and run the instant shit gets messy. Tough chicks are the hottest fucks."

She laughed. "You really think I'm tough?"

"Babe, I know it. And tonight, you're working this bed with me like it's goddamned boot camp." Growling, I pushed her hand down to my cock, tightened her fingers around my ballooning length, and squeezed.

A couple minutes later, I pulled her legs apart and pushed into her from the side. We fucked our way to paradise 'til the birds began to tweet in the trees.

Club business waited for me the next day. Ugly, bloody, unfinished business.

I thought about us fucking the whole ride in. Thinking about her hot bod convulsing all over mine sweetened the blow that was about to come.

When I got inside the clubhouse, I met up with Rabid,

and every hot, happy thought I had melted. There was nothing sexy about the grisly problem in front of me.

"Go easy on him, big guy. The fuck's already missing a whole hand. If the asshole dies before we've got a firm yes for the Prez, we're shit outta luck." Rabid walked with me down the long hall, toward the storage room, now guarded by several prospects and a full patch member twenty-four-seven.

The prospects nodded to us and the door squealed open. Gold Teeth was slouched in his chair, his arms and legs bound, everything except the bloody stump where his right hand had been. They'd saved his bum leg and taken his hand.

Blackjack and the boys carved it off two fingers at a time, a little more each day, sending the rotten meat back to Mexico with a three-line note attached.

Leave California, or he dies. No negotiations. You know how to reach us.

Seeing the asshole sick and clammy was a nasty sight. Didn't stop me from wearing the same impassable mask, or remembering this fucked up clown nearly took me away from my wife and kid way too damned soon.

If I could've resurrected Beam and killed him a few more times, I would've. Instead, this asshole was all I had, and the Prez's orders said we couldn't put him under unless the cartel's answer was a hard *fuck no.*

The don saw me and cracked his eyes, slow and groggy, like he was waking up from a dream. Really, he was coming home to a nightmare.

Those dark eyes got a whole lot wider when he saw me, recognized the man he thought he'd killed. He started sputtering some shit in rapid-fire Spanish.

I didn't understand any of it except the word *dios* – God.

I leaned down, face to sweaty face, making sure he could see the bulge underneath my cut from the gauze covering my screwed up shoulder. "You ready to talk today, boss man? The boys have done a damned good job carving meat off your sorry ass. 'Course they're only part-timers. I'm this club's Enforcer, and making assholes' tongues move is my full time job."

"That's right," Rabid growled in his other ear. "You can start by speaking English, asshole. There's nobody here who'll whisper sweet nothings in your native tongue, let alone bail you the fuck out."

I gave my brother the evil eye. He got the message and backed away. This was all me.

I walked to the little stand in the corner, where some of the brothers had set up our usual toolbox for persuasion. Wires, clamps, batteries, and about a thousand different knives.

Sometimes I actually missed the Mauler, that torture glove the evil bastards used under Fang, but I didn't miss the fact that too many good brothers ended up shredded under that fucking thing.

I'd make do. Picking up a hunting knife, I brandished it in one hand, testing the very edge. It wasn't great for taking more bone off him, but it'd do the job for peeling skin.

When I turned around, he was fully conscious, bright fear alive in his eyes. "Please. I told your men everything already. Everything about this operation, the raid, the organization…"

I rubbed my chin with my free hand, feeling the sandpaper stubble. Hm, he was weaker than the other assholes we'd captured. Or maybe more willing to squawk because he was the first one ever who actually had a chance of walking away with his life.

Not that it was his choice. It was all up to his buds in the cartel now, and we had to hope golden boy here was as bright and shiny as his teeth.

"Yeah, except you haven't given us anything we can work with. Let's make this easy. What the *fuck* do I have to ship them in the mail to get an answer?" I walked forward, slow and plodding, circling him like a damned shark. "An ear? An eye? A nut?"

He flinched and looked down. Asshole caught a glimpse of the bloody stump where his hand had been, a reminder he'd already taken serious damage. He blubbered like a baby, shaking his head in disbelief.

"I dunno, Jose. Better think hard. Loosen those lips. Maybe I should put this knife down and pick up the pliers instead, rip out every last one of those pretty fucking teeth in your mouth, and send it to your boys in little envelopes."

"They'll never give up," he spat, looking at me more sternly than before. "Whatever you do to me, we'll do a thousand times worse to your man, Blackjack."

Wrong answer.

I pushed the blade's flat edge against his head, starting near the back, one clean swipe away from taking an ear. The don lost his spunk just as quick as he'd gotten his balls back. Fuck, those rotten nuts were probably crawling up his guts right now, scared shitless I was crazy enough to take his ear right now, or something worse.

"All things are negotiable in this world, motherfucker. People change their minds. A few months ago, I'd have never believed I'd give up whores and drinking for something better. The name's Roman. I lived rough, lived to crucify sick motherfuckers in the worst ways possible. Now, all I wanna do is curl up with my wife and kid."

"Then do it," he whispered. "Go home. Finish me quickly. Spend your last few precious days with your family before the elites come for vengeance, for you and all your miserable brothers."

Fucking. Asshole.

I looked up and saw Rabid smile. Then I slid the blade in hard, listening to the bastard howl, tearing through buttery cartilage. It wasn't enough to sever his ear, but it couldn't stay hanging off his head for long without some serious attention.

Moving to the other side of his head, I spoke slow, clearly. "It's not too late for you. We can reattach that worthless flap of skin and send you home missing nothing worse than a hand and a little pride. Just tell us how to make your boys cave. Throw us a goddamned fucking bone so we don't have to grind yours into dust."

He swore, blubbered, spat such rapid fire curses I couldn't tell what language he spoke anymore. It went on for about a minute before he finally got control, sweating like a pig from the pain searing his brain. Blood pooled on his shoulder, running down his neck in rivulets from the severed ear.

"You tell them you'll hit them where they live! It's fucking obvious, is it not?" he sputtered, all he could manage before he closed his mouth again, chewing on the agony. More dark crimson stained his shoulder, almost in the same place where I'd taken a bullet.

Ironic.

"You mean in Mexico?"

He nodded. "I told you everything. You know about our ops across the border. Your President knows all about our bases in Baja, Sonora, Mexico City. You threaten them the same way we've done to you. You have to hit their homes, their families, their kids. Keep *nothing* off limits."

I pulled away. Rabid looked a little pale.

Fuck. The asshole in the torture chair had a point. Of course, the club never went after civilians, American or otherwise, and we sure as fuck weren't gonna start.

But if these fucks had killed brothers, bombed clubhouse, even wiped out a few old ladies in SoCal…

They'd threatened my fucking family, and almost tore me away from them, leaving Sally and Caleb defenseless.

No, we'd never sink to their God forsaken depths, but

we'd sure as shit pretend. The asshole whipped his head backward when I touched the blade to the opposite side of his head, threatening the good ear.

"We need more. You tell us the names and addresses of your cousins and uncles in the capital. We know you're royal blood, don. Shitty part is, you're also expendable, but they'll be singing a different tune if all the hydra's heads are threatened at once, yeah?"

"Yes. *Yes.* Anything."

For the first time since I'd stepped in, I smiled, and drew the knife away. I looked at Rabid.

"Get somebody in here to sew his shit back on. We'll put him on standby for transport as soon as the Prez gets the info he's looking for, and verifies it. Something tells me the motherfuckers will answer us next time."

I got the call when I was in town picking up some grub for dinner. The cartel blinked.

The boys were putting a hood over our don's head that second and getting him ready for a ride down to San Diego. The Nomads working down there would handle the rest as soon as we passed him off, and we'd all oversee the cartels withdrawal from our home state as soon as the ink was dry on the truce.

Thank Christ. Even better, my girl went out to try on dresses today, and she'd left me some texts about 'em being fucking hot.

I couldn't wait to get home. Neither could the hard-on hammering in my pants. My wound felt better by the hour. By the time we tied the knot in a couple weeks, I'd be good as new, ready for some serious horizontal gymnastics on our honeymoon.

She thought I'd already fucked her every way I knew how. And I was ready as hell to show her she was wrong. I'd be training her to come on my cock better than any woman ever had, until the pulled every last drop of seed from my balls.

I loaded a couple pizzas on my bike and took off for home, loving the crisp air blowing in my face. The house was quiet when I pulled up. Sally's car was in the driveway, and I didn't hear shit when I stepped inside.

Missy and Jackie wouldn't drop off the kid 'til later. That gave us a few hours to talk plans for the big day, feed our faces, maybe even pick up where we'd left off last night.

"Babe?" I called it twice when I got in, louder on the third time when I reached the staircase.

She wasn't a heavy sleeper. Something was fucked up in all this silence. The hair tingled on the back of my neck, and so did my hand, poised over the nine millimeter on my hip.

"Sally? Where the fuck are you?" Our bedroom door was half-closed.

I swept it open quick, expecting to hear her in the bathroom, deafened by a hissing shower or something. Fuck's sake, I'd have *killed* to hear either of those sounds, or just to see her sleeping peacefully in our big bed.

Lady Luck wasn't so kind. Not today.

Instead, I walked in on a man crouching in the corner, a gun already trained on me, his other hand holding my girl by the neck. She was on the floor struggling, a pillowcase over her head.

"Finally! Took you forever to show up, bear boy," he growled, his dark eyes and the hint of an accent betraying his origin.

I didn't back down. I'd catch a fucking bullet through my heart before I let up, aiming the gun right at his nasty little brain. I didn't know who the fuck he was or what he was doing in our house.

None of that mattered, not even the fact that he'd obviously come from the cartel.

What mattered was that he had my woman, my love, holding her a hostage in our own damned bedroom.

"Let. Her. Go."

Three simple words. They never listened. They never did.

This asshole was no exception – but why the fuck should he when I'd decided he was dead before I opened my mouth?

"I can do that, gringo. That's what I'm here for, yeah? Just as soon as you tell me where you've got Don Meza."

"He's on his way home." The demon's eyes lit up. "No bullshit. Call your boys back home in Mexico City if you don't believe it. You fuck up anything here, you kill the peace we're about to make, even though it's the bitterest goddamned peace I've ever seen. You shoot me, you kill my girl, and your don's a dead man. So is every other *capo* fuck south of the border."

We stared for several seconds. Sally whimpered on the floor, and kicked her legs again. My heart thundered pure adrenaline, fighting the urge to look at her, and lose my focus.

Make your move, asshole. Just one. I'll blow your fucking brains out your ears.

"You take half a step, I shoot her. Let me call your bluff." He eyeballed me the whole time, reaching into his pocket for his phone.

For the next minute or two, fiery Spanish flew outta his mouth like a machine gun, coming to an abrupt end when he snapped it shut. A sinister smile crossed his lips.

"You're a lucky man, grizzly bear. Count the stars tonight and thank every one of them. I will go, in peace, as long as you let me."

"Fine. Take the fucking hood off her head first, and let her back away. I'm not letting you outta this room 'til you do."

He shrugged, and began to do exactly what I said. Sally crawled into the corner, red faced and shaking her head. Those soft blue eyes were huge, terrified.

I wished like hell I'd brought the shit from the club home. I'd use every tool I had on this pig fucker to make him scream, finish him with a Colombian necktie, after I'd fried his nuts to a crisp.

Yeah, I'd be violating the imminent truce, but there were no rules 'til it was all official.

"Just breathe, baby girl," I mouthed, watching as he

stood up.

I backed into the opposite corner and watched the fucker move to the door. I'd wait 'til he was next to the stairs before I pulled the trigger to be safe.

It was dangerous as fuck, especially when he had me in his sights, slowly backing toward the stairs, his gun up and ready. He'd get distracted before he took the first step. He'd pause, giving me the perfect opening to punch the trigger.

I started counting his slow, creeping steps in the hall. When I was down to three, my fingers burned, ready to snuff him the fuck out forever, even if I risked another bullet landing in my –

Sally moved like a blur. She rushed to the wall next to the door, and I only caught a flash of something large and bulky in her hand before I heard the deafening bang.

"Babe!" I screamed, ready to tell her to get the fuck down, but she'd already hit the floor, crashing on the carpet simultaneously with me.

I didn't realize the explosion was her gun 'til the Mexican dropped. I caught a flash of blood spraying from his throat, heard him make that choking sound, and his gun tottered down the stairs. He fell in the hall, staining the carpet a deep red.

I ran forward, scooped her up, held her so fucking tight she couldn't cry.

"In our house…our house…our fucking house!" she screamed, over and over, like something inside her was broken. "I'm sorry…I didn't know what to do. I couldn't let him walk away."

"You did good, babe. It's done. Don't think. Just breathe." I exhaled pure relief, then leaned down and kissed her forehead. "Fucking hell. I said you were tough, but I had no idea. You proved me right. Again. You're gonna make the best wife an outlaw could hope for."

I called the boys over to clean up the fucking mess while I sent Sally over to Brass' place. Jackie and Missy could keep her company while she calmed down, and hold onto our kid for a little while longer.

This shit was too close for comfort. I wasn't gonna be content stripping out the carpet and dumping this fucker off in a cement grave.

It couldn't happen again. *Ever.*

I'd wire the house up with cameras, wires, and alarms galore, install bullet proof glass if I fucking had to.

What would've happened if the cartel man hadn't listened to his higher ups? What if he'd slit my girl's throat before I even got here, or walked to my sleeping son's crib?

All the bloody, pitch black possibilities flashed in my mind. They gave me a rage like nothing else, and an energy like I was on cocaine, espresso, and that yerba mate shit all at once.

Asphalt and Southpaw showed up in minutes to deal with the body. I stood by growling orders at the prospects, taking my tools and stripping up the bloodied carpet myself. Good thing half the guys in this club had some carpentry experience.

We never had to rely on outsiders, thank fuck.

Loose lips always sink ships, and the club had almost struck an iceberg over the years. Covering our tracks the right way and keeping as much talent as we could in-house went a long way toward keeping our asses outta prison.

Fuck, prison. I'd never go back. Just like I'd never allow another armed man to come in here and threaten my family.

It took all night to finish the job, working non-stop. When Southpaw and Asphalt finally came home from dumping off the Mexican's carcass, they looked at me like I'd lost my fucking mind, stapling shit in place like I was a mad man.

"Christ, brother. Settle the fuck down before you have a heart attack. You realize we can all help wire this place up in a couple more days?"

"No!" I pointed my finger like a dagger at Asphalt. "Truce or no truce, I don't trust the cartel motherfuckers 'til every last one of 'ems gone. This shit almost went rotten because their own right hand didn't know what the left was doing. I'm not risking my old lady and my kid again. You can either help or keep your damned mouth shut."

Asphalt clenched his jaw, but he didn't bark back. He marched up and got to work, helping me run wire over all the doors, perfect for installing the new security cams the prospects picked up at a twenty-four hour department store.

Everything human leaves a man when his family's

under the gun. It was like I had a goddamned second sun burning in my guts, turning my blood to pure fire, hellbound to finish the job so she never, ever had to worry again.

'Course, Sally's trigger finger just might've saved my ass in the end too. But she'd also put herself in harm's way, and I'd be a dead man before I *ever* let that happen again.

We worked like dogs past sunup. When we were close to finished, I got the call, and so did the rest of the brothers. We needed to get to the clubhouse by eleven.

Just enough time to test the shit. It all worked, minus a few finishing touches, and I'd polish that off later. There was also time to make a quick stop by Brass and Missy's place.

I rode in, parked my bike, and knocked on the door. The Veep let me in, and nodded.

"Hurry up. It took my girl half the night to calm her down. Fucking shit, Roman, you realize you almost wound up like those poor bastards who get themselves shot after the war's technically over?"

"He broke into my house. He threatened my girl. You wanna give me any shit about the truce, Veep, then that's on you. I'd have blown his fucking brains out if Sally hadn't beat me to it."

He shook his head. "No, brother. You made the right call. Truce wasn't official 'til this morning. The cartel's not gonna do shit about a missing grunt as long as they've got their golden boy back."

I stepped into the house as he walked off into the kitchen. I found her sleeping on a fold out sofa, baby in her arms, both of 'em making soft, peaceful sounds.

Sitting on the sofa, I stretched out, wrapping one hand around her shoulder and pulling her tight. The movement caused her eyes to open.

"You're here!" She whispered. "Is it safe to go home yet?"

"Soon, babe. I'm gonna ask you to put 'til we know this thing's locked down with the cartel. I'll be welcoming you home in the evening to see a few home improvements?"

She cocked her head. "God. Don't tell me you've thrown up barbed wire in the yard or something."

"Just cameras and some really earsplitting burglar alarms. Trust me, woman, *nobody's* ever getting in our home again. Knowing it happened once makes me fucking sick."

It really did. My guts churned, but what I really meant was *sick in the head.* Dismembering anybody who actually hurt her or Caleb crowded by head, alongside a thousand other tortures I'd inflict on the twisted fuckers.

"It's all over, isn't it? I can't believe it." She sighed. "I'll have to help Norm back to the farm next week. He's going to need a lot of help while he gets back on his feet."

"Sure, once we're done combing those fields. Your cousin's a stubborn SOB, babe. I'll wire up his place too on the off chance those damned jackals are dumb enough to come back someday. Otherwise, tell him to get the hell ready for our wedding."

She swallowed, her big blue eyes shining like gems. "You really think we can do this? After all that's happened? I mean, I want it too, but we can wait if it makes you feel –"

"Better? Fuck that. The only thing's that's gonna make me feel whole is watching you come down the aisle. You've been through hell, babe. We all have. There's nothing either of us need to worry about now except *this*."

I didn't give her another chance to speak. My lips found hers, and they didn't let up, not 'til the Veep and his old lady walked in a few minutes later.

By then, it was time for us to go, and Caleb was ready for his breakfast. I shook his little hand and kissed him on the forehead, then headed for my bike outside.

No, I wasn't a hundred percent whole 'til the wedding, just like I'd told her. But something about waking up with a bombshell next to me and a kid who shared my blood was pretty damned close.

This time, church was outside. We all gathered around the fire pit in the back. The inferno normally blazed late at night when we had our rowdy hog roasts and guests came in, or sometimes to entertain high level brothers from other charters.

Not today. This morning, we had the rite of grievances, a first for this charter, and something that had only been used in a couple times before aross the entire Grizzlies MC.

"Step forward, son." Blackjack waited for me next to

the flame, side by side with Stryker.

He passed me the dagger, and I slid it across my palm. Hot blood seeped through the burn, the pain meant to wipe away all the wrongs we'd done to our man.

Blackjack nodded, took back the blade, and I stepped up, looking Stryker in the eye. "I'm sorry as hell, brother. These mistakes are never gonna happen again."

The tension on the younger man's face melted. He took my hand, gave it a firm squeeze. He felt my blood on his palm, and then gave me a zen-like nod.

"You're forgiven, Roman. It's already ancient history."

I passed by and waited for everybody else near the fire. Each full patch brother stepped up, plus a few prospects who'd been there before we killed the real rat and a whole lotta cartel assholes. Everyone made the same apology, dripping blood into Stryker's hand and then into the fire, killing the bitterness and guilt we'd summoned with our fuck up.

Blackjack was the last, and he sliced into both his hands. Deep, brutal cuts wept blood on the concrete patio underneath us. He gripped Stryker's hand tight, before reaching up and grabbing him by the neck, pulling him close to the old man's chest.

"I'm sorry, son. Never again. If we ever fuck up this bad, you kill me first."

The kid had tears in his eyes at the end of it as the Prez stormed away, reaching for the bandages Brass had waiting. Blackjack wrapped his hand like it was nothing, and carried on with the rest of the meeting.

"Brothers, I signed off on the treaty this morning. The cartel's got their man back, and they've already begun to pull out of LA, with our men watching them like hawks. We won't let up 'til they're all back across the US border. It's over."

Brothers jeered. They clapped their bloodied hands together, pounded each other on the shoulders, or just quietly smiled. Asphalt and Rabid looked the most relieved, but we all felt it in our chests, like a damned gorilla just crawled up outta our skins.

"Don't turn your backs yet. These bastards across the border will never be our friends. They're rivals. Competitors. Killers." He paused. "Let that sink in, and get ready to watch them with every ounce of vigilance we have. We don't let up until every last goon with an eagle patch is *out*. We don't quit before our territory's really ours again. I know I can count on you. Every man here's put his heart and soul into this club, and we made a grave mistake doubting it."

He stopped and looked at Stryker. "Whatever happens from here, we'll keep this club tight. We've made friends with the Devils and smashed the greatest threat we've ever faced. There'll always be new ones, bastards who pop up like weeds, threatening to strangle everything we've fought for. But as long as we never let bad blood come between brothers, and no man sinks a dagger into his brother's patch, we're whole. We're alive. We're men."

I nodded. The Prez looked down and pulled one of his bandages tighter.

"You can count on everybody here," I said. "I'll do my damnedest to make sure every last one of those fuckers is outta Redding's city limits next week, on their way to San Diego and gone."

"You'll do no such thing, son," Blackjack snapped. "You're taking the next two weeks off to make sure your woman's the happiest old lady in the world before the big day. I won't risk that thing on your shoulder opening up again either. We've got the manpower to deal with anything, Roman, and you've already given us your brains and your courage. Now, stop working like a maniac and smell the goddamned roses. That's an order. Your only job right now's making sure this club has the best damned wedding we've ever seen."

God help me, I grinned. So did everybody else, even Stryker, the first time I'd seen him smile since we almost skinned him alive.

"Anybody else?" Blackjack asked, slowly scanning over the ranks of brothers.

Nobody said a word. The shitstorm threatening to blow the club to pieces hadn't let up for a second since I'd walked outta the pen.

Now, at last, the end was in sight. Every brother here might actually get a chance to ride off into the sunset, and I'd keep the peace for the club as a married man, happier than every other day I'd ever been alive and breathing on this planet.

XV: 'Til the End of Time (Sally)

Shit. I didn't dare breathe a word of panic. Only in my own head, and I really wished I'd practiced walking in these high white heels a little longer.

It was going to be embarrassing as hell if I tipped over and landed on my butt in front of all the guys and the grinning old ladies, my whole extended family. Then I stopped in my tracks.

Seriously, if this was the *only* problem today, we'd come a long way. Walking in my wedding shoes was a universe away from worrying about bullets flying.

Pick yourself up, I thought. *Keep walking. Smile like you mean it. The sun's shining on you today, girl, and you've already walked through hell on hot coals to get here.*

I smiled as I sashayed down the narrow aisle in the clubhouse. And I actually meant it too. By the time I got to the makeshift altar where they were waiting, I was positively beaming, and my face burned a few degrees hotter when I finally looked up.

Blackjack looked neater than ever. He locked eyes with me, smiled, and nodded, adding a few more wrinkles to his tough old face.

When I took a good, long look at the man I was about to marry for the first time, my heart stopped.

Remember to breathe. Remember to beat, heart.

Yeah, I really needed to remind myself. I had to remember how to *live* through the biggest day of my entire life without going into a coma.

The clubhouse fell silent as Blackjack waited for the last of the chatter to die down. A thin, wiry brother I didn't recognize from some other charter stood behind him – probably the man who'd observe and make it official for the state of California.

I barely noticed anything else because my eyes were glued to Roman. I'd never seen him in an honest-to-God suit before. Wet didn't begin to describe how my body responded.

I burned. I ached. I pressed my thighs together uncomfortably, holding back tears at the crazy lengths he'd gone to go traditional.

It wasn't exact, of course. He still had his club jacket on over it, and a small Grizzlies MC pin fixed to his lapel. But seeing him outside his cut and jeans made this all *real*, reminded me I was really about to take this man as my husband, 'til death do us part.

"Ladies, brothers, friends," Blackjack began. "I could say a lot of things about these two. I could prattle on about how they were meant to be, fated to have a life, a love, and a child together by some wild magic sent from Valhalla. But this club's always had more eloquent ways to celebrate two of our own tying the knot, and so do I."

A couple men snickered in the audience. "Roman, today you become a man. You become whole. You've proved yourself to this club over and over again, and nobody will ever doubt you. I know you'll do the same with this woman."

I watched Roman's eyes lock tight to Blackjack's as the Prez spoke louder. "Defend her. Love her. Own her. This day, you take your old lady in the last way, the best way, the deepest way. You take her as your wife. Last chance to back out, son."

"No fucking way," Roman growled, grabbing my hand. "I want this forever. I do."

I smiled. A thousand degrees of heat raged through me, especially when Blackjack's dark, serious eyes turned on me.

"Sally, I don't need to talk about your duties. You already know you're obliged to help our brother, love him, no matter what may come. In blood, in sweat, in death, he's your husband. Your old man. In life, he's the best damned friend and lover you'll ever have."

I lost it there, reached up to wipe one eye. I looked between Blackjack and Roman. Each time the President spoke his stern words, Roman nodded sharply, all incredible promises flashing in his eyes.

"Squeeze his hand tighter. Take a moment to feel him. Remember, lady, this thing's going to be forever. You're already bound by blood, the first child of many you'll have. Are you ready to be bound by law and brotherhood too?"

"Yes," I croaked, taking a second to stabilize my voice. "Of course I am. He's the only one I'll ever want. I love you, Roman. I do."

The old man nodded, his gray hair tied back neatly. We knew what was coming next.

I watched as Roman reached into the little box Brass held out next to him, already open. He plucked out the ring. I didn't realize how crazy big and bright it was until he pushed it on my finger.

The thing was almost *heavy*, studded in sharp cut diamonds like stars in a halo of golden sunlight. My knees almost dropped out, but I held on, forced myself to squeeze my old man's fingers tight.

"Thank you," I whispered. "It's amazing."

Smiling, Blackjack turned to the stranger behind him. "Angus, get up here. Finish it off for these kids."

The thin man cupped his hands over his mouth, covering his long mustache. "By the power vested in me by the state of California, you're man and wife. Start locking lips so we can kick off this party!"

Brothers cheered. Roman didn't wait for another word.

In a flash, his hands locked around me tight, pulled me in, buried me in his eager, powerful heat. The storm on my lips drowned out all the manic celebrations surrounding us.

I didn't think he had it in him to kiss me harder than all the times before, but he did. Oh, yes.

His lips plowed mine, possessed me, took total control

of what was eternally *his.*

And I kissed him, shoving my tongue against his, feeling him as he led me on a dizzying taste of everything to come. Everything below my waist tensed as his tongue pistoned in and out of my mouth, conquering me, promising me hell between the sheets for the honeymoon.

I couldn't come up for air. His hands kept me hooked to his body, the same as his lips, and he kissed me so long and hard my nails raked his jacket.

"Fuck, babe," he snarled, coming up for air at last. "You kiss me like that again, and we won't even stick around for the reception."

I was about to do it, just to tease him, when Brass and Missy got up between us. Missy rubbed against me like an overgrown kitten. She couldn't hug me with Caleb smiling in her arms.

"Congratulations, girl! I can't believe this. Thanks for taking charge too. You know there's probably going to be a few more weddings around here now that somebody's finally tied the knot?" She flashed Brass a wicked look.

I laughed, and reached out to stroke my son's little chin. Caleb giggled, grabbing at my fingers. It was strange to think my new husband and I had already created the greatest gift two people could.

Jesus, my husband. I looked at him, and I still couldn't believe it.

But the crazy scene in front of us didn't lie, and neither did the bank busting ring on my finger. I knew he did well for himself when he got the house, but I didn't know the club's profit share went so far.

"Fucking congrats, brother." I walked up next to Roman just in time to hear Brass talking. "You sure you wanna take that limo ride after all? You're gonna be driving that truck a helluva lot more once you pump out a few more kids."

I laughed and rolled my eyes. "That'll take some time. Besides, he's got to keep up on riding for the MC, and I won't get in the way. We're pretty happy getting used to all this with just Caleb. It's not like we'll be a huge family overnight."

Roman shot me a wild look like I'd just said the sky was pink. "Babe, it's happening a lot quicker than you think. We'll adjust. We're gonna have the biggest family in this town."

I laughed, even though I knew he was deadly serious. Hell, so was I. He'd find out soon about the surprise I had waiting for him. I reached for his hand and squeezed, wiggling my fingers against his.

Love can be a powerful thing. Here, it was so potent I'd really try to give him as many kids as he wanted. He'd already saved our lives several times over, and it only seemed right that he got to take charge of a few more.

"Unbe-fucking-lievable!" Rabid bounced forward with Christa at his side, shoving aside the VP, grasping Roman's huge free hand in both of his and shaking it like mad. "You're a married man! You got any idea what that means?"

Roman chuckled. "I think I do after being up here at

the altar. You'd better be next in line, brother."

He looked at Christa. She wrinkled her scarred face, but something about the glint in her eyes told me she wanted it.

"It'll happen soon," he growled, pulling on her hand. "Shit, it's all roses from here, isn't it? The cartel's off our ass, and business is ready to boom! We're finally living the dream, bro. Fucking *finally.*"

They shared a long, intense look, and it was like I could see a hundred terrifying old battles unfolding in their eyes. A hundred battles, won and buried, but never forgotten.

All the sweat, all the blood, all the pain had brought us all together.

Then somebody started tugging on my long white skirt, and I swirled around. A small ball of excitement jumped up and threw her arms around my neck.

"My daughter! Welcome to the family!" Julie Forker nearly put her giant son to shame with the choke hold she had on me.

I nearly tripped on my heels after all and went crashing to the ground. Roman noticed at the last second and pulled me up by the waist, swatting his mother's greedy hands away.

"Ah, ma! Let her breathe."

"I'm just so excited! Somebody pinch me!" she squealed. "I never thought I'd see my son…married."

"Well, you got a grandkid quicker too, ma, and Caleb's gonna be the first of many. Hope you're ready for him tonight."

"Oh, where is the little angel? I want to pick him up now, if that's all right. I promise I'll keep him fed and happy while you're gone for the next week. I raised you, didn't I?"

Something about her smile made me laugh. Roman clenched his jaw, suppressing a smile, and pointed to the baby in Missy's arms.

"He's over there. Go get him, grandma."

She took a few quick steps away, and then stopped and looked back at us over her shoulder. "Wow. I wish your father could see all this, son."

"So do I," Roman said, barely a whisper.

Roman looked at me and stopped. Next thing I knew, those huge, world lifting hands were around me again, but this time they were lifting me up. I howled and kicked my heels, trying not to lose them.

He carried me through the last of the crowd. I reached out and cupped hands with a few grinning cousins, tears in the women's eyes. The wire cage Norm still had around his head bobbed over everybody, and he got his hand into mine too. I smiled when I saw the genuine happiness in his eyes, the giddy and proud spark that said, *congratulations, cuz.*

"Hey, hey! Not so hard. You don't want to tear this thing, do you?" I whimpered in Roman's ear.

"Babe, we'd better head to the car right now, or else I'm gonna tear it off and fuck you on the floor. No lie."

I leaned up and we shared another long kiss. Honestly,

his crude as hell suggestion didn't sound half bad.

As pretty as this ivory white dress with the bitch heels could be, it was starting to feel like an over-fastened corset, and it was definitely coming off tonight, one way or another.

The limo jerked forward about ten minutes later, surrounded by the roar of our escort from the brothers on their bikes. Blackjack rode in front, and everybody else on the sides, behind him, or else several paces back, forming a long line to the luxury lodge just outside Redding.

I watched Roman chug down a glass of champagne in one swoop, while I'd barely touched mine. "Uh, you know you're supposed to savor the flavor, right? That stuff's like three hundred dollars a bottle!"

He laughed. "Whatever. Doesn't go down half as hot as Jack."

"Give me a chance. I'll make you a little more civilized now that you're my husband," I said with a wink, sipping the drink. The sweet, fizzy bubbles swirled in my mouth, mingling with his lingering taste, deliciously pleasant.

"Put that shit down, babe," he said, unfastening my seat belt and jerking me onto his lap. "You think I've got no taste? That I don't know how to savor anything? I'll show you right fucking now how wrong you are. Just because we're married doesn't mean you know everything about me, woman."

Holy shit. I tried to guard my dress as he reached up it, his rough hand brushing my thigh, passing above the sleek white stockings clinging to my skin. He went straight for my panties, and had them down in one rough jerk.

"Lay the fuck down. Put your legs up." He pushed two stiff fingers inside me, and I groaned, trying to close my thighs and completely failing.

"Roman! The driver...it's not that long to get to this place either. You really think this is a good idea?"

You really think it's not happening? the look he wore told me.

"Open up, Sally, and keep sipping that gold stuff in the crystal. Unless you want me to keep these in my pocket all through the reception." He held my panties up, balled in his hand, white lace that was already soaked.

I almost died at the thought. My trembling legs parted, and his hands cupped my ass, squeezing me and dragging me to his face.

I prayed the driver couldn't see us behind the dark tinted privacy glass. I also wished to God the heavens would open up and explain how he made me feel like a blushing virgin all the time, even after we'd fucked close to a hundred times and he'd knocked me up.

Yep, I kept count too. Tonight, we'd be on number eighty-seven, and well over the hundred mark by the time the week was over.

I knew his appetites. He knew mine. And right now, he dug in, forcing his rough face between my legs, sliding his tongue up and down my folds. His teeth found my clit, pulled it tight, and all my concerns melted like the carbonated elegance rippling in my mouth.

Time distorted as his tongue worked my pussy, edging me closer and closer to climax. It didn't take long. I'd never get tired of this man's mouth on my clit.

Something about seeing him in that suit, thrusting against me with the same mad vigor he'd always had, sent me over the edge.

I came hot, fast, and *hard*.

I reached up, careful to avoid the shiny new ring on my finger, and stuffed my fist into my mouth. It was all I could do not to scream.

Roman didn't care about staying silent. He growled his satisfaction as my muscles convulsed, sending me to ecstasy, making me squirm and rock and thrash against his face. His powerful hands held me down, held me open, kept the pleasure coming strong.

It took what seemed like forever to come out of the hot white heat. When I did, an insatiable fire tore through my veins. I wanted him inside me.

My mouth, my pussy, my ass. Anything was game. *Everything* belonged to my old man now, and I wanted to give it to him in spades.

I reached between my legs and felt the massive bulge beneath his trousers. I shifted my legs, fumbling with his zipper.

"Babe, we're almost there…" Roman looked out the window.

I looked at him and winked. "I know you need it. Now, who's getting camera shy?"

Jesus, he was hard, like warm steel, and I wanted him

inside me until he melted into slag. I brought my lips to his, flicking my tongue into his mouth, feeling for the zipper.

Then there was a clicking sound, and we were bathed in evening light. The neat dressed man who'd been hired to play chauffeur coughed uncomfortably.

"Fucking hell." Roman gently pushed me away, and handed my panties to me. "Put those things back on, babe. You've earned it. We've gotta go."

On our way out of the car, he leaned over to me, and grinned. "Better Jeeves here than the brothers. They'd have never stopped giving me shit for fucking you in the backseat on a ten minute ride. Not that they'll do any better when they finally get hitched."

Arm in arm, we smiled for the brothers and old ladies flashing cameras, and went inside.

Our first dinner as a married couple went by in a blur. The men were getting rowdy by the end, hitting the dance floor with their girls.

Even the whores like Twinkie got in on the action, swinging around and giggling as Asphalt hurled her around the floor, snatching her close for a thick, drunken kiss.

Everybody congratulated us again. We waited for the liquor to keep flowing so we could make our exit unseen. By the end, things were turning *really* wild.

Harsh biker laughter cut through the booming music, and all the dark corners had couples together, caving to the passion and revelry building in the air. I watched

Roman take one last swig of his tall beer, before he grabbed my hand and leaned over.

"Time to go, babe. Let everybody else have their fun, and we'll have ours. No bullshit – I'm gonna fuck you 'til sunup, 'til you scream, 'til the whole damned bed's soaked in our come."

His hand reached for my thigh, squeezing it through my dress. I thought for sure my sweet white bridal gown would combust.

He didn't have to ask twice. With a snarl, he grabbed me, and carried me over his shoulder all the way down the hall to the elevators. Our room was attached, high up on the top floor. The place had an awesome view Rabid and Christa told us about when they'd stayed here in the summer.

But by the time we pushed into our room, the only view I cared about was the one in front of me. Roman threw me into the bed and pinned me down, smothering me with his lips, stamping fiery kisses down my neck.

His fingers went straight between my legs, cupped my wet mound through my panties, and squeezed. I couldn't take it. I wasn't even sure why I'd bothered to put them on.

I pushed against him, trying to find room to take it all off. I'd never wanted us naked and joined so fucking bad before. Every nerve ached, and the swelling fire in my womb made my fingers nimble gymnasts. I was halfway stripped in less than a minute, only stopping to struggle with the zipper on the back.

Growling, Roman turned me around. I shivered with delight when his thick fingers found the zipper and yanked it down. He grabbed my shoulders and pushed everything down, unwrapping me, baring the gift he'd claimed. His hands slid back up, cupping my breasts, squeezing them so hard my nipples puckered.

"Hurry," I begged. "I. Need. This."

"Stand up and let it drop, babe. Everything except the stockings and those heels. It's all you get to fucking wear for the next twenty-four hours."

He stood up with me. I barely shuffled out of the dress and unclasped my bra, freeing my breasts, before I was transfixed on him undressing.

The jacket dropped, and so did the suit, piece by piece. The bad boy underneath emerged in all his glory, the furious ink all over his hard torso rippling like a canvass in the evening light. When he shoved down his boxers, the bead in his cock shined, making it a target my lips couldn't resist for anything.

He smiled, watching me sink to my knees. I wrapped my hand around his length, feeling his hardness, and squeezed.

Holy hell.

His fingers reached for my chin, clasped it, and closed the distance between my mouth and his cock. "Suck it like I taught you, babe. These are the only lips I ever wanna feel wrapped around this dick."

As if I needed any encouragement. I lowered my lips slowly down on him, teasing him, taking in his taste. His masculine scent stroked all my senses, a hypnotic majesty that took over each time I was this close to him, making me hornier.

Slow, gentle strokes, rapidly turning fiercer as the fire in my pussy roared. One hand snuck down and I played with my clit. I might have died with my mouth full of his cock if I didn't.

The thunder in his throat rolled out, building with his pleasure. His stern fingers fisted my hair, moving me faster on his cock, and his hips began to meet my strokes. I shoved my tongue deep into his crown, tonguing him in his most vulnerable spot, begging him to fill me.

If he came down my throat, then I'd lose it too. Hell, I'd finger myself senseless if I saw him shoot anywhere right now.

What the hell was happening? Why hadn't anyone told me the sex gets a hundred degrees hotter with that ring on my hand?

And it looked awfully good wrapped around his rock hard length. Roman's huge chest swelled, taking in breath, cursing it back out again as my lips quickened.

"Fuck. Shit. Goddamn, babe. Stop." He wasn't asking. His rough fist tugged me away, until his cock popped out of my mouth. "You suck like a good wife. I wanna see you fuck like one too."

"You seriously don't want to come in my mouth?" I bit my bottom lip, teasing him. *Please.*

He paused, his eyes bright, considering it. Then he shook his head, giving my hair a jerk to make me stand up.

"You've got a month to get off those damned pills, Sally. I'm not coming anywhere except your hot, wet cunt 'til Caleb's got a brother or sister on the way. Might as well practice."

Practice. Yeah.

I couldn't argue with that, as insane as it sounded. Hell, I wouldn't be arguing with his insane desire to knock me up again soon. I hadn't told him, but I'd already stopped taking my pills two days before.

The holidays were a good time to get pregnant, right?

I wanted it to be a surprise, big news to break near Thanksgiving or Christmas for both him and Julie. I was also a little afraid of what he'd do to me when he found out there was nothing between his seed and my womb.

I had a feeling it involved rope, sore legs, and weeks of being bound while he fucked me and came inside me, until he'd claimed my womb for the second time.

He pushed me down at the edge of the bed, standing up while he pushed his length to my entrance. The fingers in my hair grew softer, sifting through my blonde locks, sliding down my neck.

"Fuck. You're the hottest old lady, the hottest wife, a man could ever ask for. And I'm gonna fuck you 'til you believe it too, babe."

"Do it."

Two words. It was all he needed to push inside me with a growl, and then the steady creak of the bed crashed into the pleasure surging through my body, drowning out everything.

It wasn't twenty thrusts in before my body tensed up and jerked. I wrapped my legs around him, clawed at the sheets, and screamed.

I came for the second time that night, and then I couldn't stop. Something inside me broke that night, and I shuddered through three mind blowing climaxes, each one harder than the last. I saw stars before he came, and not just in my eyes.

Outside, the huge window showed the bright lights beginning to sparkle in the sky. He pushed me higher onto the bed and climbed on, throwing my legs over my shoulders, the better to fuck me harder.

"You're not done yet. You're coming with me this time, baby girl. Milk every inch of my dick dry."

My eyes narrowed and I locked my arms and legs around him, tight as they could go. I was growling with him by the time his thrusts quickened, pounding into me so hard they shook me like an earthquake, hammering me from the inside out.

"Fucking come inside me, Roman. I need to feel your heat. I love you, Travis." I sounded desperate as all hell, like a different person, whispering those words.

It didn't matter. I sounded like his *wife,* the one who'd love him more than anyone else in this world.

My words caused his hips go completely berserk. He fucked me like a huge, tattooed snarling bull, slapping my ass with his balls and grinding into my clit. I started to worry I'd lose control again, become another gushing, screaming mess before he finally pierced deep and emptied himself inside me.

No, I need his come this time.
Fucking. Need. It.

My fingernails dug deep into his skin. His expression matched the bear tattooed on his chest by the end, and he roared just as loud, stabbing deep inside me and swelling.

"Here's my dick. Here's my come. Take it, take it, and don't you fucking stop, woman."

I wouldn't dream of it. Especially when his cock swelled more than ever, and he ran his teeth into my neck, holding me down like a vessel as he erupted.

We writhed together forever, locked in an embrace so fiery we matched the stars through the window, twinkling on the horizon. I came so hard I lost my breath, my voice, my everything, fused to the only man whose heartbeat could match mine.

The wedding ring on my finger turned molten hot, and I swore it was the *only* thing I felt as my body became a foundry, every inch of me melting, unraveling, merging into him.

His heavy breath and the gentler tickle of his stubble brought me back to life. That sweet sandpaper on his face always grew back so fast. Not that I'd expected anything less from a walking cannon of testosterone.

"You feel that heartbeat, babe?" I grabbed my hand, pulled it to his chest, right over the furious Grizzlies MC bear. "That's my love. That's what's gonna keep us up all night. That's what's gonna shake off the fuck-haze tomorrow and keep us riding to the orchards."

"It's supposed to be a beautiful day," I said, swooning a little bit when I imagined us riding on his bike along the rows of apple trees. The prospects had brought his Harley to the lodge, all we'd need to enjoy our special week.

"Here," I whispered, pulling on his fingers until they hovered over my breast. "Feel mine. That's my life. That's everything I'm going to keep alive for you, baby."

"And you'd better keep it going a long time, babe. We've got a lotta decades to blaze. I'm gonna make the most of it before shit slows down and we're staring at our grandkids."

I slid my legs up and down his calves, reaching for his cock. "You'll just have to fuck me harder, I guess."

He grinned, taking his hand off my breast to reach for my ass. A couple seconds later, he had me on all fours, dangerously close to round two.

"Careful, babe," he rumbled in my ear. "You tease me like that, you just might get everything you ever wished for."

The joke was on him. I already had, and the rest of our lives were rolling out before us like a slow moving sunrise.

Thanks!

Want more Nicole Snow? Sign up for my newsletter to hear about new releases, subscriber only goodies, and other fun stuff!

JOIN THE NICOLE SNOW NEWSLETTER! - http://eepurl.com/HwFW1

Thank you so much for buying this book. I hope my romances will brighten your mornings and darken your evenings with total pleasure. Sensuality makes everything more vivid, doesn't it?

If you liked this book, please consider leaving a review and checking out my other erotic romance tales.

Got a comment on my work? Email me at nicolesnowerotica@gmail.com. I love hearing from my fans!

Kisses,
Nicole Snow

More Erotic Romance by Nicole Snow

FIGHT FOR HER HEART

BIG BAD DARE: TATTOOS AND SUBMISSION

MERCILESS LOVE: A DARK ROMANCE

LOVE SCARS: BAD BOY'S BRIDE

RECKLESSLY HIS: A BAD BOY MAFIA ROMANCE

STEPBROTHER CHARMING: A BILLIONAIRE BAD BOY ROMANCE

Outlaw Love/Prairie Devils MC Books

OUTLAW KIND OF LOVE

NOMAD KIND OF LOVE

SAVAGE KIND OF LOVE

WICKED KIND OF LOVE

BITTER KIND OF LOVE

Outlaw Love/ Grizzlies MC Books

OUTLAW'S KISS

OUTLAW'S OBSESSION

OUTLAW'S BRIDE

SEXY SAMPLES: OUTLAW'S OBSESSION

I: Some Wounds Don't Fade

It was hard to say goodbye to the kid because I knew what was waiting for me up the street.

Martin made tutoring easy. Only eight years old and obsessed with Napoleon, he wouldn't have needed me at all if the schools did a better job kindling his interests.

"His grades are already coming up! I dunno how you do it, lady, but you earned this. Here." His mother, Shirley, gushed all over me, pushing the check in my hands.

"Thanks." I was careful to make sure she didn't see how hard I pinched the scrap of paper when I stuffed it into my purse.

I didn't even take a second look to verify the right amount. There was no point when every single cent was going to an utter bastard who'd have me by the throat for the next ten years, no matter how much I earned.

Shirley gave me one last wave and I headed for my crappy old beater parked near the curb.

I got in my car and tried to collect my wits. It wasn't easy with the evening sun setting over Redding, casting its light across the dashboard. If there was one thing I hated as much as getting paid and forking it over to Big Ed, it was seeing my face in the rear view mirror.

The scars were still there. Visible reminders that the Grizzlies Motorcycle Club had wrecked my whole life, and it wasn't going to let up anytime soon.

Sure, they'd healed about as much as they were going to after a couple months, but my skin would never be the same. Fang robbed away what little beauty I had, torturing me in the back room of their clubhouse, all over an internal war I didn't even know about until he began to slice into my face and whisper death threats in my ear.

I pulled away from the curb and set off toward the nursing home, trying not to let my scars summon old ghosts. I'd survived Fang. Hell, I'd helped his own men kill him.

Missy, Brass, and that other man I didn't dare think about saved me from an agonizing end. And I returned the favor by marching out with them as living, breathing proof of everything the Grizzlies MC's old President had done.

Half his men couldn't take seeing me standing with Brass and his buddy, cut to pieces. They turned on the devil and his flock of demons. Rabid barely had time to escort me to safety when the shots started going off.

When it was all over, the man who pressed the knife into my face was dead. The Grizzlies MC chapter here in Redding began to change with new guys in charge.

Maybe their lives changed – I didn't care to know.

Mine didn't. Fang's death didn't change a thing. I was still knee deep in the same old shit that began long before the monster pressed his blade to my cheeks.

Big Ed answered to Redding, but he obviously wasn't

interested in listening to the new crew leading their mother charter. He had his own agenda. All the bastards in the Klamath charter did, and they were going to make me pay until I was destitute and bloodless.

His bike was already parked outside the nursing home when I got there. A quick stop at the bank turned my hundred dollar check into cold cash, the only thing he'd accept. I added it to a couple hundred more I had waiting for him, hoping it'd be enough to make up for the payments I'd missed last month.

I parked and headed inside. Walking up those stairs was like going into hell. Without Ed, it would've been hard enough seeing my dad screwed up.

With the nasty looking biker hovering in the room like a total thug, it was much worse.

How bad would it be today? Would I have to listen to dad ask me who I was for the thousandth time while Ed stood by, cold and calculating, a grim reminder that there were worse things waiting for my dad than early onset Alzheimer's if I didn't pay up?

They sat in their usual spots when I opened the door to my father's room. There was dad, staring out the window in his wheelchair. Big Ed was sprawled out on the bed. He bounced up with a muscular jerk. His large gut got in the way, and his trademark handlebar mustache twitched angrily, the only thing drawing attention away from his dark eyes.

"What the fuck took so long? I got another run to make before I head home to Klamath tonight. Fucking bitch." He spat on the floor. "You've been keeping me here all evening."

I stepped over his spit and reached into my purse, digging for the money as quickly as I could. He watched me while I pulled out the little stash and tore off the money clip. I shoved it into his face, trying not to shake.

"Here. Count it. Everything I promised."

He flipped through the twenties, letting out a loud snort when he finished counting. "That's it? Babe, you'd better start coughing up a whole lot more if you ever wanna skip these little visits. You're about one dollar over the threshold that keeps me from knocking his fucking teeth out. One."

Ed growled, pointing to my father. Dad stayed mercifully oblivious, muttering to himself as a little bird landed on a tree branch outside.

"It's everything I have this week," I whispered, trying to stay calm for my father's sake. "Don't know how I'm even going to make rent, to be honest. I'll have more for you later."

Big Ed shot up, grabbed me by the shoulders. His hot breath reeked tobacco, sour whiskey, and something else I could never quite identify. It stank plenty.

I was scared for dad, but not for me. Not anymore. Surviving Fang's torture drove away the terror I used to feel when he got up in my face or slammed me against the nearest wall.

"Stop being such an ungrateful cunt! You know I'm doing you a big fucking favor, right? Because we could do things much differently, babe. Trust me."

"Ed, please." I pushed against his fat chest, but he only tightened his grip.

Bastard. I pushed harder, the way he always made me struggle, before he finally cut me loose. Too bad it never shut him up.

"I could shut the door behind you, cut his fucking throat, and take you for a ride north on my bike. Shit, we'd probably be doing the old fart a favor. It's not like he knows who the fuck either of us are or what we're up to." He paused.

My eyelids fluttered shut. I quietly prayed he'd stop. He never did.

"You're a little worn to be a good whore, Christa, but there are plenty brothers in Oregon who'd love to use that firecracker cunt between your legs. A redhead's still a redhead. Doesn't matter if she's got a few scrapes and scratches." He licked his lips, eyeing the shameful lines on my face.

I shook my head. I was used to crude comments about my natural hair forever, but hearing about the scars was new. Hearing it from Ed's foul mouth was the worse.

"Tell me I'm being a good guy, Chrissy. I wanna hear you say it. You know how fucking easy I'm letting you off? I'm not even asking you to pay for the gas it takes to get down here just to put your tits into a vise. My bros would kick my ass if they knew what a softie I'm being."

My head snapped up, and we locked eyes. Was he fucking serious? As if this wasn't humiliating enough…

Sigh. I had to spit it out, if only to make him leave sooner.

"You're doing me a favor. You're playing nice. You're the best debt collector a girl could ask for." I could barely force the words through my clenched teeth.

There. Is that what you wanted, you fucking asshole? I hated when my brain felt like burning coal. Every thought hurt, hot and fierce as moving fire.

Big Ed laughed. He walked past me though, moving through the narrow space between dad's bed and the TV stand. His arm went out and gave me a rough shove on his way out.

"Don't you fucking forget it, bitch!" I steadied myself against the wall, hoping I wouldn't have to turn around before he was finally gone. Then he opened his fat mouth again, and I knew luck wasn't on my side today.

"Oh, and don't you dare think about going to any of the Redding boys with this. It won't help your ass – it'll just be more trouble. Rip's never backing down. He doesn't give a fucking shit what Blackjack or any of those other cocksuckers say. We don't take our orders from this town. We're free men. And if you stir up trouble, you'll just cause a damned war on your doorstep. Your job's easy. Fucking remember it."

Easy? Easy?!

Now, I had to turn around. I wanted to throw myself at him, scream, jab my fingernails into his eyeballs and tear his stupid mustache off.

But it wouldn't do any good.

If I somehow survived and got him arrested, his brothers would come to town. They'd know who did it. And everything I'd heard said the bastard was right – the new Grizzlies leadership in Redding was too busy finding its footing.

My problems weren't theirs, if they even cared. Besides, I wouldn't dare drag Rabid and his brothers into this, though he'd jump at the chance. They saved me once. I'd already screwed over my dad, and I'd rather die than see anybody else get killed for my screw ups, my debt.

"Ed – we're done. Please." He wanted me to beg him, so I did.

The asshole stopped, stood up straight, pulled on his cut. He was coming toward me again.

No, no, no…

"What'sa matter, Chrissy? Seriously?" His voice was so soft, but the way he grabbed my chin and tilted my head revealed his inner demon. "You ought to work your little ass off and go on a retreat. You're so fuckin' stressed. It's no good for your heart, you know."

He thumped his chest. The sound was the first thing to really make me shake. It reminded me how huge, dangerous, and ruthless these men really were.

"Life gives do overs if you play your cards right. Keep coughing up the dough. Keep doing everything I say. The old fuck over there'll get to live out his days in peace. You'll get to live another week without my boys running a train on your sweet ass, wearing nothing but their cuts. God, I bet you fuck *good* – even if you look like you stuck your fucking face into a cat fight."

Laughing, he reached for my ass, pulled me to him. I had to fight to make sure his disgusting tongue never contacted my skin.

Ass. Hole.

He let me go at just the right time. I went spinning toward the wall and crashed, hit the TV hard with my hip. Big Ed roared, stomping past me again, this time ripping open the door to the hall.

"You take care of yourself, Chrissy. Who the fuck knows. The universe works in mysterious ways. You keep working with a fire under your ass, maybe you'll get to have a little biker bar up by Crater Lake again one of these days. We'd *love* to give you the fucking money to get it off the ground again, soon as you pay this shit off."

I closed my eyes. Finally, he was gone, leaving the thunderous echo of the door slamming behind him in his wake. Just before he disappeared, I caught the roaring grizzly bear on his back, hateful symbol of all my terrible mistakes.

Christ. Seriously. He'd gotten to me again, even though it took a lot these days. My hand was squeezing my purse for dear life, and that made me realize how fucking empty it was. Just then, dad chose to turn around and look at me with his vacant eyes.

"You lost, lady? Can I help you?"

I stopped and stared up at the ceiling for a full minute. There was one more thing in my purse, something I'd bought with a couple bucks I hadn't forked over to Big

Ed.

"Here, dad. Your favorite candy." It was a dark chocolate bar I'd gotten at the gas station, something he always liked in better times when he could still fish and ride his bike.

With any luck, it might slow the weight melting off him too. Dad didn't look like the man who raised me anymore. He used to be big and strong and muscular, ready to lift the world. Now, he couldn't even lift his own legs to walk.

He sniffed, gave me the look that hurt the most – the vacant one that reminded me he really had no clue who I was, and probably never would again. The lucid moments were so rare these days. It wasn't fair, damn it.

He wasn't even sixty. Four or five years ago, he'd been enjoying his first year of early retirement, and now everything he'd scrimped and saved was being used to support him while every last light went out in his head forever.

"Hm." He unwrapped the chocolate slowly, something that had become our ritual for the last six months. "Oh, yeah. Hell yeah. Tastes good."

He chewed a square and looked up at me, wonder in his eyes. I sniffed back more tears. He didn't remember his daughter, but I'd managed to make him truly happy with this little thing.

That counted for something wherever my worldly karma was being tallied up, right?

"What was your name again, dear?"

"Christa. Christa Kimmel. You can count on me to be here next week, dad, same as always." I leaned down and gave him a quick peck on the forehead as his lips formed a confused smile. "I don't care how hard anybody makes it. I'm never going to stop loving you."

That night, I stared into my empty refrigerator. My stomach growled, pissed that I hadn't fed it anything since the roast beef sandwich Shirley gave me. I turned away in disgust, gulping two big cups of water to take the edge off.

Dad was safe for another week, the only thing that really mattered. But I couldn't stop wondering how *I* was going to keep living like this.

Something had to give. It always did. Bad luck caught up to me with trouble right by its side, always wearing a Grizzlies MC cut.

I'd been in deep before I got into trouble with the Redding club. Fang and his monstrous brothers tortured me because I'd been tutoring this teenager, Jackie, younger sister to Missy, who'd been claimed by Brass. He was the VP now, but he'd been one of the main traitors then, leader among the men who ended up destroying Fang and taking over the club.

Well, at least there was one less demon in the world. Not that it did me much good.

The awful memories weren't the only thing that kept haunting me. Every few weeks, Rabid came by, quite possibly the only man I didn't mind seeing with the murderous bear patch on his leather. His club sent him around to make sure I wasn't going to go to the cops about anything that happened during Fang's overthrow.

They didn't have a clue I'd been avoiding pigs since I was fifteen. I'd been wild, and I'd made dad's life a living hell for the next few years. Guess it went with the territory growing up a biker's daughter without a mother to straighten me out.

The stupid shit I'd gotten into wouldn't have wrapped around my neck like a noose if it didn't keep compounding. At eighteen, I hitchhiked my way up to Klamath Falls and made the greatest mistake of my life.

I was young and stupid. I thought I understood outlaw motorcycle clubs since dad was in one, but I didn't really know crap. My teenage brain couldn't even compute borrowing six figures from one with double digit interest.

I thought I was tough and wild. Thought I could run a bar without letting the Grizzlies MC walk all over me. I completely wilted the first time they wanted me to launder money through them.

Their President, Rip, got in my face, close enough to feel his beard's tangled bristles. He reminded me exactly what I was – their bitch, not a real businesswoman.

I had to get out. I ran, and ran the bar into the ground, leaving a real accounting mess behind. The whole thing fell apart within a year, but the debt remained.

I should've seen it coming. I'd been a smart girl, a trophy winner and a gifted kid before I flushed my brains down the toilet for adventure. I'd still managed a perfect score on the SAT even when I was fucking off.

I should've seen it coming, but I was too young, too naïve. Too strung out on hope and smarts. I didn't realize I was missing the magic ingredient – bravado – until it was too late. Some lessons have to be learned on the streets instead of in schools, I guess.

My head knew it. My heart refused to listen.

The years after Klamath went by in a blur of failures and intimidation, and there I was at twenty-three, slaving away for these savages I'd never escape.

God, what I would've done for a good drink to knock me on my ass. The gifted brain I'd never done anything good with sure loved to think. It never shut up unless it was doused in poison. And so, I suffered another evening alone, resisting the urge to pick up my cheap pay-as-you-go phone and call up Rabid.

I still had his number – he'd insisted on me taking it, the same way he made me promise to call him if anything came up between his visits.

He tempted me to pour my heart out. Maybe more than that too.

The boy – no, the *man* – was handsome. Six feet tall, broad shoulders, short dark hair and pristine hazel eyes to match. Lickable was too weak a word for how his clothes clung to the sculpted muscle underneath, the kinda hard, rugged strength a man gets with violence, rather than pumping iron.

He couldn't have been much older than me, but his face had experience and wisdom. He wore a confidence that said he'd avoided all the stupid things I'd done in my youth.

When I let it all lay out, Rabid was a fucking conundrum.

He excited me as much as he scared the hell out of me.

I hated being attracted to a brother in the Grizzlies MC at all. Too bad loathing the dark men behind the bear patch hadn't stopped me from admiring anything dark, masculine, and heavily tattooed.

That was Rabid to a tee. Rabid the brave, Rabid the biker bastard, Rabid the enigma who got into my head during dark hours like these, nudging me to learn more about him.

Thank God he wasn't perfect.

It didn't take hanging around him long to realize he was a crazy, womanizing biker who partied, drank, and fucked as hard as the rest of them. I had a pretty good idea what men like him did behind closed doors after the bar, and what happened in outlaw clubhouses was ten times worse.

I didn't care if Rabid melted my panties off. I wouldn't let myself get an inch deeper into his wicked world. And even if he wanted me, scarred cheeks and all, there was no way in *hell* I'd end up in his bed and become one more notch on the bedpost.

There were bigger problems to deal with than a silly cat-and-mouse crush. There always were.

Welcome to my life.

Look for Outlaw's Obession at your favorite retailer!

Printed in Great Britain
by Amazon